BLOWN

He dumped his mag targets, with Flanagan and Burgess moving and in the open, they needed some suppressive fire. The long burst stopped abruptly as his bullets smashed through the door and the shattered window, and he might have heard a shouted curse in Russian.

Flanagan and Burgess passed him, following Kristof and the rest of Dalca's people into the woods. Brannigan reloaded but held his fire since he didn't have a target and got ready to move.

Fortunately, he hadn't gotten too sucked into the target zone in the doorway. He had resumed his scan of their surroundings as he'd reloaded and spotted one of the bad guys as he'd jumped the brick fence in the back yard behind the neighboring house, then ducked behind a tree. While a part of him wanted to hold his fire until he had a target, the reality of their situation meant that getting lead downrange was more important. He blasted chunks of bark and splinters off the tree, then turned and ran as Flanagan took up the fire from above him.

Just before he got moving, though, a figure loomed in the open doorway. He was off target and out of position, but Santelli wasn't.

The stout, balding man put three rounds into the Russian's chest. Red puckered holes burst through his track suit jacket, and he fell on his face. Then Brannigan was running as Burgess started shooting at the house from above and off to the east.

BRANNIGAN'S BLACKHEARTS

CONCRETE JUNGLE

PETER NEALEN

CHAPTER 1

Tomas Fiero was nervous.

Short, built like a fireplug, and with cauliflower ears and a nose that had been mashed flat more than once, Fiero didn't seem like the kind of guy who should *get* nervous. Especially not when he had an HK VP9, three knives, and a garrote under his suit jacket. He was the kind of man who made *other* people nervous.

Something about this setup bothered him, though, in a way that he hadn't experienced since he'd been a simple street enforcer, almost twenty years before.

The meeting place was the first part he didn't like.

He turned in his seat to address the stunning blond woman in the back seat. "Signora, this is a bad place. After everything that has happened between us and Garin over the last two weeks, we should be meeting in a public place, with lots of eyes around."

Erika Dalca, CEO of Ciela International and also the queen bee of one of the biggest and most secretive underworld networks on the face of the planet, was a woman of somewhere between thirty and fifty years of age. Her skin was flawless, her slightly angular face as perfectly symmetrical and lovely as it was possible for a woman to get without surgery. She was stunning, she knew it, and she used it as a weapon more often than not.

Right at the moment, she looked completely unconcerned, and as she turned her glittering green eyes on him, he knew that she was turning that weapon on him, if only to get him to shelve his suspicions and trust her.

"That is why we have an overwatch element up, Tomas." She smiled faintly, and even that expression was enough to make a younger man forget where he was. Fiero, however, had worked for Dalca for years, and he'd learned to detach himself enough that her charms only had the vaguest effect on him. The part of him that had grown up with fairy tales wondered sometimes if she wasn't some sort of siren or other mythical creature. "Gaston is watching our backs."

Fiero just sighed. He wouldn't even have agreed to the meeting, but Dalca wasn't a woman you said no to, especially not when you owed her as much as he did. She'd been determined, after the events of the last few weeks, to handle this as peacefully as possible.

She was like that. While she could be extremely ruthless, all the same, she had a practical streak that made her determined not to waste resources and lives in violence if she could avoid it. In Fiero's mind, that made her more willing to talk when they should be fighting.

He didn't trust Artyom Garin to abide by the terms that had been worked out just for the meeting, never mind anything they came up with during said meeting.

Turning back to the front, Fiero nodded to the driver, semi-consciously touching the VP9 at his waist. There was nothing for it.

Putting the Land Rover into gear, young Kristof started them rolling down the flagstone road between the residential houses on the right and the open fields to the left. Fiero's eyes flicked momentarily to the partially wooded rise on the south of the field. Gaston was supposed to be up there, in a ghillie suit, along with Murray and Yakob, watching the last house in the

2

small neighborhood, where they were supposed to meet with Garin and his chief lieutenant.

He couldn't *see* any threats. Everything was quiet, and there was even an older Czech lady walking her dog on the street. There were no Russian thugs hanging out near the white brick and white picket fences around the brightly colored houses. No guns. No suspicious vehicles.

Something was still off, but there was nothing he could do about it except keep his eyes open, his hand close to his gun, and his ears pricked. Dalca was too determined for anything else.

Kristof pulled the vehicle around the corner and in front of the gate. He didn't park right at the gate itself, but pulled a couple of car lengths past it, then parked on the far side of the road, halfway into the field.

Dalca might have been dressed to the nines, but she didn't complain in the slightest about the fact that her door was opening up on a recently harvested field. She just slid to the other side of the vehicle—though Fiero would much have preferred if she *had* gotten out on that side, putting the bulk of the subtly armored Range Rover between her and any of Garin's people, at least for a moment—but he'd learned to roll with the punches. She wasn't going to hide when the reality of the situation *demanded* that she show no fear in front of the Russians.

Fiero was well practiced at staying one step ahead of Dalca. He was already out of the vehicle and halfway across the street when she got out, glancing over his shoulder at the men getting out of their trail vehicle with some irritation. They were slow, and Dalca had nearly caught up with him by the time he reached the gate, while the younger enforcers were still only halfway across the street.

He opened the gate. The door remained closed, the windows dark. He stopped just inside and put out a hand to stop Dalca in her tracks. "Something's wrong."

She halted, stepping behind the brick column that supported the gate. She was relentless and determined, but she wasn't stupid, and while she might have overruled him on attending the meeting at all, she wasn't going to ignore his instincts when it came to actual security on site. Fiero had worked for Dalca's father, after all, even before she had stepped into the old man's vacant shoes and started to steer the network in her own, more subtle direction. He'd earned that trust.

There was a bush growing just inside the gate, and he slid partway behind it as he watched the windows and the front door. It wouldn't provide him any actual cover, but it might keep any enemy inside guessing as to exactly where he was, which might buy him the crucial second or two to get Dalca to safety.

The door creaked open then, and a thickset man with practically no neck and a balding head, wearing a suit that was ever so slightly too small, stepped out. "You are late."

Fiero felt a flash of anger. They weren't late. He knew exactly the game this Russian thug was playing, and he didn't like it. It didn't bode well for any hope that they could resolve this problem between Dalca's network and Garin's Mafiya cell peacefully.

Still, at least it wasn't gunfire. Not yet anyway. And Dalca wasn't going to let strongarm mind games get in her way. She stepped out from behind the brick column and strode toward the house, sparing the Russian guard a withering, icy glare.

"Don't try to tell me what time it is, Vasili." The tone of her voice was as cold as her expression as she brushed past the man. There might have been a flicker of surprise on his face that she'd known his name, and Fiero suppressed a gloating smirk as he followed Dalca inside.

That smirk died completely as they came into the living room, or what had been the living room.

There was plastic on the floor, all of the furniture had been moved to the walls, and none of the men in dark track suits standing around the room were Garin. In fact, none of them were even any of his senior lieutenants. These were all mid- to low-level *brodyagas*. And they were all armed.

Fiero just pushed a button on his smart watch, glad that he'd thought ahead and hoping that he survived the next few seconds.

The Russian standing in front, a wiry, beak-nosed man with tattoos crawling up his neck, lifted his Skorpion machine pistol with a leering grin just before the first .50 caliber bullet smashed through the window and took the heavyset thug behind him in the head.

Blood and brains splashed across the wall as the thunderclap of the weapon's report and the crash of shattering glass echoed through the room. The Russians all ducked, as did Dalca, though Fiero had been through enough violence that he hardly blinked as he snatched his VP9 out of his waistband and shot the tattooed thug with the Skorpion through the chest.

Gaston continued to mag dump his GM6 Lynx through the windows and the walls as Fiero grabbed Dalca and dragged her back toward the door.

The thickset gangster who had let them in was in the way, though. He'd ducked at the first report of the Lynx, but now he was coming back up with a Laugo Alien pistol in his fist. He was a split second too slow, though, as Henri appeared behind him, put the muzzle of his own Glock to the Russian's temple, and blew his brains out.

Then Fiero was hauling Dalca out the door, running over the still-twitching body of the Russian and heading for the Range Rover. The meeting hadn't been a meeting at all, but a trap.

Garin's people might not have seen Gaston's overwatch with a .50 caliber rifle coming, but they still hadn't expected that the ambush would go entirely smoothly. Even as Fiero got Dalca halfway to the Range Rover, an Alfa Romeo Stelvio SUV came roaring down the road, pivoting with a screech of tires to block the entire street as men with submachineguns piled out and opened fire.

Henri went down immediately, several bloody holes torn in his suit coat, and hit the bricks with a limp finality. Robert was hit as well, though he threw himself back into the yard, clutching a bloody side while he shot back with his own Glock.

Fiero, for his part, picked up the pace even as he shoved Dalca to the side, putting himself between her and the gunfire. That was his job, after all. He fired the VP9, almost without aiming, just dumping the mag at the SUV. Window glass shattered, and he saw briefly that he'd punched a couple new, shiny holes in the body work. He didn't hit any of the gunmen, but the incoming fire slackened, especially as the thunder of a carbine opened up from Dalca's Range Rover. Kristof had entered the fray.

Panting, Fiero yanked the rear door open and unceremoniously shoved his boss inside. For her part, she made it look more graceful than it was, reaching into the go bag in the back seat for a weapon of her own, snatching the USP compact that she tended to prefer out of the integral holster and pivoting around, her businesslike yet fashionable dress hiked up to allow her to move more easily.

If Fiero had had less common sense and less history with her, he might have gawked at the sheer amount of leg she was showing, but he had much more pressing matters on his mind. He yanked open his own door as Dalca fired back at the Russian gunmen, pulling his 10-inch HK 416 out of the passenger seat as he yelled at Kristof. "Get in!"

He pivoted, put the red dot on the first head he saw peering over the hood behind a TMP-9, and put two bullets in it as fast as he could rock the trigger. Then Kristof was yelling at him, and he swung into the passenger seat, twisting around to face the back, pulling the door almost shut, pinning the rifle's forearm between it and the door column. "Erika! Get inside!"

Dalca was already pulling her door shut as Kristof started the Range Rover moving. After a moment, Fiero had to do the same, as Kristof stomped on the accelerator and got the up-armored vehicle moving faster than Fiero could control the door.

He didn't turn around just yet but jammed the rifle between his seat and the center console before reaching into the back seat and running a hand over Dalca's body. There was nothing erotic about it, even if he'd had any such thoughts about her. He was checking for bleeds. "Were you hit at all?"

"No." She'd already been running a hand over herself, showing the same cool assurance under fire that she always had in the boardroom or during more *discreet* business dealings. "Henri was hit."

"So was Robert. Henri is dead." He had no doubt about that. Turning back forward, satisfied that his employer wasn't going to bleed out in the back seat, he heard the thunderous reports of Gaston's GM6 again, as the overwatch opened fire on the Russian gangsters now that Dalca's vehicle was out of the kill zone. "We will have to make them pay for this."

"We will." If she was suffering any shock over what had happened, Fiero couldn't tell. She was as cold and collected as ever. "I know just the man to call about it, too."

8

CHAPTER 2

John Brannigan looked down at the phone on the seat beside him as it buzzed. The glower on his face had little to do with the unknown number on the small screen and far more to do with the phone's presence at all.

Following his practically involuntary retirement from the Marine Corps, not long after which his wife died from cancer, he'd essentially gone completely off grid. There had been no one he'd been interested in talking to, aside from his son Hank, who'd been off on his own Marine officer career at the time, so he'd just sort of disappeared into his mountain refuge.

It had taken Hector Chavez a long time to find him, but find him he had. Life had never been the same since.

He couldn't say he minded being the commander of the secretive mercenary team known amongst themselves as Brannigan's Blackhearts. It had gotten him back in the game, in a way he'd never have been able to dream of as a flag officer. And it had given him a sense of purpose again, when he'd simply been *existing*, marking time until he followed his wife in death.

There were drawbacks, though. The cell phone was one of the most obnoxious.

It kept buzzing, though, despite his glare. He finally pulled off the road and reached for it. This was going to be a brief conversation, whoever it was. Not only was he uninterested in talking to a solicitor, but he had supplies in the back of the truck that needed to get into the root cellar up at the cabin soon.

"Hello, John."

The woman with the faintly accented, honeyed voice on the other end didn't identify herself, but she didn't need to. He recognized her immediately. "Erika Dalca."

"I hope I didn't catch you at a bad time." She sounded a little like she was pouting that he hadn't immediately greeted her like an old friend. It was one of her games, one he was, unfortunately, getting somewhat used to.

He still wasn't sure how much of her flirting was genuine and how much was just another of her mind games. He *thought* it was the latter, but every now and again—whenever they'd had to deal with her, which was more often than he might have liked—she did or said something that made him wonder if she really did have feelings of some sort for him.

That was part of what made her so dangerous.

The majority of the handful of people who had heard of Erika Dalca knew her as the CEO of the global logistics company Ciela International. She even had her own website. She was one of the more low-key millionaires—or billionaires—in the world, but she could easily move around in the circles of high-powered executives and politicians.

Brannigan knew more about her, though. She had a hand in all sorts of illegal activities, mostly revolving around information brokering, though he suspected that she was involved in any number of other things. She always swore to him that she wasn't into the *really* dirty stuff, and that she'd steered her father's underworld network away from things like drugs, human trafficking, and suchlike to more "victimless" crimes. Yet a criminal queenpin she still remained.

That was the biggest reason he didn't trust her, despite the intel and logistics support she'd lent the Blackhearts over the last few years. The biggest *rational* reason he could put his

10

finger on, anyway. There was something about her that always put him on his guard.

Maybe it was her undeniable sex appeal, and the particular attention she always paid to him when they were in the same place. It would be entirely too easy to succumb to her charms, which was why he always got a little angry when she turned them on him.

"I'm on the road." Sure, he'd pulled over, so he wasn't exactly at risk of getting into an accident because he was on the phone, but she didn't need to know that.

"Well, I won't take too much of your time. I need you, John. You and the rest of your boys." Given her choice of words, he'd more than half expected that to be a double entendre, but the tone of her voice was suddenly deadly serious. "I'm in trouble, and your expertise is the best I can call on."

He frowned as he stared down the road in front of him, lined with dark evergreen trees on either side, not really seeing any of it. "We're not exactly hired muscle, Erika."

"I wouldn't dream of calling you for anything like that." She actually sounded genuinely offended. "I have other avenues for such things." He was sure she did. "No, this is something far more serious. There was an attempt on my life, and I need shooters. Professional soldiers. You and your men are my best hope."

Brannigan's eyes narrowed as he thought this over. He didn't answer right away, and his silence seemed to have affected Dalca on the other end of the call.

"John?" Her voice had become slightly plaintive. More feminine, if that was possible. "I can't give you details over the phone. You know that. But trust me that I wouldn't call you for help unless I *really* needed it." She paused for a moment, and he could almost see her chewing her lip, as if thinking it over. "There's more going on here than just a threat to me. I've dealt with those before. But I think that what's going on has to do with matters of our mutual interest."

11

He still didn't answer. Truth be told, he was somewhat intrigued. She *wasn't* the sort to call him on a lark. Every other time she'd made contact, it had been about a legit target. First had been Eugen Codreanu, the underworld arms dealer who had arranged the Humanity Front's getaway from the Tourmaline Delta platform. Then she'd put him on Jason Bevan, a Front financier who had fled to Argentina, a bit of intel that had resulted in the destruction of a Front base high in the Altiplano, where the Humanity Front had been working on a super soldier program. She'd only ever bothered him with legitimate intel. Only the knowledge of just what her line of work was, plus his uneasiness with her flirtation, made him not trust her.

"John?"

"I'm listening."

She sighed. "I can't be sure that this line is secure. Please, John. Just come to Prague. I will take care of anything else you need. I will make sure you get paid; I am not asking for charity. I *do* need your help. I am in danger, but that's not all there is to it." She hesitated again. "I also do know a great deal about your operations. If I am taken, I cannot promise that I will be able to conceal everything that I know, and there are people involved in this who might be *very* interested in such information."

Brannigan clenched his jaw. It was blackmail, plain and simple, but it could be very effective blackmail. They'd run into trouble Stateside before. Sam Childers was a permanent invalid in large part because of such trouble. If even a roster and some idea of the operations the Blackhearts had conducted over the years got into the wrong hands, they could be in a world of hurt. He *thought*, from past experience, that Abernathy's mysterious black ops group might help them, but he didn't want to rely too heavily on them, either.

"It sounds like you've got me up against a wall, Erika."

"I'm sorry, John." She sounded genuinely apologetic, but that might just be tradecraft. She was certainly a good enough actress. "I don't want it to be like that between us, but I

12

am in a very bad position right now. I *need* you, and I cannot afford to neglect *any* leverage that I might have at my disposal." Her voice dropped, sounding somewhat small. "I hope you can forgive me."

And there she was, doing it again. He took a deep breath. "I can't just order it. I'll have to run it past the others." He knew he was temporizing, but it was also equally likely that the other Blackhearts would kibosh the whole idea. On the other hand, they hadn't had much action since they'd fought those pirates in the Atlantic, and while Dalca might not be the most trustworthy client, the others all knew that she *had* hooked them up in the past.

Whether that would be enough remained to be seen.

"Please, John. Don't take too long. I'll be in and around Prague, though you'll have to make contact after you land. I can't afford to stay in one place for more than a few hours." That did sound ominous, though again, was she telling the truth, or was she trying to tug on heartstrings?

Maybe it was both. If there was one thing about Erika Dalca that he was sure of, it was that she never did anything without a purpose.

"I'll be in touch. This number?"

"Yes." There was almost a note of relief in her voice, relief that he hadn't just hung up on her, that he might, indeed be coming to the rescue. Not for the first time, Brannigan wondered just how much of her persona was faked and how much was simply a matter of carefully calculating what she dared to show to anyone around her. She'd expressed her interest in him before, more than once. With any other woman, he'd have been sure that it was ham-fisted emotional manipulation, but Dalca always managed to make him wonder. "Thank you, John."

"I haven't committed to anything yet."

"No, but you are you. If you *weren't* being cautious then I'd be worried. You'll do the right thing." A faint hint of a smile worked its way into her tone. "I'll see you soon."

The connection was cut and Brannigan tossed the phone on the seat next to him with a grimace.

That woman's going to be the death of me.

He put the truck back in gear and pulled back onto the road.

***

Carlo Santelli wiped his hands on a shop rag that he didn't really need, but it felt like the right thing to do as he watched his latest project roll out of the shop with a very happy customer behind the wheel. It hadn't even been that big a project. Just a couple of repairs and some touch-up paint, but it had meant a lot to the customer.

It hadn't really been what Santelli had had in mind when he'd set up the shop. Not even when he'd brought Pardo aboard to help out, as the business had grown. It had started as a hobby/side gig while he was home in between missions with Colonel Brannigan and the Blackhearts. Then it had become something more, possibly a replacement for those missions, a way to stay home with Melissa and the kids—Carlo Jr was running around like a wild man now, and their second child was due in a couple of months—but that hadn't worked out. Not because the business had failed. Not even because of tensions in the marriage—Melissa was as comfortable with his double life now as she ever had been—but simply because he couldn't bear to stay behind when the boys went out into harm's way. It had been a rough lesson to learn, but while he'd always maintained that he was a slow learner, he *could* still learn.

Resuming his deployments with the Blackhearts, though, hadn't slowed down the business. Pardo was a hell of a businessman, as well as a hell of a mechanic, and he'd begun expanding things as soon as he'd come aboard. Not to the point of taking over, but certainly to such a degree that they were probably going to have to hire another mechanic.

Under different circumstances Santelli might have grumbled about that. Given the state of the economy, though, a

14

growing business wasn't something to dismiss easily. And if they could help someone else earn a living, so much the better.

Still, as the cherry red Camaro disappeared around the corner, and he turned to look at the projects that needed attention behind it, Santelli couldn't help but think that *maybe* it wouldn't be bad for the expansion to slow down *just a little*.

He'd barely thought it when the phone rang. He never would have done it himself, but Vincent Bianco had changed his ringtone to the A-Team theme for Brannigan's number. It fit, somehow, and it meant he knew the Colonel was calling before he could see the phone, which was sometimes helpful for getting his mind right.

He snatched it up. It *had*, after all, been a while since the counter-piracy op.

"Yessir." His Boston accent had only gotten thicker after he'd retired from the Marine Corps as a Sergeant Major. Moving back to the old neighborhood had only accelerated the shift.

"Got an interesting one, Carlo. Time sensitive."

Santelli's eyes narrowed. "Vinnie installed some kind of encrypted program on this phone." If time was of the essence, it might not be practical to fly halfway across the country to meet in person. Encrypted comms might be the next best thing.

Brannigan growled something he couldn't quite make out. "He did it with mine too. Hang on." He hung up.

Santelli waited, the phone in his hand. It took about as long as he figured he'd have taken before the encrypted app announced an incoming call.

"I think we can talk securely this way, sir."

"I hope so." Brannigan sighed. "I got a call from Dalca."

Santelli frowned. He knew considerably less about Erika Dalca than Brannigan did, but he knew enough to be *extremely* wary when she came up. He also knew that the Colonel was, if anything, even more wary. "What'd she want?"

"From the way she told it, she wants to hire us to get her ass out of a crack." The fact that Brannigan used that particular turn of phrase illustrated how annoyed and uncomfortable he

15

was with the whole situation. "She hinted at all sorts of dire stuff going on in the background, and she's desperate enough that she tried to blackmail me. Said that if she was 'taken,' whatever that means, she might not be able to keep her mouth shut about us."

"Who's after her who would even give a damn about us?" Santelli asked, his frown deepening.

"That's the question, isn't it?" Brannigan left the words hanging in the air, and Santelli didn't need to think too hard to see where he was going with it.

"The last few times we've dealt with her, it's been about the Front." He was pretty sure he knew that was what Brannigan was thinking, but many years as a Senior NCO had taught Santelli the value of making sure everything is out in the open, with as few assumptions as possible. He might have said otherwise when he'd been a Drill Instructor on Parris Island, but he still firmly believed in the old adage, *When you assume, you make an ass out of you and me*. "She hasn't otherwise involved us in any of her…extracurricular activities." Even over an encrypted connection, it didn't feel like coming right out and saying that she was an underworld information broker and shadow facilitator was a good idea. Almost as if she or one of her people just *might* be listening in. Or any number of three-letter agencies that might be very interested in a group of American mercenaries who might have been in contact with such a person. "You think that's why she's trying to call us in? The Front's surfaced again?"

"It's possible." If Santelli hadn't known Brannigan for so many years, he might not have picked up on the subtext. Brannigan had had time to think about this, and he thought it wasn't just possible. It was probable. "Without more information—which she's not willing to give over the phone—I can't say for sure. If this *is* one of her games, I really don't want to get any more entangled with her than we already are."

"Which might just make her more inclined to lean into that 'blackmail' angle," Santelli mused. He harrumphed. He was getting old enough he found that he did that a lot. It was a little unnerving to notice from time to time. "Well, given our past history, sir, I think that it's probably a good bet to at least follow up on it. It should only be a small team at first, though. Just in case." He thought for a second. "What did Joe say?"

Brannigan chuckled faintly. "I haven't talked to him yet."

Santelli's eyebrows climbed toward his receding hairline, though he didn't say anything.

"Joe's a good man and a good XO, but you've been my right hand for a very, very long time, Carlo. You may have backed off and handed that Number Two spot to Joe, but you're still the Sergeant Major I trusted to keep the boys out of trouble and on task. I needed your insight first. I'll call Joe next."

Santelli felt his chest swell just a little at that. Old and fat he might have gotten—though he was still a fireplug of a man who could just about tear a phone book in half with his bare hands—but the Colonel still trusted him, even after those rocky times when he couldn't commit wholly to the Blackhearts. "Well, when you go, Colonel, you'd better not go without me."

"Wouldn't dream of it, Carlo."

He suddenly thought of something. "By the way, where are we going?"

"Prague."

CHAPTER 3

Joe Flanagan sat down in the booth at the back of the Rocking K. He'd been close enough that Brannigan had asked for a face-to-face. While the encrypted phone app might have been acceptable for talking to Santelli, neither man trusted it entirely. They were much more comfortable sitting down in a place they were reasonably certain no one was going to be listening too hard.

Minding one's own business was a local pastime in Junction City.

Of course, Brannigan had met with clients often enough in the diner —either retired General Van Zandt, Hector Chavez, the mysterious Clayton Abernathy, or all three—that it was possible that someone had snuck in a plant or a bug, but Flanagan wouldn't have put it past Mama Taft to have the place swept and any new clientele discreetly checked out from time to time. She was old-fashioned, but she was smart, and nobody around the area wanted to cross her, because then they might be banned from the diner.

That was a fate worse than death to most of the locals. Flanagan had eaten there often enough that he understood why.

Leaning on his elbows, he watched Colonel Brannigan closely. The Old Man was disturbed by whatever they had to talk about, that much was clear. Which both worried Flanagan and piqued his curiosity. It took a lot to put Brannigan off his poise. "What's the job?"

"Dalca called me this morning." At Flanagan's raised eyebrow, Brannigan nodded. "Yeah. I had about the same reaction."

He proceeded to lay out the job as he'd understood it. Flanagan listened in silence, just taking it in. It was his way. He always strove to listen more than he talked, and this was definitely a time to listen.

"Carlo thinks we should send a small team in advance, just in case this turns out to either be a trap, or one of Dalca's underworld power plays." Brannigan smoothed his gray handlebar. "She hasn't played that sort of game with us yet, at least not overtly, but there's a first time for everything. It *seems* like she's tangled with the Front again. So far, it's the only reason she's ever called on us. But we won't know until we get there."

Flanagan looked down at his plate as Ginger Taft slid it in front of him with a smile. He returned her smile, though his own turned into a grin as Ginger put Brannigan's plate in front of him and touched his shoulder with an even wider smile before she left.

Ginger's got a bit of a crush on the Colonel, or so it seems.

They both waited until Ginger was out of earshot to continue the conversation. She was Mama Taft's granddaughter, young enough to be Brannigan's daughter, and a bright, cheery young woman who would never have talked about anything she heard, but it wasn't necessary to take chances. What she didn't hear couldn't hurt her.

"So, who do you have in mind?" Flanagan was already thinking his way down the roster. He'd taken over—somewhat reluctantly—as the Blackhearts' second in command after Roger Hancock had been killed in Argentina, and that put him most often in the position of sending out the calls to bring the team together from half a dozen scattered areas around the country.

20

"I was hoping you might have some ideas." Brannigan shrugged as he dug into his steak. "I'm going. Carlo's going. I don't know if we *should* bring anyone else, frankly. At least, not at the start."

Flanagan thought it over. He really didn't want to leave Rachel at this stage of her pregnancy, but all the same, he really didn't want to let Brannigan and Santelli go on a trip like this on their own. "I think we'd better at least have four. That way we've got a little bit more backup if things get weird."

Brannigan looked up at him from under a single raised eyebrow. "I heard that 'we,' Joe."

Flanagan sighed. "I can't let you and Carlo go by yourselves. You know that. It's not the same as if we were sending Kevin..." Brannigan snorted. "But still. As soon as you announced you were going, you had to know that I was, too, unless you specifically ordered me not to."

Brannigan nodded. "Okay, that's three. Who should be our number four?"

Flanagan chewed his steak as he thought it over. "Where did you say we were going?"

"Prague."

"Czech Republic." Flanagan grimaced. "The closest we had to an Eastern Europe guy was Herc." Erekle "Herc" Javakhishvili had been killed in Kyrgyzstan.

Brannigan frowned thoughtfully, his eyes narrowed, as his fork hung over his plate. "Well, Herc might be gone, but we know he had a good friend with a thing for Eastern Europe..."

***

Tom Burgess leaned on the cab of the truck, his hand on the AK that was one of the three firearms in the village. He had a pretty good view of the hills and the fields around the village, though he was most concerned with the roads. The jihadis and bandits around this part of Africa weren't usually the most motivated, so he rarely saw any of the bad guys coming cross country. The Janjaweed up north didn't usually make it down into Kenya these days, anyway. It was mostly IS and Al

Shabaab. And from what he'd heard, even the Janjaweed, such as were left, had mostly switched to trucks instead of horses.

So, he was watching the approaches to the village of Kitengela and the small Eastern Orthodox mission at the outskirts. They'd had trouble before, back when he'd been here with Herc, but the fight that he and their late, lamented Georgian medic had taken to the jihadis had quieted things down considerably.

That didn't mean that they could relax. It was Africa.

It was hot, but Burgess had been all over the world, first as a SEAL, then as a contractor, finally as one of Brannigan's Blackhearts. The discomfort didn't bother him. Even the lack of money didn't bother him. He was in Kitengela in more of a volunteer capacity, but he was something of a terminal bachelor, so he could afford it.

A flicker of movement caught his eye. Leaving the rifle where it lay on the roof of the cab, he lifted his binoculars. They were old, the black paint chipped and scratched to show the silver of the aluminum underneath, but they were good glass. He'd had them for a *long* time.

He lowered them with a faint smile behind his neatly trimmed, salt and pepper beard. He recognized the old man with the cart. No threat there.

There was always the possibility that someone had taken Gitonga hostage and threatened him and his family—which was of considerable size, when accounting for all of his children, grandchildren, cousins, nieces, and nephews—as leverage to get him to sneak them into the village, but there wouldn't be much point. It wasn't like Burgess was there with a solid militia, let alone a full team of armed, trained, and experienced contractors.

It was just him and Ignatius Kirk, with two AKs and one SKS. And he wasn't sure if he trusted that SKS not to jam up after the first couple of rounds. A full raid would be a lot easier and more efficient than trying to take the sneaky way in.

"Behind you, Tom." Kirk's growl had gotten steadily more gravelly over the years. His equally steady diet of whiskey and tobacco use accounted for a lot of it, along with the fact that they were all just getting older.

Burgess gave the horizon one more scan before he turned to his old friend. There was nothing but Gitonga and his cart in view—except for the boys with the herd up in the northern field—and even if that changed in the next few seconds, they would still have time to react.

Kirk was dressed a little more for the heat than Burgess was, in a sleeveless shirt above his fatigue trousers. While Burgess was fairly sure that Kirk was pushing fifty, if not past it, he was still powerfully built, and his arms bulged, red though they were since he didn't tend to tan like some of their old compatriots did. He'd trimmed his beard back for this trip, because of the heat, and for the first time in a long time he looked like an average Joe with a reddish beard shot through with gray, instead of a second cousin to ZZ Top.

"What's up?" Burgess glanced at his watch. It still wasn't time for shift change. That was in another hour.

Kirk held up the sat phone. "The Colonel's on the line. Wants to talk to you."

Burgess reached down to give Kirk a hand up into the bed. They might have some time, but he wasn't going to leave the watch completely uncovered while he talked on the phone. "What's cooking?"

"Not sure yet." Kirk moved up to the cab, checked the AK out of sheer habit, and then stood, his legs splayed, his arms crossed over his chest. It was a little too hot to lean on the roof with no sleeves, which was why Burgess was wearing a long-sleeved shirt, as lightweight as it was. "He said he wanted to talk to you, specifically, but that both of us should probably be ready to move."

Burgess frowned as he took the phone from Kirk and put it to his ear. "Colonel? It's Tom."

"Hey, Tom." There was a faint delay, and the sound was pretty scratchy, but that was to be expected with a satellite phone. "Got a potential job coming up, but it's a little sensitive and we need to proceed carefully. How soon do you think you can fly out of Africa without leaving your people in the lurch?"

"It might take a couple days." Burgess had sat down on the edge of the truck bed and scratched his beard as he thought it over. "We've got a rotating pool of volunteers for this little overwatch operation. It'll just take a few calls and some last-minute flights to get someone else out here." He glanced up at the horizon again. "To be fair, it's been pretty quiet out here since the first time Herc and I worked this gig."

"Good to know. Okay, I don't want to go into too much detail over this connection, but Joe, Carlo, and I are heading to Prague to do some advance recon for this, see if we can determine if it's a job we really want to pursue, or if we need to pop smoke altogether. I will say that it involves Ciela International."

It took Burgess a second to place the name, then he nodded gravely. *Dalca*. He didn't know as much about her as some of the others did, but he knew enough to understand why Brannigan was being wary.

"Now, since you're the closest we've got to an Eastern Europe guy since we lost Herc, I'd like you along, if you can make it."

Burgess glanced up at Kirk, who was half turned toward him. It was quiet enough out there that Kirk could probably hear the phone. The big man shrugged. *Fine with me.*

"When are you looking at leaving?"

"This is apparently a little time-sensitive, so we're planning to fly out tomorrow."

Burgess grimaced a little. That was going to be tight. "I can't make it back to the States in time, but I might be able to meet you in Prague. I might be a day behind you."

"We'll meet you there, then. Can I talk to Kirk again?"

Burgess handed the phone back to his friend and took up the watch once more. Kirk traded places and put the phone to his ear. "Yessir." He listened for a moment. "Yessir. I think we can swing that. Where do you want the rest of us to meet up?"

Another pause. "Yessir. What about logistics?" He nodded. "Copy. If you think we can trust her that far…"

He listened for a few moments, then said, "Yessir. We'll get things moving. You need to talk to Tom again?" He pulled the phone away from his ear. "You got any more questions, Tom?"

"Nope." He was already planning the trip in his head, even while he continued to watch the horizon.

"All right, Colonel. We'll be moving in the next twenty-four. Out." Kirk turned off the phone and shoved it in a pocket.

"Well." Burgess glanced over his shoulder as Kirk moved up to stand next to him. "This is getting interesting."

"That's putting it mildly." Kirk launched a stream of dip spit off the side of the truck. "Not sure I like it. I've heard a few things about this Dalca chick."

"So have I." Burgess held out a hand for the phone and Kirk pulled it out and slapped it into his palm. "The others have more experience with her, but she seems like one hell of a dangerous dance partner."

"Sounds like it." Kirk shrugged. "As long as she pays, though."

"Oh, I'm sure she'll pay. Brannigan would have already told her to go jump in a lake otherwise." Burgess started to punch in the number to try to get Samuels and Branca out early. "Thing is, I'm sure we'll have to earn that pay along the way."

CHAPTER 4

John Wade walked back to his car in a combined mood of frustration and glee. Glee because he'd just gotten paid a great deal to do not a whole lot. Las Vegas might be a generally less than civilized place—not that Wade had much of a taste for "civilized" places—but it wasn't nearly as dangerous as some of the cities where he'd plied his trade. And this last gig had been quiet as could be. The principal, a corporate IT nerd who seemed to have just left his basement office for the first time in years, was a bit of a rabbit, seemingly nervous about even being in Sin City, as if he wasn't supposed to be there. That was combined with a fear of violence that had made even Wade seem scary to him.

That was the root of the frustration. John Wade had never been accused of being the most cheerful or friendly of people, and that had been among fellow Rangers and military contractors who were used to being apex predators.

Spending two days escorting a complete leaf-eater around had strained his patience nearly to the breaking point. He'd had to remind himself of his fee more than once.

It wasn't Blackhearts money, but it was still pretty damn good money. He just found himself questioning, more than once, whether it was worth the blood pressure points.

Swinging his go bag into the back seat of his truck, he blew out a pent-up breath, glad that at least the job hadn't required him to wear a suit. Or even a sport jacket. That would have been a humiliation too far. Ducking into the driver's seat, he pulled his phone out and checked it. He'd been tempted to check it before, but he hadn't been on a static sort of security gig; he'd needed to actually follow the principal around, and that had precluded concentration on anything but the job.

Especially since that idiot had almost wandered into some actual danger a couple of times just from sheer cluelessness, despite his obvious terror of his own shadow. Wade's lip curled in a grimace at the memory as his phone started up. He'd actually found himself rooting for something bad to happen, both to snap the soft little man out of his complacency and to furnish Wade himself with a little bit of action to break up the monotony.

The screen in front of him lit up with a missed call in that encrypted app that Bianco had found. No voicemail, but then, Brannigan rarely left voicemail messages. Wade could appreciate that. He didn't bother with them, either. He called back and lifted the phone to his ear.

"Wade." Brannigan's voice rumbled through the speaker. "How's your schedule look for the next couple of weeks?"

"Clear as a bell if we've got work, Colonel." Wade leaned back in the seat and watched the parking lot. This might not be the high-crime part of Vegas—there was no way the client would have been going anywhere near those parts, even if he'd known where they were—but it never paid off to get complacent, *especially* if they had a Blackhearts job coming up.

"We *might*." Wade frowned a little at the caution in Brannigan's voice. "Our old friend from Ciela International is the client."

"Oh." Wade could appreciate Dalca's looks, but if anything, he trusted her less than Brannigan did. "Her."

"Yeah. That's why I'm heading to Prague tomorrow with Joe and Carlo. Tom's meeting us there. He's in Africa." Wade blinked a little at that. He'd known that Burgess and Herc had been doing some side work for some missionaries or something, but he hadn't known it was in Africa. *Maybe I should have signed on with them. Might be more action. On the other hand, I doubt missionaries pay that well.* "The rest of you I want on standby, in case this is something we decide to move on. She made it sound like it might be our old 'humanitarian' friends at work again."

Wade suppressed a snarl. He didn't need that bit of euphemistic phrasing spelled out for him.

The Humanity Front was still, to most of the world, the biggest and most influential humanitarian NGO on the face of the planet. Their star had fallen a little bit over the last few years, but they'd hobnobbed with—and gotten a *lot* of money from—just about every major celebrity, politician, multinational corporation, and monarch that was important in any way from across the globe. They were the darlings of media and governments alike, the people with the vision to bring about a shining new future.

The trouble was—even if Wade hadn't been inherently skeptical of any and every such idealistic bunch of starry-eyed dreamers in the first place—that they had their own ideas about what constituted a shining new future, and it generally involved a lot of dead people and complete control over the remainder, even down to their genetic code. They were a high-tech, very well-funded, global terrorist organization with a nightmare vision of the future that required everyone who didn't bend the knee—or even had the wrong bits of DNA in their bodies—to die.

They'd been fairly quiet since the Blackhearts had destroyed their super-soldier lab on the Altiplano in Argentina, though they hadn't stopped working on things, as the team had found out in Kyrgyzstan. If they were in the middle of Europe, though, that could mean they were getting up to their old tricks again.

He was looking forward to the day when the Blackhearts just got complete carte blanche to hunt them all down and murder them in their penthouses. He knew, on an intellectual level, that it was going to take a lot of time, intel, resources, and top cover to make that happen, but a man could dream.

"I can go now, if it's those assholes." Most of his reticence at the mention of Dalca's involvement had fled as soon as he'd smelled the Front.

"I know, but we need to play this cautiously. That's why only four of us are going at first. I was ready to go with just me and Carlo, but Joe talked me into at least making it a four-man team." Brannigan sighed. "You're in Vegas?"

"Yeah." He wasn't sure exactly how Brannigan knew that, but the Old Man had his ways.

He suddenly had a sinking feeling as he answered the question. He knew what was coming next. If Flanagan was flying out to Prague in the morning...

"I hate to ask this, John, but somebody needs to track Curtis down. He hasn't answered his phone so far today." Brannigan *almost* sounded apologetic.

Wade sighed heavily, almost a growl. "I guess that's what I get for taking a job in his stomping grounds. Do we at least have an idea where he might be?"

"Joe gave me a list of his preferred haunts. You might have to check around. He might be a wild man, but he rarely follows the same pattern."

Wade looked at his watch with a tightening of his jaw. It was already late in the day. He was probably in for a long night. He'd heard a few of Flanagan's stories and their accompanying gripes.

For all his grumbling and antisocial attitude, though, John Wade was still a responsible man and a team player. He'd do the job, because he was there, and it had to get done. "Give me the list. The sooner I get started, the sooner I can get this over with."

***

It was getting close to one in the morning, and Wade's rage was nearing white-hot.

He'd already been to Kevin Curtis's apartment several times, just in case. As the night wore on, he hoped that *maybe* the man might have circled back to crash out. After all, he *was* newly married. Wade had even been at the wedding, as cringeworthy as so much of it had been. *What the hell is he doing still out on the town when he could be in bed with that hot young wife of his?*

If he had been the worrying kind, Wade might have started to get concerned, the longer he looked for Curtis. After all, the woman—girl, really—he'd married had been a mobster's daughter. If Curtis had gotten sloppy and had been rolled up…

This is the last place. Then I'm going to get some sleep and try to call him in the morning. He's probably just drunk. Curtis acted the clown more often than not, but he was still a lot more cunning than his outward behavior would suggest. Even drunk, he'd have watched his back and planned his route to avoid ambushes. He had a talent for getting into trouble, if Flanagan was to be believed, but he was almost as adept at sliding out of it, smelling like a rose.

Wade was hardly as staid as Flanagan was, but this place was garish even to him. The entire front was blue and purple neon, and the windows were tinted. Wade knew a seedy nightclub when he saw one, and this was one of the seediest.

Strangely, it seemed like just the sort of place Kevin Curtis would be drawn to.

He paid the cover, grudgingly, and glared at the bouncer who tried to intimidate him by looming in the doorway. The guy probably had fifty pounds on him, but it wasn't exactly muscle. *Try me, fat boy.* Fortunately or unfortunately, the bouncer backed down, and he brushed past him and into pandemonium.

31

Most of the noise was deliberate. The bass vibrated in his chest and the electronic music assaulted his ears. He didn't mind it; he'd hooked up in more than one place like this. He didn't especially *like* it, and he knew that the longer he was in there, the more it was going to grind on his nerves.

The loud EDM, however, couldn't entirely mask the commotion over in the far corner, near the dance floor.

He didn't immediately recognize the girl dancing on the table. She wasn't wearing that much, but that was to be expected in Vegas, anyway. Only when he got closer, he saw that she was Curtis's wife.

She wasn't so much dancing for the sake of display, despite the tight, cropped and low-cut top and miniskirt she was wearing. She was dancing more out of drunken glee as Kevin Curtis brawled with three other dudes next to the table.

With a sigh that was almost a feral snarl, Wade dove in.

He grabbed one of them, who was trying to beat on Curtis while the short, stocky bodybuilder held his friend in a headlock, leaning back to put some serious tension on the man's neck. Hauling the guy backward, Wade spun him around and delivered a thunderous elbow strike to his face. The blow snapped the man's head halfway around and mashed his nose. Blood spurted, and the brawler immediately lost interest in the fight, slumping half-conscious to the sticky floor.

The guy Curtis had his arms around was tapping furiously, but Curtis wasn't letting up. The other guy who was trying to stomp on him probably had something to do with that. Wade went over the guy in the headlock, feeling something *pop* under him as he did so, and slammed into the stomper, a burly type in a rumpled shirt that might have been silk. They went down hard, Wade on top, and he heaved himself into a mount, proceeding to hammer his fists into the man's face for a few moments. The ground and pound didn't take long, as the man went limp after the first couple of punches.

Curtis rolled the man he'd been grappling with off him as Wade got up, barely glanced at his teammate, and held his hands up to his wife. "Come on, baby, we gotta go."

"Aw, babe, it's still early!" The girl was clearly plastered out of her mind, still dancing on the table.

Of course, now that the fight was over, and the short black guy wasn't being ganged up on by three idiots, *now* the bouncers decided to get involved.

"Hey! You're going to have to leave!" The big guy who'd been at the door cracked his knuckles as he approached, but he stopped dead as Wade turned on him, that fighting gleam in his steely, ice-blue eyes. There weren't many people who wanted to tangle with John Wade after they'd looked into those unblinking points of ice.

"Don't worry, we fully intend to." He glanced down at the guy Curtis had been fighting, wondering for a moment if he'd broken the man's back when he'd vaulted over him. He was stirring faintly, though, so whatever that *pop* had been must not have been too serious. It looked like Curtis had just choked the guy out. "Kev, get your girl down and let's go."

Curtis, however, was still arguing with his wife, even as two more bouncers closed in from deeper inside the nightclub. She seemed to be oblivious to the trouble they were in, and just wanted more drinks and more time to dance.

Finally, Wade lost patience. He reached up, grabbed her by the arm, and hauled her, none too gently, to the floor, put her hand in Curtis's, and growled, "Now."

She shrieked as he pulled her off the table. In fact, she seemed to have only just noticed that he was there, despite him having battered two men senseless right in front of her. She calmed down a little as Curtis wrapped his ebony arm around her waist, but she was still protesting as Wade led the way out onto the street.

"What the hell, Kevin?" Wade ground out, as soon as the doors had closed behind them.

"What?" Curtis was clearly quite a few drinks in, himself, though he was holding his liquor better than his wife was. "It's a good night, and we felt like partying. What's the harm in that?"

If he was being honest, Wade couldn't really come up with an answer, except he was pissed off about having to drag all up and down the Strip and beyond looking for the man. Beating those two down hadn't quite taken the edge off, either. "Come on. I'll get you back to your apartment."

"Wait, what are you doing out here, anyway?" Curtis wasn't quite as sober as his words might have suggested, as he staggered when his wife couldn't quite negotiate a straight line in her stacked heels and pulled him to one side. "I thought you'd be, I dunno. Yelling at people somewhere or something."

"I am. I'm yelling at you. I'm just doing it quietly because I don't want to attract too much attention." Wade stalked toward his car, unlocking it as he went. He pulled the go bag out of the back seat and threw it in the front, leaving the back seat door open. "Don't puke in my car." It was a rental, but he still had to drive it for another day, and he didn't want that smell in there.

It took entirely too long to get both of their drunk asses in the vehicle. He didn't even bother to wait for them to buckle up before he started moving.

They weren't that far from Curtis's apartment, but even so, with the man's young wife still complaining and starting to feel sick in the back seat, it was entirely too far. He was about ready to throw them both out on the curb when he pulled up. "Are you going to need help getting in the door?" The fact that he asked the question through clenched teeth belied the helpful words.

"Nah, I think we got it." Curtis might have been about to take him up on the offer, but at the last moment, the danger of the situation got through the alcohol fog in his brain.

"Get some sleep, keep your phone on, and I would strongly suggest that you not go out drinking for a while." Wade had turned partway around but made no move to get out of the car.

"We gotta job?" Curtis's wife was now half unconscious, her head lolling on his shoulder, and he was having some difficulty getting out and bringing her with him.

"Possibly. Brannigan, Santelli, Flanagan, and Burgess are going ahead to check it out. The rest of us are on standby." He realized then that some of his foul temper was probably because he was on standby. He didn't like just sitting and twiddling his thumbs.

"Okay." Curtis got out the door and half-carried his wife out with him. "I'll be standing by."

Wade stuck his arm through the open driver's side door window and pushed the rear door shut as soon as Curtis and his wife were clear. "I'll fill you in tomorrow." He glanced at his watch. "Fuck. Today. Later."

He was too pissed to watch as Curtis and his wife staggered toward their door.

CHAPTER 5

"Where was that note?" Vincent Bianco swiveled around in his desk chair and started rifling through the papers stacked on the small folding card table that was now acting as a second desk. "No. No. No. Dammit!" He looked at the box of more loose notebook paper on the floor. "Hell. I was *sure* I put that somewhere safe."

He sighed as he heaved the box up onto the desk and started going through the random collection of notes. "'Somewhere safe.' Should have known better. *Especially* after all this time."

He had to admit, though, that he was having a lot more fun right now than he had since he and Tom Glenn had launched their epic RPG *The Legend of Morval*. He wasn't answering interminable—and often indecipherable—emails to support the game. In fact, he hadn't even checked his email more than once a day for the last two weeks. Instead, he was up to his elbows in doing what he actually loved about the business: building a new game.

Technically, it wasn't a new game, but an expansion to the original *Legend*, but that didn't really matter. He was getting back into the lore, expanding the backstory and designing entire new lands, peoples, and characters. There wasn't a whole lot of new gameplay mechanics, and those had all pretty much been nailed down already, anyway. The meat and potatoes of the work was pure imagination, and Vinnie Bianco loved it.

He stopped and started reading the scribbled note in his hand, his mind starting to head down a new fork in the road. It wasn't the note he'd been looking for, but it had just sparked a new idea. He grinned as he turned back to the notebook that he'd been working in. This was *better* than what he'd been looking for.

The phone's ringtone startled him. He'd been working in silence, since the playlist he'd been using had run out about an hour before, but he'd been too absorbed in the storytelling to restart it. The sudden noise made him jump.

It took a few panicked seconds to find the damn thing. It was buried under another stack of papers, sourcebooks, comics, and fantasy novels that he was drawing on for inspiration. He almost dropped it as he flipped it over to see who was calling.

Please don't let this be a business thing. He'd really been able to relax without worrying so much about the support side of running a game company. Glenn was better at that than he was, anyway. But every once in a while, something came up that he *had* to pay attention to.

It wasn't Glenn, though. It wasn't even the normal cell call. It was a call coming through the encrypted app he'd installed on all the Blackhearts' phones.

He hastily answered it. "Yeah."

"Vinnie, it's Joe." Flanagan's voice was a welcome one, despite how much he was enjoying the worldbuilding work.

"We got a job?" He was a little torn. He was really getting on a roll with some of the lore of the new kingdom he'd dreamed up, off to the west of the existing map they'd built for the game, but all the same, there was a part of him that always felt a little guilty about the possibility of making a living as a professional nerd. He knew he wasn't the only geek in the team. Wade was an enormous comic book nerd, and knew more about GI Joe than Bianco did, which was saying something. But sometimes a man needs to do man shit, just to ensure he still has a pair.

"We *might* have a job. The Colonel wanted the calls to go out so that everybody's at least ready to roll if it comes to it. Four of us are heading out to do some advance work, but if it comes, it's going to come fast."

Bianco sighed. He wasn't sure if that was a reprieve or a problem. He'd have more time to work on the expansion, but at the same time, if there were Blackhearts heading out into harm's way, he was going to be wondering about them the entire time.

He also felt a little put out that he was on standby. He knew it wasn't a logical or reasoned reaction, but he couldn't help it. Sure, *somebody* had to stay back if they were going to send a small team ahead to scope things out, but why did it have to be him?

He was also well aware, even without Flanagan saying as much, that he wasn't the only one staying behind. That didn't actually help all that much.

"So, what do we do until we hear?" It was kind of a dumb question, but he was a little fried. He glanced at the clock as he asked and realized just how late it was getting.

"Just keep doing what you're doing but be ready to drop it and fly to Prague any time in the next two weeks," Flanagan replied. "Sorry, Vinnie, I know you're swamped, but the working vacation's going to have to wait just a bit."

Bianco laughed. "I'm actually having a pretty good time right now. This is the creative side of the business. The *fun* side. Still, wish I was going with you."

"Not yet, you don't. Have a good one, Vinnie. We'll be in touch."

***

Mario Gomez sat in his father's old rocking chair on the porch and looked out at the desert. The screen door slammed as his cousin Julio came out to join him, handing him a cigar before sitting down on the bench with a faint groan and lighting his own.

39

Julio was a good ten years older than Mario, and he looked it. Going to fat, he had a jowly face only partially offset by a huge mustache that Mario had jokingly compared to Saddam Hussein's.

Ordinarily, Mario Gomez was a pretty stoic sort of man, sparing of words or displayed emotion. His teammates with Brannigan's Blackhearts could attest to that, having seen little display of passion even after his mother, father, and teenage brother had been murdered and his sister kidnapped. Only among his close family—and while he considered the Blackhearts close, they weren't *that* close, not even Joe Flanagan—did he ever really let loose.

He accepted the cigar cutter from Julio, snipped the end, and lit the cigar, rotating it slowly to get the ember going well. Then he sucked in a good mouthful of smoke, held it for a moment, and blew it out toward the desert.

While he might let himself relax a bit around the family, especially Julio—the older man had been around the block, and in some of the same places Mario had worked—there were some things he didn't ever show. He didn't sigh as he stared out at the purple hills in the last dying light of day.

He didn't have to. "What is it, *mijo*?" Julio pulled on his own cigar, making the ember glow brightly.

"What is what?"

Julio snorted. "Don't bullshit me. Something's eating you. You don't usually just come out here and stare at the sunset."

Mario grimaced a little. Julio had known him since he'd been a savage little kid. There was no hiding things from him, any more than there had been from his sister, Mario's mother.

"Nothing. Just bored." He waved his cigar at the darkening desert. "Even the four-legged coyotes aren't coming close enough to hunt anymore."

Julio laughed. "You taught them the same lesson you taught the two-legged ones." He drew in another puff of fragrant smoke. "Maybe you did your job a little too well for your own good, eh, *mijo*?"

Mario just took another puff and glowered at the hills.

Julio reached out and put a heavy, calloused hand on his shoulder. "If I were your father, I'd say that there's plenty to do here on the ranch to keep you occupied. But I'm not your father. I've been a lot of the same places you have. Hell, I've been out there hunting those *pendejos* right there with you."

Mario nodded. He had, indeed. Julio's heavy build didn't slow him down that much when there were threats to the family to be dealt with.

"So, I get it. But consider this. You're not always going to get to do that kinetic sort of stuff. The day's going to come when your body just isn't up to it anymore. What are you going to do then?"

Mario frowned. It wasn't a question he really wanted to think about. Not yet. The specter of what had happened to Sam Childers was always there in the back of his mind. Sam was now under constant care by dedicated nurses because he wasn't just a paraplegic, but he had also received brain damage under a savage beating from a Humanity Front operative. He still wanted to help, but he just couldn't, not on the level that he needed to.

The phone buzzed before he had a response to his cousin. Digging the phone out of his pocket, he saw the number on the encrypted comm app and grinned. "Well, fortunately, it's not something I have to think about tonight."

***

Bob Puller got into his car and just sat for a moment, running a hand over his face.

Damn, I need a drink.

He banished the thought immediately. *None of that. You already know where that's gotten you. Last thing you need right now is to crawl back into that bottle.*

Could be worse, though. Could be heroin.

His own attempt at flippancy only made him feel more disgusted with himself. The truth was, he was struggling. Doing volunteer work seemed to be the only way back from that ambulance job he'd quit in a rage, and it wasn't an easy row to hoe, he was finding out. Word of his clash with the ambulance company had gotten around, and so he either had to swallow his pride and work his way back up, earning trust all over again—no matter whether or not he felt like it should be necessary—or else move somewhere no one knew him.

Or just find another line of work altogether. He wasn't entirely sure he could do that.

There was one possibility. He just wasn't sure if Brannigan's Blackhearts were ever going to call him in again.

He didn't think he'd done a bad job. He'd stayed sober. He'd done what he could. That trip out and the subsequent assault on the island mansion had been a bit of an eye-opener, though. He hadn't done as well as he'd thought he would. He'd always felt like he was Slack Man Number Two, always trying to catch up.

Still, he hoped to get that call again. It had been the best job he'd had since he'd left the Navy.

Almost as if in answer to a prayer, his phone started to play *Fortunate Son*.

He stared at it for a second. All sorts of questions played through his head. Was he sober enough? Fit enough? Would they really take him out again. Finally, as if in a dream, he reached out and picked up the phone. "This is Bob Puller."

"Doc, it's Joe." He'd seen that it was Flanagan's number, but he didn't dare say that, for fear that he was going to say something wrong.

"What's up, Joe?" He almost winced at his own choice of words.

"We've got a possible job. Still a little up in the air, so most of the team is going on standby. Can you be ready to fly to Prague sometime in the next two weeks?"

Brother, I can fly to Prague today if you need me. That was actually a little out of the question, given the time, but the sentiment was there. "Sure. Anything I need to know?"

"Just that it might be some urban protection, possibly even some assault and extraction," Flanagan said. "We won't know for a few days."

"I'll be ready." He was proud that there was no quaver in his voice.

"Good. We'll be in touch."

Flanagan hung up, and Doc Puller punched the air. He was still in.

***

Brannigan looked down at the phone and thought for a moment. This would be the last call, but it was hardly cut and dried. This last contact wasn't technically a Blackheart.

Still, he'd offered to help if the Humanity Front was involved, and they were down a man. Hank was working an executive protection gig back east and couldn't break away. It was worth calling him.

The phone rang for a while, then a faintly sleepy voice answered. "Hello?"

"Dan Tackett? It's John Brannigan."

There was a pause. He couldn't tell if it was simply because Tackett was waking up, or because he was debating whether or not to hang up. "What can I do for you, Colonel?" Tackett sounded considerably more alert.

"Not a lot at the moment, Dan, but we might have a line on our mutual adversaries." Even without being able to see the man he was talking to, he could sense that Tackett was paying a lot more attention.

Dan Tackett had been introduced to the Blackhearts a short time before, just before the mission in Kyrgyzstan. When the PMC magnate Mitchell Price and his picked team of problem solvers had been rolled up by the Front near a research base in the Tian Shan mountains, one of Price's men, an operator they'd worked with in Chad named Vernon White, had contacted Tackett and asked him to call the Blackhearts.

Tackett had a history with White, going back to an ill-fated mission in the South Pacific years before. He'd insisted on

43

coming along and had proved himself a solid professional soldier. And after seeing what the Humanity Front had done to his friends—using them as guinea pigs in a mind control experiment—he'd told Brannigan that if they had a line on the Front, he wanted in.

"Where?" That was all Tackett asked. He was still committed to that vendetta, at least.

"We don't know for sure that it's them yet," Brannigan told him. "I'm heading out for some advance recon tomorrow. Most of the team will be on standby until we find out more. I wanted to touch base with you and make sure you were up for it if it *does* turn out to be them." Tackett wasn't on the encrypted comms channel Bianco had set up, so he still needed to be somewhat vague.

"I'm in if it's them." Tackett's reply was firm. "I'm still not looking to get back in the business full-time, but if it's that bunch, call me and I'll come running."

"Good to know. We'll be in touch." Brannigan cut the connection. There was still a lot to do before he got on a plane in the morning.

CHAPTER 6

Brannigan didn't recognize the young man waiting for them beside the Mercedes GLS, but that was somewhat to be expected. They had no real idea of just how large Dalca's network was, and if she was as canny as he suspected, then this guy might not even really be a part of her immediate organization. He wouldn't put it past her to contract out a lot of roles like this.

Although, under these circumstances, that might not be the best choice, either.

The young man was wearing a gray flat cap with a square of red and blue plaid on it. That was what Brannigan had been warned to look for. For his part, Brannigan was wearing a black leather jacket with a red handkerchief in the right-hand pocket. They weren't terribly subtle bona fides, but they worked for rapid identification and didn't stand out *that* much.

They still probably stood out somewhat less than four men, two with beards, one with a graying handlebar mustache, all of whom were in noticeably better shape than most of the travelers around them. Most people seemed to be ignoring them, wrapped up in their devices or simply their own personal thoughts, but anyone who was really paying attention might just pick them out as something beyond the usual, everyday travelers in the Czech Republic.

He walked up to the young man, who didn't stir from where he was leaning against the SUV. "Kristof?"

With a nod, Kristof finally straightened. He was a slender, fit man, his blond hair closely cropped and a faint stubble on his jaw. "You would be John?"

Brannigan nodded as they shook hands. Kristof had a firm handshake, and from the way he carried himself, Brannigan suspected he was former military of some sort. That made sense; he doubted that Dalca would draw her elite protective details from street thugs. It didn't seem to be her style.

Kristof glanced past him and frowned slightly. "Only four?"

Brannigan met his eyes calmly. "These things don't get put together overnight." Not *strictly* true, but not strictly a lie, either. "The others are getting things together and will be along later." If *this turns out to be legit*.

Kristof didn't seem to particularly like that, but as far as Brannigan was concerned, that wasn't his business. It did tell him something about Kristof. If this guy was a contractor, he was a committed one.

He was a professional, though, and with a faint shrug, he turned back to the vehicle. "Come along, then. It can't be helped." He walked around the front of the GLS and got in the driver's side, while Brannigan got in front and the other three squeezed into the back. The Mercedes SUV wasn't tiny, but then, neither were the Blackhearts. It was still a bit of a tight fit.

"There are weapons in the bag there on the floor." Kristof pointed at Brannigan's feet as he started the vehicle and put it in gear. Brannigan had to admit that while he wasn't a huge fan of smaller SUVs, the purr of the Mercedes engine was pretty nice, and the interior was plush and spotless. "I would strongly suggest keeping them out of sight, especially if we have to deal with Czech police."

Brannigan considered telling the younger man not to try to tell old hands how to do their jobs, but he refrained. The small pack held five FN FNX pistols in 9mm, each with three 17-round magazines. The mags were all loaded. Low profile, inside-the-waistband holsters and mag carriers were tucked into the small, densely packed bag around them.

Keeping the weapons low, out of line of sight of the windows, Brannigan passed three of them back to the other Blackhearts before loading a fourth and tucking it into his waistband under the jacket.

Straightening, he watched the road as Kristof pulled out of the parking lot and headed out through the green countryside that sprawled around the Prague airport. "Where are we going?"

"We have a safehouse in the country, to the south of the city." Kristof didn't take his eyes off the road as he spoke, and he kept checking the mirrors and scanning every road they passed as they turned away from the city skyline and headed into the farmland and forest to the south. "I would have preferred an isolated farm, but there were none to be found close enough, certainly none for sale."

Brannigan glanced over his shoulder to catch Santelli's sardonic look. Neither said what they were thinking—that if Dalca had *really* wanted one, she probably could have strongarmed a farmer into letting her at least use the farm.

That might not have worked out well from the perspective of keeping a low profile, though. And Dalca was strange. She was a queen of the global underworld, but she at least affected to have certain standards and moral limits she wouldn't cross. Brannigan still wasn't sure exactly what those limits were, or how set in stone they were, but they were there.

They passed most of the rest of the drive in silence. The Blackhearts watched their surroundings and Kristof with equal interest.

For his part, Kristof kept his cool and drove like a pro. He wasn't overly slow or cautious, and he wasn't driving like a maniac. He was the penultimate gray man on the road, driving the speed of traffic and passing where it made sense but refraining from weaving in and out of traffic.

If they were being followed, it might not work out well, but if he'd run a surveillance detection route on the way to the airport, and was confident enough that he was clean, then it lessened the chance that they might attract attention and pick up a tail.

Finally, after about half an hour, they pulled into a small village nestled between tree-lined hills. The Blackhearts looked around carefully, hands close to their concealed pistols.

Most of the houses were brick, though there were a couple that might have been stone. Most were covered in whitewashed stucco, and several had red tile roofs. Nothing in that place appeared new; there was a fair bit of dinginess to the stucco and some of the brick was crumbling at the corners. Several of the small yards were partially overgrown, and as they came to the house at the end of the road, they saw several piles of junk and scrap against the leaning fence and inside the small, fenced courtyard at the front of the house.

"This is the most redneck looking place I think I've ever seen in Europe," Santelli muttered.

Burgess chuckled, while Kristof kept his expression carefully neutral. "You haven't been some of the places over here that I have."

The house was dark and silent as Kristof pulled up in front of the station wagon parked out front and shut off the engine. "We are here."

Brannigan kept an eye on him as he opened the door and got out. If this was an ambush, then Kristof would have to be a pretty ice-cold not to react in some way, like dashing for cover. While he was still alert and scanning their surroundings, though, he didn't seem to be ready to bolt, which was a good sign.

The Blackhearts got out of the SUV, spreading out while trying to look like they were just visitors there to see a friend. Kristof might have given them a little bit of a sideways look, but he went through the gate into the courtyard, walked up to the door, and knocked.

48

It took a moment before the door opened. Brannigan had seen a curtain move in the second-story window, however. They were being watched. He glanced over his shoulder, but the other houses in the little ville were still and quiet.

Kristof spoke quickly and quietly to the man at the door, then beckoned to them and disappeared inside.

Flanagan was right on his heels. The black-bearded man wasn't inclined to let their guide out of their sight for long, not until they had a better feel for the situation. Brannigan followed, with Burgess and Santelli somewhat discreetly keeping an eye on the rest of the place before collapsing on the door.

The interior was dark, but a lot neater than the outside. They found themselves in an entryway leading onto an open first floor, with a living room connected to an open kitchen, and stairs at the back leading up to the second floor.

Erika Dalca was standing in the living room, waiting for them.

She swept forward, her poise unchanged despite the setting and the circumstances, and held out her hands to Brannigan. "John. You came." She sounded genuinely relieved, even though a couple more military-aged men with the sort of edge to them that suggested they were a bit more than just hired muscle watched from the back of the room warily.

"I said I would." He kept his voice cool, though if he'd hoped that it would disarm her a little, he should have known better.

"You did." She was so apologetic that he almost believed it was genuine. "I'm sorry. I didn't mean to doubt you. It's just been a difficult time." She took him by the arm and ushered him toward the living room, once again getting a little bit too close for comfort. Yet he couldn't *quite* bring himself to try to extricate himself, especially while her shooters were watching.

"Please, sit down." She looked up toward the stairs. "Annette? Can you get some refreshments for our guests?"

A young woman came down the stairs, drawing most eyes to her. She wasn't exactly dressed to the nines; she was ready for action, and the pistol on her hip—worn openly as opposed to the rest of the muscle in the room—fit with her plain outdoor trousers and shirt. She was still quite attractive, though, and her black hair fell in waves to her shoulders. She smiled at them as she went to the kitchen and began to make tea.

Brannigan didn't doubt that her looks had been part of the criteria to get her hired. She was a hell of a distraction, but he also noticed that the rest of Dalca's shooters weren't watching her but were watching the Blackhearts, as well as the doors and windows.

The rest of the American mercenaries didn't spare her much more than a glance, too, which he found somewhat amusing. He was a widower, Santelli and Flanagan were both married, and Burgess was an old enough hand that he wasn't going to get caught up in such an obvious ploy. If Dalca's intention had been to throw them off guard, she'd failed.

If she was frustrated about it, she didn't show it. She just sat down on the couch and drew Brannigan down next to her. He found that a little irritating, but it was probably best to play her little games for the moment. He nodded to the other three, and they found seats of their own, from which they could cover all the entrances and Dalca's people at the same time.

"So, what exactly is going on?" He leaned back, simultaneously giving himself just a little distance from her nearness—despite himself, he had to admit that she was intoxicating when she turned on the charm—and a better angle to draw his pistol from the appendix carry position.

She smiled. "So, that's why you came with only three of the others? To feel the situation out before you committed?"

"Can you blame me?" he asked bluntly. "You didn't exactly give me a lot to go on, and knowing the nature of your *real* occupation, can I really afford to be blindly trusting?"

She sighed and patted his arm. Her familiarity was really starting to get on his nerves. "Of course not. Someday, I hope that we can take our relationship to the point where we do really trust each other." The subtext was about as subtle as usual, and he almost rolled his eyes.

As for her people, they maintained their poker faces for the most part, though the dark-haired, scarred up dude who had sat down in the love seat after Dalca had brought them to sit on the couch looked somewhat amused. The look he gave Brannigan said *you're doomed, buddy.*

She was suddenly more businesslike, though. He'd seen that light-switch transition before, but it never quite got any less jarring. It was a useful reminder of just how dangerous she really was.

"This all started about a month ago. I have a robust network here in Prague. It dates back to my father, though I made some changes once I took over." She'd talked about that before, though always in vague enough terms that Brannigan was never entirely sure just *how* far she'd really changed anything. She still dealt in illegal traffic. The question was just *how* illegal.

"Artyom Garin has had his own network here for almost as long. Some of my people assure me that it goes back to the Soviet days, when this was Czechoslovakia, but Garin wasn't a part of it then. He was KGB right at the end, and somehow went from a low-ranking drone in the Lubyanka to a rising *vor* in the Russian Mafiya by the end of the nineties."

She leaned back in the couch, which coincidentally put her closer to him, and looked up at the ceiling in thought. "There wasn't a lot of overlap between our operations. We had done some business in the informational realm, but we had always refused to work in some of the seedier sides of the business that Garin has always made the backbone of his own organization." Brannigan read that as meaning drugs and human trafficking. "The truce might have been uneasy from time to time, but it had held for years.

"That all changed about three and a half weeks ago. Garin's people confronted Kristof here and demanded that he provide them information on counter-narcotics operations in and

51

around Prague." She nodded to Kristof, who had taken up a position just inside the front door where he could see out the window. "Needless to say, that went against our principles."

Brannigan managed not to snort at the idea of Dalca's "principles."

She noticed his reaction, though, as hard as he'd tried to stay impassive. Either that, or she felt some defensiveness about it. "We don't do drug trafficking, and we won't facilitate other people's, either."

He nodded. She'd made that claim before, as well. He really wasn't sure just how she maintained such a massive underground empire *without* dealing drugs, but that was probably best left for another conversation.

"They didn't take the refusal well, at any rate. There were three attacks on my people in as many days. Then the real pressure started. Calls to the police. Mysterious 'accidents' that destroyed several of our safehouses. Harassment on the street. It quickly became evident that Garin was trying to push us out of Prague.

"We pushed back. No violence, but I gave Tomas permission to turn the Czech police against Garin's operation. It didn't work, though. Things got even more tense after that.

"Then Garin asked for a meeting. I'm a businesswoman. If we could settle this and get back to business without further disruption, or even bloodshed, I had to take that chance."

She got quiet for a moment, and when Brannigan looked over at her, he saw a woman who was genuinely shaken. This was no act. She might be a ruthless, efficient shadow facilitator, but whatever had happened, it had struck her to her core.

"The meeting was an ambush. Garin wasn't there, and the men he sent had orders to kill me."

"You're sure?" He'd seen things go sideways before, but the idea that someone would try to assassinate Dalca outright seemed a little off. Kidnapping, maybe.

"They had plastic over the floor in the house where the meet was supposed to happen, and they pulled guns as soon as we arrived." She eyed him as if daring him to question her again. "What would that tell *you* about their intentions?"

He spared Santelli a glance. His old Sergeant Major was frowning, his eyes narrowed, thinking it through. Something was *definitely* off, and if Dalca was telling the truth—which he thought she was—then this Garin must have either lost his mind, or he had something really bad in the works.

"Any idea why the sudden change in atmospherics?" She was too much of an information broker to be completely in the dark.

The scarred up guy with the cauliflower ears snorted. "I should say so."

"Tomas." Dalca's voice was almost placating. She turned back to Brannigan, though this time she shifted so she was facing him and the others. "What do you know about a drug called Roulette?"

"Nothing." A look at the other three got shrugs and shaking heads.

She nodded. "It's relatively new. It probably hasn't reached the States yet. No one seems to know the formula, but the reason it's called Roulette is because seventy-five percent of the time, you get the high of your life. The other twenty-five percent, it's a death sentence." She reached for a drink on the coffee table and took a sip. "That's not a one-time thing, either. The high is, apparently, extremely addictive, and so that seventy-five/twenty-five chance repeats with every new dose."

"To make matters worse," the man she'd called Tomas said, with a fairly thick Italian accent, "we are still learning about the aftereffects aside from the addiction. It seems to make the addicts somewhat passive and controllable."

A dour glance went around the group of Blackhearts. "That sure sounds like the Front, all right."

"It's possible," Dalca allowed. "I am still not sure, though. It might simply be the Mafiya. Or the Chinese."

Brannigan nodded slowly. The Chinese had advocated for "drug warfare" since the nineties, and they hadn't meant the

53

so-called "War on Drugs," either. Something about this, though, didn't feel like them.

"So, what do you hope that we can do?" It was time to get down to brass tacks. He looked around the room. "You seem to have enough muscle that my handful of shooters wouldn't make that much difference."

She actually laughed. It was a genuine sort of sound, as if he'd surprised her. "Don't sell yourselves so short, John." She sobered. "I know a few of the things you've accomplished, and the truth is that Garin probably knows most of my people. He doesn't know you." She looked up as Kristof stood, looking more intently out the window. "Kristof and Tomas have kept us a step ahead of them so far, but they are hunting me, and we cannot even get out of the country." She looked haunted for a second. "We've tried. Two of my men were killed."

"And we've been in one place too long." Kristof reached into the chest beneath the bench at the entryway, pulling out a MP-9 submachinegun. "They've found us again."

CHAPTER 7

Everyone in the room was on their feet in a moment. Flanagan and Burgess had their FNX-9s in their hands almost as if by magic, as both men got up and moved to join Kristof. "Got a van full of nasty-looking customers unloading in front of the courtyard just down the street, carrying a mix of pistols and subguns," Flanagan reported. "We've got about fifteen seconds."

"Is there a way out the back?" Brannigan put aside every suspicion, every irritation. Whatever Dalca's game was, they were now in the middle of it. He seriously doubted those were Czech police getting out of that van. Flanagan would have noticed something if they were.

"This way." Tomas was already pulling the back door open. "Hurry. We don't want a firefight in here if we can avoid it."

Brannigan wasn't sure they *could* avoid a fight, not if the Russians—presuming that was who their visitors were—had come loaded for bear. But with only pistols, he wasn't that eager for it, either. He handed Dalca off to Tomas and moved to the door, Santelli joining him as Flanagan and Burgess covered the front with Kristof and another of Dalca's contractors.

They paused at the doorway for just long enough to trade a nod, then they were going out fast. Brannigan took what he already had, pushing out through the door and covering the corner he'd already been facing, while Santelli was right behind him, bumping him slightly as he dashed through to cover his CO's back.

He found himself in a yard littered with junk, making the piles of detritus around the front look small. There was a narrow path leading up into the trees on the relatively steep slope behind the house.

There also didn't appear to be any way for the bad guys to get around the side of the house and into that yard full of crap easily. Brannigan took a step to one side, ducked around a pile of tires, and confirmed that the corner was as choked with junk as the rest of the yard, then turned toward that path leading up and out.

Tomas was already way ahead of him, another MP-9 in his fist, leading Dalca and Annette up the hill. Brannigan and Santelli fell in behind the women, though they stopped at the tree line, taking up covering positions where they could see the back of the house and the flanks. It looked to Brannigan like there *was* a way around on the left flank, through a neighboring yard, and Santelli was covering the other side, where there was nothing stopping their adversaries except the gully that ran through the middle of the tiny village and some more trees.

A crash of gunfire echoed from the front of the house, then he heard Flanagan bellow, "Friendlies coming out!"

Kristof came out first. Brannigan's eyes narrowed as he saw Dalca's facilitator dart out and head up the hill after his boss, hardly glancing back at Flanagan and Burgess as they came out behind him, both men pausing at the door to pivot and cover down on the inside. Flanagan fired twice, the bark of the 9mm sounding awfully loud in the narrow confines of the junk-riddled yard, then Burgess was moving, running to one of the bigger piles of scrap before turning and covering the back of the house.

"Turn and go!" Flanagan twisted his head to note where Burgess was and started to turn, but then dropped to a knee, leaned into the doorway for a moment, and fired three more times. Burgess opened up on the doorway, shooting over

Flanagan's head, and the younger man threw himself sideways, almost falling into another pile of random junk covered by a blue tarp before he scrambled away on his knees and one hand, his pistol held up, getting around behind the pile before turning and pointing the weapon back at the door.

Burgess's shots had probably passed within a foot of Flanagan's head, but Burgess was a hell of a good shot.

"Both of you move!" Brannigan had his own pistol leveled at the doorway, wishing for a moment that Kristof had included red dot sights with the handguns. He'd only recently begun to come around to the things, but he also wasn't getting any younger, and his eyes had an easier time with the reflex sights than the irons, especially in the play of shadow under the trees.

Flanagan looked up, then ducked and ran, forging up the hillside right behind Burgess, who had turned his head just long enough to identify where Brannigan was before he'd rolled out of his meager cover and run for the trees. A moment later, a storm of automatic fire tore through the window and the doorway, shattering glass, splintering wood, chipping stucco, and blasting bits of debris off the junk where the bullets hit. Brannigan heard a nasty whine as a 9mm bullet ricocheted off something down there and whizzed past his head.

He dumped his mag through the door. Even without targets, with Flanagan and Burgess moving and in the open, they needed some suppressive fire. The long burst stopped abruptly as his bullets smashed through the door and the shattered window, and he might have heard a shouted curse in Russian.

Flanagan and Burgess passed him, following Kristof and the rest of Dalca's people into the woods. Brannigan reloaded but held his fire since he didn't have a target and got ready to move.

Fortunately, he hadn't gotten too sucked into the target zone in the doorway. He had resumed his scan of their surroundings as he'd reloaded and spotted one of the bad guys as he'd jumped the brick fence in the back yard behind the neighboring house, then ducked behind a tree. While a part of him wanted to hold his fire until he had a target, the reality of their situation meant that getting lead downrange was more important. He blasted chunks of bark and splinters off the tree, then turned and ran as Flanagan took up the fire from above him.

Just before he got moving, though, a figure loomed in the open doorway. He was off target and out of position, but Santelli wasn't.

The stout, balding man put three rounds into the Russian's chest. Red puckered holes burst through his track suit jacket, and he fell on his face. Then Brannigan was running as Burgess started shooting at the house from above and off to the east.

Brannigan couldn't help but noticed that Dalca and her people had all disappeared.

He got higher on the hill, his heart pounding and his breath coming hard, glad that he hadn't given up on long hikes and even runs in the mountains. It was getting ever harder to stay in fighting shape as he got older, but it was worth it for times like this.

It took seconds to reach the top of the hill, which was also where the trees stopped.

The scarred man Dalca had called Tomas had halted there and was crouched behind a tree with his MP-9 braced against the trunk. So, they hadn't just run, though he could see Kristof and a couple other shooters halfway across the field between them and the next line of trees, ushering Dalca and Annette toward the woods as fast as they could move. Despite Dalca's always-fashionable clothes, she had been wearing shoes that she could move fast in, which was smart.

Tomas hadn't yet opened fire on the Russians, but as Brannigan swung behind a tree not far from him, he realized that the Blackhearts had been between the man and the bad guys.

That might be the reason he'd held his fire. The other reason might be that this was a setup, an act.

It didn't seem like Dalca's style, though. She could be ruthless but hiring men to get gunned down with real bullets, in a staged firefight, seemed a step too far even for her.

Dismissing the thought until later, when he could think it over in some semblance of safety, Brannigan looked for targets. *Then* Tomas opened fire, while Flanagan, Burgess, and Santelli ran past, Santelli sucking wind hard. Brannigan was sure the older man was still staying in shape, but he didn't have the advantage of altitude that Brannigan did.

Dalca's security man stitched bullets across the three men who were running up into the trees from the house. He controlled the submachinegun well, leaning into it and compensating for the recoil so that the line of bullets rose from the first man's hip to the third man's shoulder, tearing through fabric and flesh alike, sending all three tumbling to the litter-choked ground with screams of agony as their blood stained their shirts and jackets.

The man that Brannigan had shot at behind the tree had vanished, and he had no targets. "Move."

Tomas didn't hesitate. If he wasn't military, he had enough experience not to argue when Brannigan used that tone of voice. He turned and sprinted across the field toward where the rest had paused inside the trees on the other side.

Brannigan stayed where he was for the moment. So did Flanagan; the younger man was even less likely to be the first one to push out of harm's way as long as there were still teammates nearby. Brannigan was afraid, just for a second, that he was going to have to yell at the others, but Santelli took in the situation, grabbed Burgess, and booked it for the field, his short legs pumping and his chest heaving as he ran.

The field itself was less than a hundred yards wide, so Brannigan and Flanagan stayed put until he heard Santelli shout from the far side. Then they got up and moved, both men putting their heads down and sprinting hard. They hadn't seen any more of the opposition coming at them, but that didn't mean either one wanted to be out in the open any longer than absolutely necessary.

The entire way across that open ground, Brannigan expected to hear a shot go past his head, or worse, feel it slam into his back. Yet they reached the trees without getting shot at or, apparently, even pursued.

Dalca was huddled by a tree, surrounded by Kristof and two of her other security men, but she wasn't going fetal position and freaking out. She cut the connection on her cell phone at the same moment the Blackhearts caught up.

"We should move." She was calm and unruffled, as if getting blown out of a safehouse was something she did every day. "There's a vehicle coming to pick us up, but we'll have to meet them on the other side of the hill."

"Where?" Tomas was already starting to move, trudging up the hill behind them. Just judging by the way he moved, compared to either Gomez or Flanagan, Brannigan guessed that he wasn't all that used to the woods.

"At the end of the road, where the fields meet the trees, to the southeast." Dalca was propelling Annette, who looked a lot more shaken by this than her boss did, into the trees by an arm. "That's where Bohdan said he'd meet us."

Tomas had slowed, looking around with poorly disguised confusion. He clearly hadn't seen exactly where they were, so he wasn't entirely sure where the road was.

"Joe, take point." It wasn't just the Russians behind them that Brannigan was concerned about, but also the Czech police. The Czech Republic was a lot more open to private firearms than most European countries—they'd recently amended their Firearms Act to enshrine the right to defend life and property with firearms—but they still required licensing, which the Blackhearts didn't have.

Flanagan headed up past Tomas, clapping the shorter man on the shoulder as he went, his pistol held ready. If anyone in the group could find the quickest and stealthiest way through the woods and to the rendezvous point, it would be Joe Flanagan.

Tomas looked a little nonplused. Maybe a little pissed at being shown up. But if they could have handled this all by themselves, Dalca wouldn't have called in Brannigan's professional soldiers.

Fortunately, none of Dalca's security men decided to make an issue out of having their man card pulled. Maybe they were thinking of the fact that they'd run with Dalca while Brannigan and the others had covered them.

He hoped so. The last thing they needed was to get crossways with Dalca's organization, *especially* now that shots had been fired and there were dead men on the ground. Getting out of the Czech Republic under those circumstances would be a nightmare.

Flanagan made straight for the top of the hill, weaving through the trees and barely making a sound in the undergrowth and the carpet of leaves and needles beneath the canopy. The others following behind weren't nearly as good, and they made a fair bit of racket, but quiet had descended on the valley again as the echoes of the gunshots faded.

Pausing at the top of the hill, Flanagan took stock. With a glance behind them, Brannigan wondered just how his pointman could see through all the trees, but he'd learned to have faith in Flanagan's abilities.

A moment later, they were moving again, shading off to the left, presumably farther to the east.

It didn't take long to reach the road. The narrow, two-lane hardtop flared out into a bit of a triangle with trees on the north and south corners. Slipping his pistol into his waistband, under his shirt, Flanagan stepped to the edge of the trees, then turned and looked over his shoulder. "Tomas, you're up."

They were right on time, apparently. Brannigan had no idea whether or not Dalca had already coordinated with this Bohdan to be in the vicinity while they were holed up in that safehouse, but even if she hadn't, he'd been close enough. A white, windowless panel van pulled into the triangle, took a hard turn to present its sliding side door to the trees and the men and women under them, and then a stocky, blond man with a small strip of a goatee stuck his head out the passenger side window and yelled in Czech.

There was a moment where everyone just sort of paused, and Brannigan wondered if they hadn't just met the wrong people. He didn't speak Czech, and he was pretty sure none of the rest of his boys did, either. Burgess might know a little, but from what he knew of the old SEAL, most of his time in Eastern Europe had been down in the Balkans, not in the Czech Republic or Slovakia.

Dalca, however, stepped forward and responded with a short, curt answer in the same language, and then they were ushering her and Annette into the van.

A lot of the vans that Brannigan had ridden in on operations like this had been stripped, the back little more than a hollow shell where shooters essentially piled in on top of each other. This one still had the seats, however, which slowed down the boarding process. Brannigan and Santelli held security at the front and rear of the vehicle while the rest clambered in, then they collapsed and squeezed into the seat right behind the driver and passenger. Brannigan was the last in, pulling the door shut behind him as Dalca barked at the driver in Czech.

Then they were moving. Brannigan didn't have a window or a mirror to look through, but it looked like they'd gotten away cleanly.

For now.

CHAPTER 8

They drove around for a long time. Apparently, Bohdan didn't want to go straight to their destination. Brannigan couldn't say he blamed the man. They were already in a bad spot. However, just driving around with weapons and no licenses for said weapons wasn't what he considered a sound plan.

Dalca didn't seem too concerned, and the Blackhearts held their peace. Neither Santelli nor Flanagan were the type to second-guess their CO, and apparently Burgess wasn't, either. As long as Brannigan didn't bring up the seeming aimlessness of their wandering around the outskirts of Prague, they weren't going to, either.

Dissention in the ranks, real or apparent, would not go over well when they were working with Dalca's underworld crew. You showed weakness around such people at your peril.

Finally, as it got dark, Bohdan seemed to find a new purpose. Checking his watch, he leaned forward, took a closer look at the nearest street sign, then turned sharply left at the next intersection.

They blew past several residential neighborhoods and blocks of high-rise apartment buildings, skirting a large, mostly forested park. Bohdan was obviously working on either detecting or evading surveillance now, ducking into the neighborhoods a couple of times before weaving his way out. Finally, they circled around a large block of multi-story apartment buildings before turning inward on Bratislavskā.

Bohdan slowed down as he cruised past the first two buildings. Brannigan got the distinct impression that he was scanning the buildings and the vehicles parked outside as he went.

He tried to do the same through what he could see of the windshield, but without a baseline of who and what was normal, there was no way to tell if there was a stakeout in place or not. He twisted around in his seat to look at Dalca. "What are we looking for?"

"The next safehouse is in the building we just passed on the left." She was as collected as ever, though she'd certainly had plenty of time to reset after the stress of the firefight while they'd been driving around. "Bohdan is just making sure that we weren't followed."

Brannigan caught Flanagan's look. *Being followed isn't the only threat you need to worry about.*

Finally, though, Bohdan circled back around and parked in the narrow lot to the north, between high-rises. He shut down the van and started to get out, pausing and turning around to address the men and women in the back of the van. "Wait here. I should go check it out." His English was heavily accented, but intelligible, which drew a glare from Santelli. *Why couldn't he have spoken English before now?*

Brannigan didn't react. It was probably just more games. He didn't even think that the language issue was Dalca's doing. Again, it wasn't her style. It was probably Bohdan thinking he was being a Secret Squirrel.

That was another issue with dealing with these sorts of underworld types. They were never anywhere near as high-speed as they *thought* they were.

That could apply to some military and intel people I've known, too, though.

He glanced over the group in the back, though it was too dark to see too much. He caught a faint gleam of light from outside on gunmetal, however. "Let's keep the weapons out of sight." If they really had gotten away from the first safehouse cleanly, then there was no need for the weapons. Even if they hadn't, keeping them concealed might buy them a few extra moments in the dark. Unless the bad guys had night vision, it would be more difficult to identify the group as they got out of the van.

Presuming the bad guys were readily identifiable, themselves.

They waited in tense silence for a few moments, before Bohdan came back, opened the driver's door, and stuck his head inside. "It is clear."

Flanagan and Burgess went first, pushing their way through the sliding door and jumping out. The van rocked as they left it, but while they each turned in opposite directions, like they were clearing a room, they didn't draw their pistols. To a random observer, they were just two guys who'd been impatient to get out. It would have taken a professional to figure out that they were actually clearing the area around the van, hands close to weapons, just in case.

The lot stayed quiet, so they all got out as Bohdan led the way toward the apartment building. Their Czech interlocutor, for his part, seemed to have decided that they were completely out of danger. He was relaxed, not even looking around as he turned and sauntered toward the door.

He probably should have been a lot more alert.

Brannigan felt a jolt of adrenaline as an Audi Q5 SUV suddenly surged out of a parking space in the shadows of one of the high-rises across the street and, without turning on its headlights, suddenly darted across the street, forcing an oncoming sedan to screech to a halt with a loud, constant honk of the horn to avoid a collision, and bounced up onto the sidewalk as a man leaned out one of the side windows and opened fire. Bohdan went down in a heap as muzzle flash flickered in the dimness between buildings.

"Back to the van! Move!" Brannigan already had his FNX-9 in his hand, punching the weapon straight out with his shooting hand as he put an arm out to stop Flanagan. He picked up the faint green glow of the sights and was already taking up the slack on the trigger as they lined up right in front of the windshield.

His weapon barked at almost the same time as Flanagan's. The black-bearded woodsman had seen the oncoming vehicle at the same moment and reached the same threat assessment. He threw himself off the sidewalk, his own 9mm held in a two-handed grip, dumping three rounds into the windshield even as Brannigan hammered half his own mag—one of only one and a half he had left—into the hood and windshield himself.

The glass starred and cracked as the bullets smashed through it, and the SUV suddenly swerved hard and hit the front of the building with a *boom*. Whether the driver was dead or just wounded, he was still stomping down on the gas, and while shattered brick and concrete cascaded down and a window above shattered as the impact bent the frame of the building, the vehicle started to grind its way along the wall as the rear wheels kept spinning.

Tomas was already quickly dragging Dalca and Annette back to the van while the rest of her security detail pulled guns. The passenger side doors flew open as more bullets punched through glass and sheet metal, and three men piled out as fast as they could, dropping to the ground and returning fire.

For a moment, the narrow yard between apartment buildings was a hell of barking pistols and whizzing bullets. Projectiles smacked off concrete and metal, a few ricocheting into the surrounding night with angry whines. A few windows shattered, and someone started screaming somewhere.

The bad guys were spraying and praying, though, having been apparently caught off guard by the sudden storm of gunfire as their ambush went south. The Blackhearts, now that they had clearer targets, were not.

66

Brannigan had shifted his aim as soon as the vehicle had hit the wall and almost thrown the gunman hanging halfway out the window clear. His first shot had been too hasty and had missed, and then the doors had opened. Now, as the first bodies hit the grass, shooting wildly as they scrambled away from the SUV, he put three rounds into the closest, seeing the man in the black leather jacket jerk under the impacts. His fourth bullet punched right through the gangster's skull, which bounced once and went still.

Flanagan had just shot the man behind that one five times in the chest as he tried to get up and run. He stood for half a second, looking down at the bloody holes in his shirt, then staggered back to hit the side of the SUV and slide to the ground, leaving a smear of blood on the light-colored paint.

Santelli had swung wide and finished off the last man with a pair to the chest and a third round to the head.

The gangsters hadn't been alone, though. Two more SUVs, both big, blocky GAZ 2308 Atamans, pulled up to the curb behind the wrecked Audi. The gunmen were smart this time; they left the doors facing the Blackhearts and Dalca's people shut and started to pile out the other side, on the road.

"Get back to the van!" Brannigan was already backing up, his pistol leveled at the enemy vehicles, though he held his fire to conserve ammunition. This mag was almost done as it was. Flanagan was back on his feet, and with a glance over his shoulder, turned and ran for the vehicle.

If it had been anyone else, Brannigan might have thought he'd bolted. Since it was Flanagan, however, he had to have something else in mind.

A moment later, he heard the van's engine fire back up. At the same time, two dim figures ducked around the front of the rear Ataman, clearly armed, and he took two shots at them, forcing them both to duck back behind the vehicle even as his slide locked back on an empty mag.

"*John!*" Dalca all but screamed. "Let's go!"

He turned to see her leaning around Flanagan from the passenger's seat. Santelli was already at the rear of the van, covering his back, while Burgess was right beside him, barricaded on the corner of the building.

"Time to go, Tom." He reloaded as he turned, and the two of them sprinted for the front of the van as Santelli opened fire from the back.

Ducking around to the open side door, Brannigan bellowed at Santelli. "*Get in!*" With one final, parting shot, the stout, retired Sergeant Major rolled to the door and bounded inside, making the whole vehicle shake with the impact.

Burgess hauled the door shut and yelled, "All in!" Dalca was in the front seat, while Tomas, Kristof, and the rest of her detail—minus Bohdan and his buddy, who were now rapidly assuming ambient temperature on the grass in front of the wrecked Audi—were crammed in the back with Annette.

Flanagan already had the van in reverse and hauled it around so fast that he almost tipped it over. Then he slammed it into drive and roared for the end of the parking lot.

On the street, the gangsters piled back into their vehicles and immediately brought them around in pursuit.

CHAPTER 9

Flanagan silently cursed the memory of the fallen Bohdan for picking the van. It was a pig, with a high center of gravity, poor tires, and a considerably less than ideal amount of power. He had the pedal on the floor, and it still felt like it wasn't accelerating for crap.

That was bad, because from the drive in, he was pretty sure he was going to have to go back to Bratislavská. And it was as sure as the sunrise that those two Atamans were going to beat him to it.

"Everybody get low! This is gonna get hairy!" He was starting to build up some speed as he passed the two big, U-shaped apartment buildings on the right, but he was going to have to slow down to make the turn, or else he really *was* going to tip the van over, and then they'd all be dead.

Dalca had shifted herself low in the passenger seat, getting her head almost even with the dash. She knew what she was doing, but Flanagan really wished that there was a Blackheart up there. Even as she pulled a USP out of the bag at her feet, with an RMR red dot sight mounted on it, he still would have preferred any of the other American mercs.

Twisting the wheel to the right, he put the van up on two wheels as he brought them around the corner. He barely missed sideswiping the cars lined up on either side of the road as he put the pedal to the floor again, cursing the van all over again through clenched teeth as it sluggishly started to pick up speed again.

The two GAZ SUVs were already coming toward them, their high beams on and moving fast.

That was the bad guys' miscalculation though, and Flanagan saw it a moment after rounding the turn. "Everybody hang on." If he'd been driving anything else, he would have surged forward at that, but he couldn't even mess with the van's gears enough to increase their acceleration. It felt a little anticlimactic, but he bore down on the two enemy vehicles even as they split to block the road.

Flanagan didn't brake, didn't even slow down. He just bore down on the Ataman to the right as he picked up speed, his own headlights seeming feeble in comparison to the GAZ's headlights.

Dalca got lower in the seat, trying to cram herself behind and under the dash. "Joseph…!"

He hadn't known she knew his first name, but she was observant enough that it was probably a foregone conclusion. She'd probably made a note of it in Argentina.

For a moment, he thought that the driver was going to call his bluff, and he braced for a crash. Despite the weak, piggish engine of the van, he was up to almost forty kilometers per hour—he wasn't going to try to do the math to turn that into a real measurement right at the moment—which meant they were about to hit at close to eighty or ninety.

The bad guys' driver, however, apparently suddenly realized that Flanagan wasn't going to stop. He stomped on the brake, almost losing control of the SUV as he locked the wheels up with a screech, then, when he realized he didn't have anywhere else to go—while the van continued to bear down—he threw the vehicle into reverse and stomped on the gas.

They were bumper to bumper as Flanagan kept going and the enemy driver kept backing up. Flanagan got as low behind the wheel as he could, knowing all too well what was coming next.

The man in the GAZ's passenger seat opened fire a moment later, bullets smashing through both windshields with crashing reports, starring and spiderwebbing the automotive glass. He was aiming too high, though, as the two panes diverted the rounds upward, sending at least one through the roof of the van over Flanagan's head with a *bang*.

Flanagan, as low as he could get while still being able to see, kept steering with one hand while he drew his FNX-9 again with the other and returned fire. He couldn't be as accurate as he might have liked, but he put rounds low into the opposing windshield, hoping they'd deflect upward and into the other man's face.

The incoming fire stopped a second later, just as Dalca opened up.

She wasn't just spraying and praying. Through the corner of his eye, he saw that she'd hitched herself ever so slightly higher in the seat, just so she could engage over the top of the dash with both hands. She wasn't the greatest shot, just judging by the way the gun moved, snapping upward with every slap of the trigger, tracking more holes through the windshield, but it did the trick. The Ataman swerved suddenly as the driver desperately tried to duck beneath the bullets smashing their way through the glass in front of his face and went over the curb at the corner to smash the rear of the SUV into the steps leading up to the doors of yet another apartment building.

Flanagan almost left some paint on the SUV's bumper as he pulled himself a little higher in the driver's seat and squeezed past the vehicle. Glancing in the remaining rear-view mirror— his had been shot out—he saw the other vehicle trying to turn around to follow them.

Then he turned onto K Horkám and commenced hauling ass, at least as much as the van would allow.

It was hard to see out the smashed windshield, but he did what he could. This wasn't the time or place to try to go it on

71

foot. They couldn't drive around like this for long, though. "Everybody in one piece?"

"We're good." Brannigan must have had Santelli and Burgess checking everyone. Santelli's heavy hand reached around the driver's side seat to start checking Flanagan.

"What about you?" Santelli's examination was brief but thorough. It was uncomfortable, but it was vitally important that blood sweeps be done by someone else if possible. In the heat of the moment and the adrenaline dump, it was easy not to notice that you'd caught a round. Or even a nasty bit of flying glass.

"I'm good." Flanagan squinted as he tried to see through the spiderwebbed glass in front of him. The oncoming headlights and streetlights glittered into a myriad of sparks in the fractures, almost blinding him.

Brannigan was checking Dalca, who looked over her shoulder at him and smiled. "I knew you cared, John."

Brannigan might have growled, but he ignored the comment. "We need to ditch this vic and get something that's not shot full of holes. The cops are going to be swarming this area soon."

"I can delay that a little," Tomas said from the back. "But he's right." He worked his way up to the front, crawling over seats to get to where he could direct Flanagan.

"Unfortunately," Flanagan gritted as he looked for a way off the main road, "we have to lose these bastards first." That Ataman had gotten turned around and was coming after them now, closing in as the van struggled. There was an ominous rattle coming from under the hood now, and he wondered where a few of those bullets had gone. Apparently, they hadn't all deflected high.

"Turn north as soon as you can." Tomas was now leaning forward between the front seats, making things a little crowded with three people across the front passenger seat. He was also apparently on the phone.

"If we're trying to avoid cops, going into the middle of town doesn't seem like the best idea." Flanagan nevertheless kept to the right and started to look for a way north. He was sorely tempted to try to kick the remains of the windshield out of his way, but he couldn't think of a way to do it without crashing.

Tomas yammered into the phone in Italian before replying. "We need to get to a parking garage." He pointed. "Turn onto E65 and stay on it across the railroad tracks."

Flanagan did as Dalca's security chief had said, though when he glanced in the rear view again, things hadn't gotten any better. "We're still not going to lose these guys anytime soon."

"If we can reach the garage, we can take care of them." Tomas was getting more confident as he listened on the phone. "Nothing quite like you men might do, but it should stall them long enough for us to get away."

Flanagan spared a brief glance over his shoulder at Brannigan, but their chief just shrugged. "Don't see too many other options from here, Joe."

Gritting his teeth again, Flanagan leaned forward a little, as if he could coax just a little bit more speed out of the van.

The Ataman was closing in on them now, coming up on the driver's side. He had to crane his neck to check out the window with the side mirror shattered, but he also had to keep tabs on that vehicle. He saw movement as the passenger side window was cranked down. They were going to try to pull alongside and open fire.

Maybe we won't have to wait until the parking garage, after all. He still had his FNX-9 in his lap, though he wasn't entirely sure how many rounds were left in the magazine. He hoped and prayed there were just enough.

While the rest of the van was a pile of suck, at least it had power windows that still worked. He punched the button with his thumb, holding the pistol upside down so that he could reach it. The window cranked down with agonizing slowness, even as the GAZ pulled closer.

The angles were bad, but Flanagan had gotten used to making do and doing what needed to be done as a Blackheart.

He stuck the FNX-9 out the open window, cranking his shoulder back to point the pistol at the oncoming vehicle and let rip.

He got three rounds off before the slide locked back. It was enough, though. Even while several more bullets slammed into the side of the van, eliciting a yell of pain from one of Dalca's security men, the SUV fell back. They'd seen what had happened to the other vehicle, and they were being more cautious.

They didn't fall back far enough for the sluggish van to lose them anytime soon, though.

He kept following Tomas's directions, skipping the turnoff that led to the rest of the E65 and staying straight, crossing over the railroad tracks on what was now Chodovská.

Their tail was still behind them. They hadn't shot at the van again, which was a plus, but it was only a matter of time. Over the rush of wind through the open driver's side window and the bullet holes in the windshield, he thought he could hear the whoop of European-style sirens.

"Go past the next intersection and then turn into the parking lot," Tomas directed. "There will be an entrance ramp to the garage on your immediate right."

Flanagan waited until the absolute last second before he stomped on the brake, throwing everyone in the van forward, and twisted the wheel over. He still felt the van go up on two wheels again as he took the turn as sharply as possible, straightening out just long enough to line up the ramp leading down into the parking garage beneath the bauMax parking lot.

The bad guys in their GAZ kept pace, though. They were still hanging back far enough not to get shot, especially since Flanagan could see in the center mirror that Burgess had knocked out one of the small windows in the rear doors so he could aim his pistol at anyone behind them. They were still far too close, but at least they weren't riding the bumper.

For a moment, he was afraid that the gate might be closed, but whoever Tomas had been talking to on the phone had taken care of that. He sped inside as fast as he could make the van move, forcing himself not to duck instinctively as the vehicle's roof almost scraped the concrete ceiling. Dalca, in the seat next to him, was just holding on at that point.

As the van passed through the gate, the flicker of headlights on parked cars confirming Flanagan's suspicion that one of the headlights had been shot out. Only sheer luck had kept them from running afoul of the *policie*. Luck, or some diversion Tomas had cooked up to keep them occupied. Even in Europe, the cops couldn't be everywhere.

That wasn't all Tomas had figured out, though. Almost immediately, as soon as they'd entered the parking garage, another car came roaring out through the same gate, the headlights blazing to life as it passed the van. Flanagan had a hunch that the driver had just been sitting there waiting for them. A moment later, as he heard the squeal of tires and the *bang* of a collision, he was sure of it.

Tomas pointed over his shoulder. "Go to the end of the row and turn onto the next one. Our contact is there."

Despite his every instinct screaming for speed, Flanagan forced himself to slow as they came to the end of the row and took the turn. There was another van waiting there, almost identical to the one he was driving, and he stifled a groan. There was no way they were going to get away from these clowns in one of those.

"Park here." Tomas pointed to the open parking space next to the van. Flanagan pulled in, stopping with a lurch, and shut down the engine.

The others were already out as he pushed the door open, only then seeing the bullet hole torn through the headrest within an inch of where his neck had been. That had been close.

Brannigan was already at the rear of the van, his pistol in his hands. They could hear gunfire from up by the front of the parking garage, which meant things weren't going well for Dalca's people who had intercepted the gangsters by way of head-on collision.

"We need to go." Tomas was halfway around the second van when he realized that the Blackhearts weren't following.

"Ammo counts." Brannigan ignored Dalca's head of security.

"One mag left." Burgess was watching the way they'd come. There wasn't another lane that would give the bad guys access to the row where they stood, at least not if they stayed in the vehicle.

"Same here." Santelli, for his part, was mostly watching Dalca and her detail, though he was positioned so that he could engage anyone on foot coming between the vehicles that were between them and the entrance.

Brannigan looked at Flanagan and got a nod. Same thing.

Before he could issue orders, though, Dalca pushed past Kristof and held out the bag that had been on the floor of the van. "There are more magazines in here." She was cool as a cucumber and didn't appear to have been remotely rattled by a high-speed chase and gunfight in a panel van.

"No time." Several more shots barked outside the parking garage. "On me." The big man started toward the entrance immediately.

Tomas and Kristof both cursed at the same time, then again even more viciously when Dalca gave them a look that said without question that she expected them to back the Blackhearts up.

Flanagan wasn't thrilled with the idea of running out to get in a firefight for Dalca's outlaws, but then, whoever was out there had thrown themselves into the breach to cover the Blackhearts, so there was an obligation there.

Another shot sounded with what seemed like an awful finality. Whatever had happened out there on the ramp, it was now over.

Brannigan must have decided the same thing, because he dropped to a crouch behind a Skoda sedan, covering down on the entrance with his pistol. It wasn't a long shot, despite the dim lighting.

"Gents?" His voice was low in the sudden quiet. "I want one alive, if we can swing it."

Flanagan decided that was his cue. He tapped Burgess, pointed to the other side of the row, and got a nod. The two of them slipped between the cars and ran down the length of the garage, positioning themselves behind two smaller SUVs near the entrance, just as Flanagan heard footsteps crunch on the concrete. Maybe in shattered glass from the collision.

Two men entered the garage, pistols in their hands. One had a flashlight, though he was being smart, flashing it briefly where he wanted to look instead of just leaving it on, casting a bright cone of white illumination around him. Still not smart enough, because they were both obviously focused on looking for the van.

They paced past the two Blackhearts, who got up and followed them, keeping the line of cars between them and their targets.

Dalca's voice suddenly cracked out through the garage, and the two gunmen froze. Flanagan thought she'd shouted in Russian, but his Russian wasn't that great. He was *fairly* sure she'd told them to freeze and drop their weapons. Or maybe she'd just insulted their mothers. Either way, the two gangsters stutter-stepped and looked at each other for a moment, as if wondering what they should do. Then one of them lifted his pistol and took another step forward.

Flanagan and Burgess both shot him in the head from ten feet away at the same moment.

The second man jerked as blood and brains splashed him in the face, lifting a hand to clear his eyes of the mess just as Burgess lunged out from between the cars and slammed into him.

That tackle actually saved the man's life. Bullets whizzed overhead to smack into the landscaping outside the gate as Burgess and his target crashed the concrete.

77

Burgess was up in a flash, straddling his opponent and throwing an elbow at his head. He kept hitting the man as Brannigan's voice boomed through the garage. "Cease fire!"

Flanagan paused for just long enough to make sure Burgess wasn't going to need his help, then, his weapon leveled, moved to the entrance of the garage.

The two vehicles were mashed into the concrete rail, a tangled mess of twisted metal and shattered glass. Neither one was going anywhere anytime soon, but at least there was room to get past, so their escape wasn't cut of, so long as they got moving before the cops showed up.

He still moved up toward the wreckage, just to make sure that there were no more bad guys waiting for them to do just that, and to check on whoever Dalca had sent to cover them.

The driver of the SUV was slumped over the wheel and there was blood on the glass, clearly visible in the light from the streetlights nearby. He still carefully cleared the inside with his pistol held ready, hoping he didn't have to use it with no reloads and on his own.

The rest of the vehicle was empty.

So was the car. There was no sign of the driver. There were 9mm casings scattered on the tops of the concrete barriers, and still more in the grass, glinting in the orange light. It took a second, but Flanagan thought he had it figured out.

Apparently, their diversionary driver had decided that Dalca and her American allies weren't worth a heroic last stand. He'd run for it, though not without laying down some covering fire of his own.

An engine sounded behind him, though he'd jumped the concrete barrier, keeping the pistol close to his body and out of sight, so that he wouldn't be jumped by anyone coming out of the garage. To his relief, Tomas was driving one of two sedans instead of the van that he'd parked their bullet-riddled ride next to.

Santelli stuck his head out of the rear driver's side window of the second car. "Get in, Joe, we've gotta go."

Flanagan ran around the back and squeezed into the back seat, and then they were tearing out of the parking lot and away from the supermarket, even as blue lights flashed in the distance.

CHAPTER 10

They didn't go to a safehouse this time. It took about an hour of driving, most of it through darkened backroads in the Czech countryside, but they finally found a spot that Dalca found suitable, and pulled over in the middle of the woods, somewhere to the south of Prague.

The Blackhearts and their current allies got out and spread out into the dark under the trees, pistols topped off and eyes and ears alert for anyone who might have followed. Tomas pulled their prisoner, his face bruised, swollen, and crusted with blood from the beating Burgess had given him, out of the back seat of the lead sedan and hauled him under the trees. Dalca followed, Brannigan trailing just behind her, not sure if he liked the direction this was going.

Tomas shoved the man against a birch, hard enough that his head bounced off the trunk with a faint *clop*. That had to leave him seeing stars, even though it was cloudy out.

Brannigan had no idea what time it was. His internal clock was completely screwed by jet lag already, and it had been dark for hours. It was probably after midnight by now.

Dalca had adopted a casual, almost disinterested demeanor, and studied her fingernails in the light from Tomas's flashlight as she stood in front of the battered thug. She didn't say anything, didn't even look at him, for a moment, though when he started to lunge to his feet, Tomas pistol-whipped him with his VP9, and the man slumped back against the tree.

Now that he could see more clearly, Brannigan studied the man. He was dressed simply, in a t-shirt, jeans, and a zip-up hoodie that was currently open. He'd had no holster on his belt; he must have carried his pistol tucked into his waistband. It was a little hard to say for sure, given his current battered, blood-encrusted appearance, but he might have been in his mid-twenties. His dark hair was cropped short, and he was clean shaven, showing none of the tattoos that some Russian mobsters were known for.

"What is your name?" Dalca was speaking English, probably for his benefit. He wondered if the gangster in front of them understood it.

For a moment, it looked like he didn't. He just stared blearily up at her, then he spat blood and grabbed his crotch. *"Yub tvoyu maht, suka."*

Dalca tilted her head without her expression changing a whit. She studied the younger man like he was a particularly interesting specimen of insect for a long moment, long enough that the kid started to fidget and look scared. Then she nodded to Tomas.

Her head of security kicked the kid in the groin.

It was a snap kick, but it still had a lot of force behind it, and Tomas's aim was perfect. Furthermore, from his position the gangster couldn't move backward at all, so his nuts got crushed between Tomas's foot and the tree behind him.

He doubled over, retching, and Tomas struck out, grabbing him by the ear and hauling him back up. He screamed as Tomas twisted his ear, threatening to tear it off.

"Wrong answer." Tomas had apparently decided to follow his boss's example. Or maybe he just didn't speak Russian, either.

"I'm going to ask you again. What is your name?" Dalca sounded bored. She looked the young gangster in the eye. He looked a lot more deflated now, with vomit dribbled down his chin and front. That must have been a hell of a hit.

When he didn't answer immediately, her voice got harder. "My associate has been gentle so far. Don't make me let him pull the knives out."

The kid looked up at Tomas's face, which had to look somewhat nightmarish, lit from beneath by the flashlight's glow and silhouetted against the dark sky. For the first time, despite the beating he'd taken at Burgess's hands, he started to look scared.

He should be scared. With the Blackhearts, he might have stood a fighting chance. With Dalca's people…

Brannigan couldn't be sure. She certainly made all the right noises about trying not to be the ruthless gangster her father had been, but he'd seen enough behind the mask to have a pretty good idea of what she was capable of if she put her mind to it.

From the looks of Tomas, he had a history of violence, and probably had a lot of ideas for experimentation, if Dalca let him have his way.

Dalca turned to him, then. "If you need to walk away and not witness this, John, I'll understand. I wouldn't want to put you in a moral dilemma."

He stared at her coldly. "I'll stay."

She shrugged and turned back to the prisoner. "Suit yourself."

Am I hoping to stop Tomas before he goes too far? Or am I just deep enough already that I want to know for sure what this guy is going to say? After all, we've already got bodies on the ground. There's no going back now, not on our own.

He didn't have any answers, even as Dalca restarted her questioning. "Now, what is your name?"

The kid had stopped screaming as Tomas had let go of his ear, though now he was still partially doubled over, panting with the pain. He looked up at Tomas, then at Dalca, finally letting his eyes shift to the quiet, looming threat that was John Brannigan standing behind the two of them.

Brannigan hadn't done anything yet, or said more than two words, but he realized that his mere presence was a further bit of intimidation. He stood a head taller than either of the others and he still had a pistol in his hand. That would probably also help loosen the kid's tongue.

Especially since all of the rest of his buddies from that night were dead or a long way away.

"Luka Mikhailovich." His voice was low and hoarse. He probably smoked a lot, but Brannigan suspected that most of that scratch in his vocal cords was from fear.

"Luka Mikhailovich *What*?" Dalca's tone was even more harsh, and the kid actually flinched a little as her demand snapped out.

Brannigan wondered for a moment what the hell the kid's last name mattered, but he figured it out without needing to ask the question. She was already priming the young gangster, showing him that incomplete answers would not be tolerated.

Tomas's hand moved to his belt, and the kid flinched even more. "Luka Mikhailovich Strelkov! *Strelkov!*"

"Good." Dalca's tone mellowed. "There. That wasn't so hard, was it?" She folded her arms. "Now, Luka Mikhailovich Strelkov, what is it you do for Artyom Garin?"

"I am a problem solver." His English was pretty strongly accented but understandable.

Brannigan snorted. This kid was a soldier, a *brodyaga* or *bratok*, but even now, with his life hanging by a thread in a darkened forest, he was trying to dissemble, not to get called out for being the lowlife enforcer that he was.

Unfortunately, that probably meant they weren't going to get a lot of useful information out of him. "Were you told why you were sent after us, Luka?"

The kid shook his head, but there was a hesitancy in it that rang alarm bells in Brannigan's head. The kid knew more than he wanted to tell.

Tomas saw it, as well. He pulled a nasty little karambit out of his waist sheath with a *snick*.

The kid saw it. Of course he did. Tomas had *meant* him to see it. He jerked back against the tree and looked over his shoulder as if deciding if he could run for it into the woods, but Kristof loomed out of the dark then, his own pistol in his hand.

"They didn't *say*, really." He was still looking for a way out.

"But you know, anyway." Tomas's voice was almost gentle as he squatted down on his haunches to look the kid in the eye. The prisoner still didn't meet his gaze, though, his own stare locked on that wicked little blackened blade in the enforcer's hand. "So, why don't you tell us?"

Once more, the kid's eyes flicked from one to the other of them. Then Tomas apparently got tired of the game.

He stood suddenly, taking a step forward, and grabbed the kid by the sweatshirt, dragging him to his feet against the tree trunk. Brannigan almost winced; that had to have hurt. Like lightning, the head of Dalca's security put the edge of the karambit to the kid's throat. He had to have put just a little bit of pressure on the blade, because the kid flinched like he'd just been cut, just a little.

"Okay, okay!" The kid had his head back against the tree, just trying to get away from that edge that was threatening to cut his throat. Tomas let off a little bit of the pressure but didn't step back. "We were supposed to take the woman hostage! She was getting in the way of this new operation! Costing Mr. Garin a lot of money and making things more dangerous for all of us."

Dalca touched Tomas on the arm, and her chief of security finally let go of the kid and stepped back. In the glow of the flashlight, which was still aimed down at the ground, Brannigan saw the faint red line across the gangster's throat where he had, indeed been cut. The kid's hand started to go to it, but he froze as Tomas twitched.

"Dangerous how? Pressure from the Czech police shouldn't concern him so much that he'd try to kidnap or kill me."

The kid's eyes darted around, but there was still no escape. He was clearly scared to elaborate, but eventually he decided that he was even more scared of the killers standing around him.

"Mr. Garin has new partners. They are his chief suppliers of the new product." It almost seemed as if the mafioso was afraid to even name the drug. "They are very dangerous men. I do not know much, but they did something when they first formed the partnership with Mr. Garin, and his *vory* are now adamant that we must do nothing to offend them."

Brannigan felt his frown deepening. He didn't have a lot of experience with the Russian mob, but it struck him as unlikely that they'd be easily stampeded. Whoever was involved, they had to be some pretty powerful people with a considerable imagination when it came to violence.

That narrowed things down rather considerably.

"Has anyone told you who these people are? Or what they might have done?" His American accent drew the kid's eyes, but with Tomas looming over him with that knife, the gangster wasn't inclined to start getting too curious.

Still, their prisoner seemed a little evasive, though it was more like he was worried that he might somehow get in *more* trouble if he talked too much. He had already started to talk but, whoever was involved, they were scary enough that even facing a knife in the hands of an obviously violent man with no compunction about using it, he still hesitated.

Only when Tomas moved to bring that karambit back up did he start to talk again, talking fast. "I don't know *for sure*, but some of the guys said that all they needed to do was give Mr. Garin photos of his family from inside one of his houses. Some said that it wasn't just Mr. Garin, but all the high-level *vory*."

Brannigan glanced at Dalca, but she was watching their captive impassively. She had to understand the implications of that story. If it was even partially true, that pointed to a considerable intelligence gathering capability, not to mention a degree of ruthlessness that would be hard to find outside of the organized crime world.

Hard to find, but not impossible. There were certainly terrorist groups or even state intelligence agencies that were that ruthless. But enough pieces were starting to come together that Brannigan's suspicions were getting stronger.

It looked like the Front had a new angle they were pursuing.

There was still a lot of digging to do to be sure. It sure looked probable, though.

It also changed some of the dimensions of this contract. It wasn't just about saving Dalca's ass anymore. Someone else was involved, Humanity Front or not, someone peddling one of the deadliest poisons Brannigan had ever heard of, and ruthless enough to coerce a Russian mobster into cooperating.

He stepped back as Dalca and Tomas took over the questioning, asking more direct and immediate questions about the operation to capture Dalca herself. Those were necessary questions, but they weren't the ones chief in Brannigan's mind.

Flanagan, Santelli, and Burgess were out on the perimeter, given the low numbers that Dalca had brought out. He needed to talk this over with the three of them, especially Flanagan and Santelli, but for the moment, his mind was all but made up.

There was something dark going on here, and despite Dalca's undeniable agenda, it was worth looking into.

CHAPTER 11

It was getting close to dawn by the time Dalca and Tomas were satisfied. Tomas made another call, and they backed up to the vehicles, leaving the prisoner under Kristof's watchful and baleful gaze.

"We need a new safehouse." Dalca all but ignored the revelations the captive had made. She had to understand what they meant, but from the tight and solemn look on her face, she was compartmentalizing things carefully. She was a cool customer, there was no doubt about that. There never had been. But she was up against a threat like nothing she had faced before, to the best of Brannigan's knowledge. All of her dealings with the Front had been from the background, in her role as a shadow facilitator. She'd never really stuck her neck out. The only way she'd struck at them was through the Blackhearts, and then, there'd never been a direct line between them and her, no way that the Front, as powerful and widespread as they were, could trace her involvement.

Now, though, she was being directly targeted, and the fact that an organization with the kind of reach, money, and power that the Humanity Front could call on was looking for her head had to be daunting. After all, even when the Front had gone after the Blackhearts Stateside, they'd still been looking for descriptions, not known identities.

"Was that the last one you had in Prague?" Brannigan asked.

"No." She didn't look at him, but the flat tone of her voice spoke volumes. "But it was the last one that I can trust." She already had a phone out, though from the looks of it, it was a burner, not a primary. "I have a few contacts that can set one up, but it will probably take most of the day."

"We will have to use cutouts." Tomas clearly understood the situation perfectly, without anyone needing to say anything.

Still, Brannigan had a bad feeling about this. His earlier determination to get to the bottom of this Roulette operation, and whoever was pushing it, who could intimidate a Russian *vor* into calling a hit on one of the more powerful shadow facilitators in the world, had cooled as he'd started to think through the logistical and tactical problems involved.

"Can you handle the logistics, Tomas?" He wasn't sure *he* trusted the man, but Dalca clearly did. She gave him a sharp look, but he inclined his head toward the back of the car, and after a moment, she got it. She nodded, handed the phone to Tomas, and turned to follow Brannigan. Tomas gave the big mercenary an inscrutable look, but took the phone and turned away, bringing it to his ear.

Maybe the fight at the first safehouse had been enough that Dalca's security chief thought he could trust the Blackhearts. Maybe Dalca's own word was enough. Either way, he still spotted Flanagan, out on the perimeter across the road, his FNX-9 in his hand, positioned where he could watch the road *and* the vehicles where the meeting was happening.

Good old Joe. Flanagan was a quiet, unassuming man who nevertheless missed next to nothing and trusted even less.

Dalca rounded the trunk of the car and turned to face him, her back to the woods and her arms folded. She was still stone-faced, but he could see the brittleness behind it. She was scared. Scared in a way that he'd never seen her, never even imagined. "What is it, John?"

"Well, it certainly looks like you didn't call us just because you wanted a little more muscle for a dispute over spheres of influence." He folded his own arms, though he leaned against the nearest tree so that he could face her without turning his own back completely to the road. "I still can't quite be sure, not without more intel, but this really does look like people we've got a vested interest in taking out."

She seemed to relax, just a little. Almost as if she'd been afraid that the four-man team was all that Brannigan had or would bring. He held up a finger, though, forestalling her sigh of relief. "But. You've got a leak. And before I bring the rest of the boys in on this, that leak's got to be plugged."

He'd been thinking about it after he'd backed off from the interrogation. The hit on the first safehouse might have been a coincidence. The ambush at the second, however, had been the red flag that had set off alarm bells in his head. There was an old saying. *Once is happenstance, twice is coincidence, three times is enemy action.* That wasn't applicable here, though. There were too many indicators. Either the bad guys had figured out where Dalca's safehouses were and had set watchers on all of them, or they'd known exactly where their targets were going. Either way meant that Dalca's organization was compromised.

He almost expected her to protest. She was a professional in this world, after all. She might be an actual, real-world CEO of an international shipping company, but she was also a very dangerous underworld figure in her own right. The idea that she might have an enemy spy in her own organization was a potential indictment of her own abilities and power.

Instead, she nodded. "I know. And I'm sorry that I didn't see it and clean house before you arrived." She looked up at him, finally actually locking eyes with him. She seemed to have found some new strength from his engagement. "Unfortunately, I cannot say for certain who the leak might be."

"We'll have to narrow it down quick, then." He glanced at where Tomas was still on the phone. "We won't be able to do much if we're dodging ambushes at every turn and the bad guys know when and where we're coming for them."

She smiled faintly, and a bit of the old Dalca, the shadow facilitator cum femme fatale, was back. "I have some idea of just how to do that. It *will* require us to trust a few of my people, but there will be a certain degree of testing involved in that trust, as well." She glanced over his shoulder and then stepped closer, lowering her voice. "Here is what I have in mind…"

***

Wade wasn't going to admit that he was bored and practically chewing nails, but when the phone buzzed, he almost jumped to answer it. Sure enough, it was an encrypted call from somewhere in Europe.

"Talk to me." He glanced around the room as he lifted the phone to his ear. Kirk had been doing most of the coordination, but when it came down to it, Curtis was the only other man on the standby team who'd been an original Blackheart, and even Curtis had to admit that he wasn't the leadership type. Nobody had said much about it, one way or another, but once the seven of them had met in the hotel near Reagan National Airport, he'd just sort of stepped in as team leader.

It wasn't even a role he particularly *wanted*, but between him, Kirk, Puller, Bianco, Curtis, Tackett, and Gomez, he was kind of the natural pick.

Tackett, Bianco, and Kirk had been playing Spades, while Curtis didn't *quite* sulk at having to stay put in the hotel room, Puller had mostly slept or watched TV, and Gomez was, well, Gomez. Now, though, every eye was on him.

"We're a go, but you'll need to put off the flights for another day." Brannigan's tone was terse, and he was clearly doing what he could not to say too much over the phone, encryption or no. "We've got a bit of a security situation that needs to get ironed out before we can meet up."

Wade gritted his teeth. Another day in this hotel room with nothing to do but watch the awfulness that was hotel room cable or try to find the end of the internet. Still, he was all too aware of just how much damage impatience over security issues had done over the years.

Sam Childress's fate alone was a graphic enough reminder.

"Roger. I'll start getting the flights lined up. Probably won't be able to get on anything before tomorrow, anyway." He might have hated it, and he hated dealing with travel arrangements even more, but it was something that needed to be done. "Anything else we need to know?"

Brannigan paused for a moment. "Contact Tackett and tell him that it looks very much like the opposition is just who we suspected."

"I'll pass the word." He glanced up at their second-newest teammate. "He's actually here, already."

"Is he?" Brannigan sounded a little surprised, but not as surprised as he might have been. "That's interesting. Well, let him know, and we'll see you in a couple of days." He cut the connection.

Wade took the phone away from his ear and immediately started in on the airline tickets. There was going to be a lot to get all of them over there. It was a good thing that their previous jobs had paid as well as they had.

"We on?" Kirk asked. Of all of them, he was probably the closest to Flanagan in his utterly phlegmatic, almost bored approach.

"Looks like it." Wade glanced up from the phone at Tackett. "Looks like you didn't waste your time either, Dan."

The quiet man, who had almost reluctantly joined the Blackhearts to rescue his friends in Kyrgyzstan, just nodded and went back to studying his cards. Tackett was a man of few words, but he was a solid enough operator that Wade wasn't going to complain. He'd take Tackett's silence over Curtis.

"That's it?" Curtis had stood up from his spot in the armchair next to the wall as soon as the phone had gone off. "No brief? Just 'let's go?'"

Wade gave him that icy, unblinking stare of his. "Yeah. That's it. Apparently, the Colonel doesn't trust the encryption *that* far. Which tells me all I need to know about who we're up against, even before he told me to tell Tackett here that he wasn't wasting his time."

"Which is fine with me," Tackett said without looking up. "I understand OPSEC."

Curtis sputtered a little at the implication that *he* didn't, but let it go. Tackett wasn't Flanagan, and while Wade still found Curtis annoying, all the same he recognized that the other man wasn't quite as much of a clown when he didn't have Flanagan around as a straight man. It was an odd brotherhood the two had, and sometimes, when he let himself, Wade wondered just what would happen when one or the other went down.

He shrugged off the irrelevant thought. There was work to do, as annoying as it was. He got back to booking flights.

CHAPTER 12

It would have been better if they'd had camouflage and full recon setups. Flanagan would much rather have been ghillied up in the weeds to watch the two-story, gray stucco building. Instead, he was sitting in a tiny Skoda Fabia that he could barely squeeze into, parked just down the street where he could just barely see the entryway.

Most of the people he'd seen so far hadn't seemed to be all that interested in ducking down to look closely at the inside of a car parked on the street. The longer he was there, however, the more obvious it was going to be that he was just sitting and waiting. It gets hard to disguise a man sitting in a parked car. And even if he was watching one of the dry holes, the locals might start to get antsy and call the cops.

He had a rehearsed story for the *policie*, about waiting for a friend who'd told him to meet him there. The location he would describe was even a block away, which would explain his loitering—he was lost. The lie wasn't something he was all that happy about, but it was still rather necessary under the circumstances.

The problem with cover stories is the more fake they are, the faster they unravel. And while Flanagan had been a Marine, not a spook, his common sense told him that.

He was a hunter, which meant he was patient. Still, the longer this went on, the more he wished he could move. Or even get out of the car and book it into the woods. This was getting untenable.

Barely after he'd thought it, the curtains stirred in a window above, and he spotted a face peering out at the car. Someone was definitely starting to get uncomfortable with his presence. Yet he didn't dare take his eyes off the target house. If something was going to go down, it was going to go down in the next thirty minutes.

All the same, he started to think that he should just get out and climb up into the woods above the road. That might take some of the heat off his position, as well as let him stretch his legs. The Fabia was hardly built with a man his size in mind.

He could only imagine how much pain Brannigan would be in if he'd squeezed into the tiny car.

Just before he made the decision that he was at least going to get out and walk around the block, maybe making a show of looking at his phone and the numbers on the buildings, a pair of dark sedans rolled past him and pulled over onto the little cutout in front of a corrugated metal shed set against the hillside, across the street from the gray building.

Here we go. Looks like we might have figured out our leaker.

It was possible, of course, that these were just locals or even visitors. When the doors opened and six men in dark leather jackets got out, however, he was pretty sure they were neither.

They stayed together, looking around carefully before they hurried across the street, at least two of them with hands inside their jackets. If they thought they were being subtle or low-profile, it was a rather pathetic showing.

Flanagan waited until they went over the fence on the back side, then looked down at the phone in his lap. He sent a single-word text. *Jackpot.* Then he started the Fabia, put it in gear, and backed up the street, going around the bend before backing partway up a gravel road that split off from the main street and headed up into the woods above. He braked, put the car in drive, and then finished the three-point turn and sped away.

Provided this was the only prospective safehouse where the brute squad had showed up, they should have their leaker.

***

Dalca's expression was bleak, though she didn't otherwise react as the reports came in. Because they only had four Blackhearts in the country, and she didn't trust anyone else in her organization this far except Tomas, there were only so many traps they could set, and therefore only so many of her lieutenants she could test. It was almost sheer, dumb luck that they'd hit on one.

Almost. She'd had to have had suspicions, so she'd picked those most likely to have sold her out.

Burgess reported in that he'd stayed in place for fifteen minutes after the window, and there was no movement. He was heading back.

They still didn't have a safehouse, though Tomas had reported that his cutouts were busy setting one up. They were moving from rendezvous to rendezvous in the various parks around Prague. They were all starting to look a little disheveled, and Brannigan had to admit that he was looking forward to a shower, but it was hardly the most austere field op he'd ever been on, either.

"Burgess's house is clean." He dropped the phone on the car's dashboard and looked across the car at Dalca. "That leaves just Flanagan's target."

She nodded, though her eyes were far away. Not wistful, not quite. Despite the show of femininity she put on—particularly, it seemed, when the two of them were in private, or close to it—she wasn't the wistful type. She was thinking, and there was a fair bit of anger and hatred in those thoughts, too.

"Well, that seals it, doesn't it?" She took a deep breath as she touched the USP on her lap. "I guess we'd better not stretch this out too long."

"I guess not." Brannigan couldn't quite read her at that moment. There was definitely a good hint of that ruthlessness he'd always known had lurked beneath her seductive exterior. But there was something else there, a sort of deep-seated pain. One of her people had sold her out, tried to get her killed or kidnapped. And that *hurt*.

She might be a high-powered CEO and an extremely powerful underworld facilitator, but she was still human, still a woman, and as hard as she tried to keep that fact from affecting her behavior, sometimes it still showed through.

"Where are we going?" He found that, despite himself, he felt the urge to try to comfort her. *She's certainly been working on you long enough. Hell, this little display, as subtle as it might be, might be just one more step.* He forced the compulsion down. She was a grown woman who commanded a great deal more power than he did. Besides, there was a mission to accomplish, and he had the rest of the team coming in. They needed a bit more than a series of parking lots to operate out of if they were going to take on the Front *and* Garin's organization.

He might have objected to the latter, but if Garin was working hand-in-glove with the Humanity Front, then that made him a target, regardless of the conflict of interest involving Dalca.

She seemed to shake herself. "Here." She brought up a tablet displaying a photo map. There was already a pin displayed on it, marking an apartment building to the north of them, closer to the center of the city. "We should move quickly. As soon as he finds out that we weren't there, he will know what has happened and will attempt to run. He is not a stupid man."

Brannigan put the car in gear. "Oh, I think he is."

***

Dalca's assessment had been spot on. So was their timing, though it was awfully close.

Libor Kozel was a fat man with a buzzed head and a couple days' worth of stubble and, while it was starting to get cool, he was visibly sweating as he hustled down the steps with a

98

suitcase in his hand. He wasn't looking up as he came out into the parking garage, but had his face glued to his phone until he was all the way out into the garage.

He only looked up after he was about ten paces from the stairs. It wasn't a scan like someone looking for threats, but the look of a man getting his bearings, as if he wasn't entirely sure where he'd left his car.

His eyes roved past Brannigan, Tomas, and Dalca as they walked toward him, while Kristof, Burgess, Santelli, and two more of Dalca's local hires named Mătej and Nikola stood back behind them, spread out across the lane between parked cars. No one was showing a weapon, but the threat was still hard to miss.

Kozel missed it on the first pass anyway, but then something clicked in his brain and his eyes snapped back to Dalca's icy stare as she walked toward him, her heels clicking loudly on the concrete, the sound echoing through the parking garage. He started panting even harder, froze like a deer in the headlights for a second, then dropped the suitcase, turned, and ran for the exit.

He didn't get far. Tomas broke into a dead sprint from a standing start and was on him in a dozen strides. He grabbed the fat man by the collar, and while Kozel looked like he outweighed Tomas by a good hundred pounds, he still stopped the traitor dead as he yanked backward. A moment later, he kicked Kozel's feet out from under him, sending him crashing onto his back on the concrete floor. The breath went out of the fat man with a *whump*, and he let out a low moan, in too much pain to even writhe.

Dalca hadn't missed a stride, and now came up to stand next to Tomas, looking down at Kozel coldly. Nikola pulled a car up behind them. "Put him in the trunk. If he will fit." Kozel finally managed to writhe a little under her icy stare. "If he won't, cut off enough of him that he will."

Brannigan rejoined Santelli and Burgess. This could get ugly, but he had little sympathy for the man. Kozel had turned on

99

his boss, not to the authorities, but to the Russian mob, and possibly even to the Humanity Front.

He didn't especially like the thought of what Dalca's people were probably going to do to Kozel. He wouldn't be afforded the courtesy of a bullet in the back of the head and a quick burial. No, unless he was reading the situation entirely wrong, Tomas was going to have some very pointed questions for old Libor before the end.

Besides, given their current situation, there was little they *could* do. There were currently three of the four of them present, and while they'd gotten reloads for their 9mms, they were still outgunned if Dalca's people decided to push this.

It had crossed his mind that *he* might be able to put some personal pressure on Dalca, but he wasn't sure that was a good idea, either. It might not work. Worse, it might work, in which case she'd call in another favor for it.

Besides, this man had tried to get them killed, presumably for money. He was all out of sympathy.

As it turned out, they didn't need to cut any of Kozel's appendages off, though it looked like Kristof would have liked to. It was still a tight fit as they crammed him into the trunk, and Tomas had to jump on the lid to get it to latch.

Dalca turned and walked back to where Brannigan stood next to their car. "Tomas will take care of that filth." She looked up at Brannigan. "Unless you wanted to interrogate him yourself, I think we should go to the safehouse and get ready for the rest of your team to get here." She looked over at Santelli. "I can provide you with more weapons, ammunition, and any other gear you will need."

Brannigan didn't ask how she knew to go to Santelli for that. She knew entirely too much about entirely too many things.

"Actually, I would like to talk to him." He ducked to get into the car, which sagged slightly under his weight. Not as much as that other one had when they'd thrown Kozel into the trunk, but enough to be noticeable. "If he knows anything about the Front being involved here, I want to hear it."

Dalca slid into the seat next to him as he started the car and put it in gear to follow Tomas. "Fair enough. We don't have a lot of time, though."

"We've got until tomorrow night," Brannigan growled as they rolled out of the parking garage and turned east. "We've got all the time we'll need."

***

The woods looked an awful lot like the same forest where they'd interrogated the Russian gangster, but this park was on the far side of Prague, outside of a village called Nouzov. It was really more of a tree farm than a forest or even a park, but it would do the job for now. They were deep enough back in the woods that they'd be hard to find, even if Kozel started yelling and people started looking for them.

Kozel was down on his knees behind the car that had brought him to the spot, shaking and looking around pleadingly at the hard faces around him.

"Now, Libor, you're going to tell me everything about your deal with Garin and about his new partners." Tomas had taken over from the get-go, and wasn't going to wait around, though the fact he was speaking English told Brannigan that he was still doing this for the sake of his audience, as well. Of course, there might be the factor that Ciela was an *international* company, and so not all of Dalca's people could be expected to speak Czech, either.

Kozel shook his head, his lips pressed slightly together. Brannigan studied him carefully. Something was off about this. This was one of Dalca's people who had sold her out. He wouldn't have expected to-the-death *omerta* from someone like that.

Tomas tilted his head slightly to one side as he pulled out that karambit. "I've asked as nicely as I ever intend to, Libor. Either you start talking now, and we can end this quickly and relatively painlessly, or I start cutting bits off you, and you tell me what I want to know anyway, with a lot more pain and screaming."

101

Kozel spoke for the first time, then. "You don't know what you're asking." He looked around him like a rat looking for an escape route. "I *can't* tell you."

Tomas stepped closer with that claw of a knife in his hand, poised to strike. Kozel couldn't take his eyes off the blade, but he still wasn't giving in, either. "Wait! You don't understand!"

"We picked up the suitcase you dropped." Dalca's voice was as cold as it had been when she'd ordered Kozel put in the trunk. "We saw how much money you had in it. Don't tell me you 'can't.'"

"Yes, they paid me!" Kozel was cowering back from the knife, holding up his hands in front of his face. Tomas must have been plenty confident that he could handle Kozel, because he hadn't secured the man's hands. "But that was just a bonus! They'd kill my family if I told you anything!"

"What makes you think they won't do that anyway?" Dalca still didn't show an ounce of sympathy. "They must know that we caught you by now."

Under different circumstances, that might have done the trick. But with Kozel, it had the opposite effect.

A flash of horror crossed his features, and then he lunged for Tomas, moving a lot faster than a man of his bulk should have been able to without being driven by utter desperation. He grabbed for Tomas's knife hand, missed, and then threw himself at the enforcer's legs. Tomas, caught by surprise, didn't get out of the way fast enough, and both men went down in a heap.

Kozel was grabbing for the knife again, as a bunch of VP9s, FNX-9s, and Glock 19s and 17s were pointed at him, but no one fired for fear of hitting Tomas. Kozel was punching him, trying desperately to keep him off balance while he tried to gain control of the knife, but Tomas, despite the fact that he'd been caught off guard, was doing an admirable job of keeping the weapon out of Kozel's hands.

Brannigan was moving in to intervene, holstering his pistol, when Tomas found his opening.

He twisted, then bucked as he got partway out from under Kozel's mass. Getting a leg free, he kneed Kozel in the side of the thigh, hard enough that the man jerked and yelled in pain. The shock made the big man lose some of his momentum, and then Tomas twisted again, got a hand on his 9mm, drew it with some difficulty, and put the first round into Kozel's guts.

The fat man screamed and rolled off Tomas, who simply rolled toward him, emptying the pistol at contact distance into the bulk of the traitor's guts and chest. Bloody fabric blew away from the weapon's muzzle blast, and Kozel jerked and screamed under the onslaught, bloody froth spewing from his mouth and nose as Tomas's bullets tore through his lungs. He tried to crawl away, got about three feet, shuddered, and went still.

Tomas, spattered with Kozel's blood, struggled to his feet, his pistol still pointed at the traitor's body, the slide locked back on an empty magazine. He realized it a moment later, and hastily reloaded, letting the empty fall to the blood-soaked loam underneath him.

By the time he sent the slide home, he'd calmed down and realized that Kozel was dead. He holstered the VP9 and turned to Dalca. "Well, *Signora*, we might not have found out anything more, but we have plugged the leak."

"For now." Brannigan looked down at the corpse with a frown. "If the people I think are involved in this are the ones he was scared of, I wouldn't put it past them to try again with somebody else." He turned back toward the car. "We'd better be ready to move fast."

CHAPTER 13

Brannigan paced the floor as he waited for the team.

The jet lag hadn't really gotten much better. They hadn't been on the ground long enough. He was still alert, though, mainly out of sheer necessity. There had certainly been enough violence in the couple of days since the advance team had landed to keep them on their toes.

Tires crunched on gravel outside, and he moved to the window, staying to one side and out of sight. The lights in the house were off for a reason, aside from the fact that they weren't needed on this clear, sunny day.

Two Skoda SUVs rolled up to the gate, one green and the other dark blue. They looked like they were probably airport rentals, which made sense and would also divert some attention.

Wade got out of the lead vehicle, and Brannigan's eyes immediately rose to scan the surroundings. The blocky, very modern white house with its walled compound was surrounded largely by trees, with a field behind and a construction site to the south. There were enough trees that sight lines on the house itself were limited, which meant that they were pretty well situated not only to hide, but to spot anyone who might take an inordinate interest in their presence.

The streets were empty and quiet, and if there was anyone watching from the bushes, he couldn't see them, which made it unlikely that they could see much of the house.

He turned away from the window and headed downstairs to meet with the rest of the team.

They looked like they'd just gotten off a transatlantic flight. None of them were particularly disheveled, but there was an aura of weariness, and Curtis's eyes were bloodshot. Wade didn't step in through the door so much as he made entry, moving out of the fatal funnel and scanning the living room and most of the rest of the first floor while his eyes adjusted to the dimness inside. He only stepped forward to shake Brannigan's hand after he'd finished his assessment.

"How was the flight?" Brannigan greeted each of the men as they came in, hustling them inside and closing the door, just in case there *were* probing eyes outside. He hadn't seen much drone traffic, but there definitely were civilian quadcopters flying around, and while the Czechs had some fairly restrictive laws about registration and licensing for such things, it was entirely possible that their opposition had more than a few in service. They *shouldn't* be connected to this place, since Tomas had used at least three layers of cutouts to rent it, but it never paid to be complacent. *Especially* if the Front was involved.

"Long and boring." Curtis dropped his carryon on the floor and threw himself on the couch. "Wade couldn't even get us business class seats, so there wasn't much rest on the way."

Wade glared at him. "Didn't see you shelling out for an upgrade that it was too late to get."

Curtis didn't even open his eyes. "Wasn't my job."

Wade snarled silently. He was clearly about as tired as all the rest, and Wade hadn't gotten his callsign of "Angry Ragnar" for nothing. He turned back to Brannigan. "How have things been going here?"

Brannigan nodded to Kirk as the old Special Forces soldier checked their six one more time before pulling the door shut. "Eventful." He filled them in on everything that had happened so far, from the hit on the first safehouse, the ambush at the second, and then the way they'd ferreted out Kozel's role as informant for the enemy.

Tackett was rubbing his chin. He'd grown a short beard since the Kyrgyzstan mission. "You don't think that this Kozel guy was the only rat they've got, do you?"

Brannigan shook his head. "No, I don't. There's only so much we can do about it, though, which is why I've made it clear that with a few notable exceptions that we can't avoid, we'll be doing most of this ourselves. I don't want a lot of Dalca's people around us." He waved to indicate the safehouse. "Only three of them should know where this is."

"You sure that they're the trustworthy ones?" Bianco had stationed himself near the kitchen and was leaning on the counter, his arms folded, a pensive look on his boyish face. "I mean, this *is* Dalca we're talking about."

"Am I sure?" Brannigan snorted. "No. But that's been par for the course on most of these jobs we've taken. At least the ones that haven't just been a matter of 'go in, smash, grab, get out.' We'll just have to keep our heads on a swivel and guns at hand."

"Speaking of." Curtis finally raised his head and looked around. "What do we have for guns?"

"Tom and Carlo are out lining that up right now." Brannigan gave Curtis a look that brooked no complaints. "We are probably not going to have belt-feds. Dalca's chief of security had a possible location of an old Spetsnaz cache from the Cold War, but I turned him down."

"They might have had RPKs or PKMs, though!" Curtis, as always, ignored the warning glare.

"Those things probably wouldn't function half the time, if they've been buried as long as I think they probably have been." Kirk was poking around the kitchen for something to eat. "Cosmoline only goes so far."

"But they're Russian weapons, so they should still work even if they've been at the bottom of a swamp for thirty years." Curtis had sat up now. "We *could* still have belt-feds!"

"No." Brannigan didn't want to discuss it. He'd already been over it with Flanagan, Burgess, and Santelli, and they'd decided not to try it. The mix and match with different ammunition was the primary reason, Flanagan's dislike for Russian weapons aside. Better to have everyone using the same rounds and the same mags as much as possible. They'd done the mix and match thing before, most notably in Transnistria, but it was considerably less than ideal.

For a moment, it looked like Curtis was going to argue, but he subsided after he glanced up and took in the look on Brannigan's face.

"Just saying, the firepower would be nice. But I guess if we're trying to stay low profile…" He trailed off and then got up, grabbing his carryon as he did so. Curtis could be a handful, but he was enough of a social butterfly to know when he needed to stop pushing. "Where are we bedding down?"

Brannigan pointed up the stairs. There were a couple of bedrooms on the ground floor, but most were in the oddly spaced rooms on the second story. "I'll show you around. Don't get too comfortable, though. The bad guys know that *somebody* has entered the game on Dalca's side, and things are probably going to start moving quickly now."

***

Santelli leaned against the back of the car, trying not to fidget. He never had cared for this sort of cloak-and-dagger stuff, though it was increasingly up the Blackhearts' alley, particularly as they moved against the Humanity Front. Still, he felt exposed as all hell, and the 9mm under his jacket only went so far to make him feel better.

The fact that Burgess wasn't far away, in the second car, watching with his own FNX-9 in his lap, ready to intervene, if need be, also wasn't as much of a comfort as it might have been.

You've already done this twice. Why are you even more nervous now than you were six hours ago? He hardly needed to even think that much about it. He knew that the longer this went on, the greater the likelihood that something was going to go sideways.

Sunlight glinted off window glass, and he watched the oncoming sedan slowly roll along the road that ran through the center of the park before stopping not far away.

They'd been doing a lot in parks on this job, but there were a lot of them in and around Prague, and they made for good places to disappear into the trees, even if only for a few minutes.

He didn't recognize the man who got out of the sedan with a duffel. The man didn't even look at him but, instead, walked into the trees and disappeared for a few minutes, before coming back out without the duffel, getting back into the sedan and driving off, not sparing Santelli so much as a glance as he passed. For his part, Santelli kept looking at his phone, watching all this unfold out of the corner of his eye.

As tradecraft went, it left quite a bit to be desired. They seemed to have picked the right place, though, if they were going to be this amateurish and sloppy. The park appeared to be completely abandoned and, so far, Burgess had confirmed with each passing vehicle that they appeared to be clean. Nobody was paying them the least bit of attention.

He still waited until well after the car had disappeared into the woods before he heaved off the trunk of his own car and, with what he hoped was a casual glance around him, walked into the woods. The message from Burgess was still up on his phone: *Clear.*

It took a little doing to find where the contact had stashed the duffel bag. It had been a slightly different position each time, in no small part because there hadn't *been* a specific spot where they were supposed to leave the bags. The instructions had been simple and vague. *Drive into the park until you see a man leaning against a blue Dacia Duster. Stop short, go into the woods on your right, leave the duffel, and then drive away.*

That was the main reason the tradecraft was so iffy. That, and the time constraints they were working under. So, he had to do a little searching.

He finally found the bag under a leafy bush at the base of some of the trees. He looked around once more as he took a knee and then, as comfortable that he was unobserved as he could get, he carefully unzipped the duffel.

Three more CZ 805 Bren A2s lay inside, their stocks folded, along with six magazines for each. He scowled a little. There were supposed to be a couple more FNX-9s in this drop, but all that was in the bag were the rifles.

With a sigh, he zipped the bag back up and headed for the car. A glance at his watch sped up his pace for a moment, until he was within view of the road again, at which point he slowed and carefully checked that there was no one around. The woods and the road appeared as deserted as they had before. He dug one hand in his pocket, found the remote, and popped the back hatch as he approached the Duster.

It was a matter of seconds to put the duffel in and shut the hatch. Even if there had been someone else on the road, they shouldn't have seen much. Not enough to see two other big duffels already sitting in the back.

Without pausing, he moved forward and got in, starting the vehicle as he tapped out a quick message to Burgess. *Done.* Then he was driving out of the park, watching his mirrors carefully, wanting nothing more than to breathe a deep sigh of relief but knowing that it was still far too early to relax. He still might get intercepted by the Czech police.

Ten minutes later, though, with no sign of pursuit or even anyone giving him a sideways look, he really did start to relax. It was still possible that he was being watched via security camera or drone, but it didn't seem that likely from what he'd seen so far. He'd seen a few cameras on gateways, and a few drones flying in public places, but there didn't appear to be too much of a surveillance net around Prague. That was good.

I just hope that Joe has had as much success with the ammo.

***

Flanagan had, in fact, already picked up the ammo. He paused as he turned onto the street in front of the safehouse, noticing the two vehicles out front. Easing over to the side of the road, he pulled up the phone and opened the secure messenger.

On the way in. Everything clear?

It took a second. *Clear. Come ahead.*

Those vehicles must be the rest of the team, then. He relaxed ever so slightly and moved up, parking nose to nose with the green Skoda Yeti. He still made sure he could get to his pistol quickly as he got out, locked the car, and moved to the gate.

Wade was waiting just inside. A brief, one-armed bear hug was the only greeting the two men exchanged before Flanagan turned back toward the car. "You want to give me a hand? Six cases of 5.56 get heavy."

"You ain't lying." Wade turned back toward the front door of the house. "Hey, Kevin! Come here and put those show muscles to use."

Curtis came out and groaned. "Joe's been here for days! He's had time to get over his jet lag!" He rubbed his eyes theatrically. "I need a nap."

"You need to work out." Flanagan turned as he pulled a case of ammunition out of the back of the car and tossed it at Curtis, who had followed even as he'd bitched. "This'll help you sleep when it's time. Get you on schedule. In fact, I should probably just leave the whole load to you."

Curtis, despite his professed exhaustion, was still quick enough on his feet to retort, even as he caught the box. "And deprive you of a chance to start to get muscles like mine? I wouldn't dream of taking that opportunity away from you, Joe."

111

"Just take the stuff inside." Wade was already halfway to the gate, and obviously didn't have a lot of patience left. "We've got intel to go over as soon as Carlo gets here with the weapons."

Flanagan handed another case to Bianco, who grinned and jerked his head at him to greet him.

It was good to have the team together again.

Now it was time to really get to work.

CHAPTER 14

"Okay, here's what we've got." Brannigan had spread a street map of Prague on the kitchen table. The Blackhearts were all gathered around, except for Santelli and Burgess, who were on security at the front and back of the house. They'd already gotten the high points of the brief, anyway. "Dalca has limited intelligence on this operation, at least the part that we suspect the Front is involved with. So, the plan is to go after Garin's Roulette operation hammer and tongs, in the hope that we can draw our old friends out of hiding."

He looked around the table. "I'll be honest. I couldn't care less about Garin, no matter what Dalca thinks we owe her. He's a thug, and if we end up taking him out, I won't cry about it, but we're here because of the Front."

When no one objected, he nodded. He'd figured that would be the way it would go. None of the Blackhearts had ever been entirely comfortable with their relationship with Dalca—least of all Brannigan himself—but there was enough blood between them and the Humanity Front that none would balk for a second at taking them on. Most of these men would happily burn down an organization like the Front anyway, just on general principles, but there was enough of a history there that it was personal for the Blackhearts.

"Dalca has no leads on Garin's Front contact, or whatever cutout is trafficking the drug they're calling Roulette. So, we're going to have to move up the kill chain a bit." He pointed to an industrial district on the eastern edge of Prague. "Right off the bat, we've got two potential targets that Dalca's put in our laps. One is a guy named Abrasha Yurasov. He's apparently Garin's chief lieutenant in Prague, and if there's anyone in his organization who's read in on the whole Roulette operation, it's probably him. *However*." He tapped the same spot on the map. "While he's reportedly a bit of a playboy, he's also an elusive bastard, and never telegraphs where he's going to be from night to night. It'll be hard to pin him down. This place, though, is a warehouse belonging to Garin's organization, and from what Dalca's been able to figure out, it's been used as a distribution point for drugs. All sorts of drugs: heroin, coke, meth, Krokodil, marijuana. But, also, Roulette."

"You're thinking if we hit the warehouse, it might draw this Yurasov out?" Wade rubbed his chin as he stared at the map without blinking.

Brannigan nodded. "It seems likely. Tomas agreed, as well. Apparently, he's met with Yurasov, and while Tomas might look like a street thug, he's smart as hell, at least judging by what I saw over the last few days. He says that Yurasov tends to be a very hands-on sort of guy. In more than one way."

It didn't take long for the meaning of that last statement to get through. None of these guys were exactly babes in the woods.

"So, the warehouse it is." Flanagan craned his neck to look at the map as Brannigan pulled out some printed out overhead imagery. The place was nothing special from the looks of it. It was a warehouse, just on the south side of the railroad tracks, inside a gated complex that might present some difficulties getting in and out. There was no way to tell from overhead imagery just how much security was on site, but that only meant that they needed to do what they would anyway: boots on the ground reconnaissance.

***

"That's a lot of security." Flanagan and Burgess had taken the Fabia, despite Flanagan's disgust, just because it was probably the most unobtrusive of their vehicles, and now that it looked like they were going to have to pull a U-turn on the narrow street leading toward the warehouse, it was actually probably a good thing.

The images of the gate leading onto the compound that they'd found online had showed a green-painted steel gate with a drop arm behind it. The gate had been open in all the photos they'd been able to dig up, with the drop arm down, presumably with a remote that authorized personnel could use. None of the photos had indicated guards.

Something had someone with property in there spooked, though. Two men in dark fatigues and military-style sweaters stood outside the closed gate with slung vz.58 rifles. They didn't appear to have body armor on, but the rifles alone presented enough of a threat.

He made the turn, thankfully before either of the security guards seemed to take notice, and headed back the way they'd come. They were behind the trees that lined the road a few seconds later.

Since they still needed to get to a spot where they could get eyes on the warehouse, he didn't go far. There was a small parking lot just around the corner at the end of the short lane they'd taken toward the gate, and he turned into it, finding a shadowed spot alongside the barbed-wire-topped fence that surrounded yet another secured commercial compound. The Czechs took corporate security seriously.

Both men got out as soon as he put the car in park and shut off the engine, carefully looking around for any observers or cameras. Everything looked a little run down and dingy, and there were some considerable cracks in the pavement under their feet. The Czechs had gone a long way to get over their history with Communism, but some of the marks were definitely still there.

115

Since there wasn't anyone in sight, the two men, dressed in drab civilian clothes that weren't camouflaged, but would still blend in pretty well, slipped across the road and into the trees.

There wasn't a lot of concealment there, but it was getting dark, and neither of those security guards had appeared to have night vision. They'd make do, and the terrain helped as well, giving them a low hill to hide behind as they worked their way up around the outside of the target compound.

The woods didn't go right up to the fence, unfortunately. By the time they'd found their likeliest line of approach, they were still a hundred yards from the fence, and it was all open ground in front of them.

"Be nice if we had a drone right now," Burgess whispered. "One of the little, quiet ones that we could fly over the compound."

Flanagan wasn't sure how well that would work under the best of circumstances, but they didn't have the option, anyway. He just shrugged as he watched the compound.

The lights were going to be the hardest part. They weren't right on the fence, but they surrounded what looked like a central operations building that stood between them and the warehouse that was their target. There was very little cover or concealment around that compound.

He rubbed his bearded chin. There was a low wall to the north side, around what looked like a scrapyard. That might provide *some* cover and concealment but moving through that without making noise was probably going to be next to impossible.

For a long moment, the two of them just sat and watched. Flanagan was most interested, in addition to the layout and the lighting, in seeing whether or not there were any roving patrols. The two security guards at the gate had been a nasty surprise. So far, he hadn't seen any, but things were just shutting down for the day, with people who looked like ordinary workers getting into their cars and driving out, probably forcing the security guards with their vz.58 rifles to open the gate for a while.

"That might be a way in." Burgess's whisper echoed Flanagan's own thoughts. "Trojan horse it inside in the morning as local workers."

"Maybe, but what if they're checking IDs?" Flanagan countered. "We don't have Czech IDs, and if they know who's supposed to be here and who isn't, it's a firefight at the gate."

Burgess squinted at the fence. "That might actually work as a diversion, give the rest of the team a chance to get over the fence while all eyes are on the gate."

Flanagan grimaced a little at that. Such a diversion was almost guaranteed to get the cops involved. He wouldn't put it past Garin's gangsters to have the audacity to call the *policie* to get intruders off their backs. As long as they had a cover—which they almost certainly did, operating in the middle of Prague— they'd have no trouble calling on law enforcement to protect their illegal activities.

It was *possible* that they'd get some of Dalca's people to run that rabbit. Possible, but he didn't think it was probable or even wise. As Brannigan had said in the brief, the less Dalca's people were involved, the better.

He shook off the reverie. They were there to scope the place out, not conduct the final mission planning. That could wait until they got all the information back to the safehouse.

Hopefully. He'd been on missions where recon had led right into the assault. He sincerely hoped that would not turn out to be the case here. All he had on him was his FNX-9 and four spare mags.

Fading back into the weeds, he and Burgess continued their circuit around the compound.

***

The two of them took a moment to make sure that they weren't going to run out in front of a train once they crossed the tracks. It quickly became obvious that they needn't have worried, though. The railroad tracks split from two into about six tracks, but they were mostly overgrown and rusted over, without any of the telltale shininess that active train wheels left. There hadn't been a train on those tracks in a long time.

That worked in their favor. The overgrown tracks were surrounded by more trees, and they were able to move fairly quickly without fear of being spotted.

"Holy shit," Burgess whispered.

Flanagan had to agree. For all the security up front, they had now found themselves, by following the leftmost track, right between another warehouse and the wall of the scrapyard, with no obstacles in sight between them and the end of the wall. Furthermore, it was dark back there, with only a few flickering sodium lights up ahead, and plenty of shadows to hide from them in between.

There was no way he was going to leave it at that, though. They had to be sure, if they were going to slip an assault force through that gap. There might still be a fence up ahead that he couldn't see, or the lights might make it untenable to move all the way to the end of the wall. He kept following the tracks.

It felt harrowing as hell. He'd done recon in some sketchy places but getting this close to the target had been practically anathema in the military. He kept expecting someone to appear right at their elbow, or worse, just pop out and start shooting.

It was that time of day, though, and even as they worked their way along the crumbling, abandoned loading dock alongside the nearest warehouse, he saw headlights come on, swing around across the wall ahead of them, and then disappear as the car that cast the twin cones of illumination sped away. People were going home. They weren't worried about two Americans skulking in the shadows along the long-disused railroad tracks.

The hardest part was moving silently. The tracks were littered with trash; cans, bottles, plastic bags, and the other detritus that gathered in undisturbed parts of a crumbling

118

infrastructure. Clearly, this area wasn't high on the city's priority list.

Nearing the end of the row of warehouses, he slowed down, hugging the ramshackle, corrugated metal and concrete structures as much to stay in the shadows as to give himself a better angle on the corner of the wall around the scrapyard ahead. An old railroad car that looked like it hadn't moved in decades stood on the tracks just past the corner, with yet another just past it. They both cast long shadows in the flickering orange light from the lamps over the parking lot to the north.

Hardly daring to make a sound, Flanagan turned and signaled Burgess to hold where they were. He got a nod, then, despite the risk of the light, he moved across the tracks and hugged the wall, moving toward the corner.

He'd almost reached it when he heard footsteps. He froze, not even daring to turn his head to look back at Burgess. Six more paces and he'd reach the corner, but there was no cover, no concealment. The nearest shadow was cast by the derelict railroad car, a good fifty yards away.

Voices murmured in the evening air as the footsteps crunched closer. He couldn't tell whether they were speaking Czech or Russian; his ear for languages wasn't that well-tuned. Either way, they weren't anyone he wanted to meet that evening.

Don't come around that corner. Don't come around that corner. He knew that just thinking it real loud wasn't going to do anything, but he tried it, anyway.

They didn't. He heard them stop and talk, and he could smell cheap tobacco smoke. Then a glowing ember arced out over the tracks and their footsteps resumed their crunching progress.

He started to breathe again. The question of course was, were they a patrol, or just a couple of workers grabbing a smoke before they headed home? Or was there an evening shift that they didn't know about?

Catfooting it to the corner, he eased one eye around, hoping that he wasn't about to find himself staring at some dude who had decided to linger for a couple more minutes.

There were only two men, and they were walking away, one still puffing on a cigarette. They weren't just random workers, either. Both were dressed in the same dark clothing, and both carried vz.58s.

He let out a breath he hadn't quite realized he'd been holding, and ducked back behind the wall, turning to retrace his steps and rejoin Burgess.

He'd seen what he'd needed to see. There might not be a good spot to set up an overwatch position nearby, but there had also been no fence or other obstacle between the tracks and the target warehouse.

They had their infiltration route.

CHAPTER 15

Time *was* somewhat pressing, but they still didn't move on the warehouse until the following night. Dalca had contacted them to see how things were going, expressing her regret over the phone that Brannigan had insisted on separate safehouses, but all they'd told her was that things were progressing.

Most of the rest of the team had prepped their gear and weapons while Flanagan and Burgess had been scouting the target. The gear was pretty easy, even though most of it was little more than chest rigs and load bearing vests. They hadn't gotten any body armor or night vision goggles. Those would have raised too many red flags.

The weapons were another matter. They all *seemed* to be in good operating condition, but when it all came down to it, none of them trusted them without a test fire.

Test fire and zero. A rifle that goes *bang* is still useless if it won't hit what it's pointed at.

That had taken some hemming and hawing. Tomas had provided them all with firearms licenses—forged, of course—so they didn't need to worry so much about being stopped by the police with weapons. Still, showing up at a local range with a bunch of FNX-9s and Bren A2s might raise some eyebrows. And finding enough such ranges that they could spread out in pairs was a logistical nightmare.

Finally, while he'd begrudged the contact, Brannigan had called Dalca and asked if there was a place where they could zero the weapons without being observed. Or at least without drawing undue attention.

That had led them to a farm well out in the countryside, almost two hours' drive from the city. The farmer had some connection with Dalca's organization, whether he was aware of it or not, and he showed them his little range tucked away in the woods at the edge of his fields. It wasn't much, but they were able to set up and get each of the rifles sighted in with a fifty-yard zero, which should give them point-of-aim/point-of-impact out to around two hundred yards.

Brannigan and Wade had zeroed Flanagan's and Burgess's rifles for them. There wouldn't be time to go out there again.

So, by the time the two scouts returned to the safehouse, everything was prepped and ready to go.

They finished planning, then set security and settled in to get some rest and try to catch up on sleep before the sun went down and it was time to go to work.

***

Wade followed Flanagan down the tracks, wishing he had NVGs with one part of his mind but acknowledging that they couldn't have everything, and the bright, orange sodium lights would have presented a bit of a problem for them, anyway, whiting the tubes out as they moved.

He split off with Tackett, moving around the front of the warehouses just to make sure that they weren't about to get blindsided. Flanagan and Burgess hadn't reported much movement around there, but it didn't pay to get lazy.

Slinging his rifle, he drew his knife, opening the Bowie-shaped blade as silently as he could. They hadn't gotten suppressors for the rifles or the pistols, so if he was going to keep this quiet, he was going to have to get up close and personal. It wasn't time to go loud just yet if they could help it.

He paused at the corner and eased his head around to check. No movement. No sounds. Tackett gave his shoulder a squeeze, and then he moved out.

The front of the warehouse was in shadow, in part because of the overhang of the roof, in part because there was another, smaller warehouse built onto the corner, standing between them and the lights over the parking lot.

The two of them padded quietly to the door. There was a window in it, but no lights on inside. Wade put his ear to the crack as they stacked up outside, listening for any movement or voices.

Nothing.

He tested the door, just in case, and was surprised to find it unlocked. Given the security on the compound immediately to the south, he would have expected any doors around here to be secured, but he wasn't going to complain. Easing the door open, he slipped inside with Tackett on his heels.

He still hadn't gotten to know Tackett all that well—the man was almost quieter than Flanagan or Gomez—but the dude knew what he was about.

They spread out as they entered the darkened interior, straining their eyes to see. Wade had a flashlight in his pocket, but he was loathe to use it any sooner than absolutely necessary.

The warehouse was mostly empty, orange light spilling through a few shattered windows high up in the wall to dimly illuminate a couple of pallets stacked in the middle of the cracked concrete floor. There was no movement, no sign of anyone inside. Wade and Tackett still moved along the outer walls, Wade having folded his knife and returned it to his pocket as he brought his Bren back up. There was no way he was going to be able to close the distance fast enough to use the knife in there.

They swept through, coming to the roll-up doors at the end, with another pedestrian door next to them. The door was steel, and when Wade tested the knob, it was also unlocked. He eased it open, then froze.

A man in jeans and a track suit jacket was leaning against the wall, staring at his phone, not six feet away from the door. He hadn't looked up as Wade had cracked the door open, but that was probably only because he'd opened the latch very slowly and, so far, hadn't made a sound.

For a brief moment, he considered just backing off. As aggressive and belligerent as John Wade could be, he wasn't going to risk the mission just to make sure there were no witnesses. If they knew that there was someone back here, that might be enough.

This guy wasn't just a rando hanging out, though, he realized. He was armed; there was an AKM leaning against the wall next to him. It was also well after midnight. There was no reason for anyone to be hanging out near a warehouse, especially not this close to a drug warehouse, at that time of night, if they were just harmless bystanders.

This guy was a lookout. Which meant that the bad guys were nervous.

Unfortunately, while they had gotten radios, they were all commercial black gear jobs, and he didn't dare make a call this close to the lookout.

He turned to Tackett, pointed to his eyes, then out the door, lifting up a single finger. He was *fairly* sure that there was just the one. From what he'd seen so far—and what Flanagan and Burgess had reported—he expected that there would be a conversation going on if there were two.

Tackett nodded as Wade once again drew his knife. They needed to be quiet, and the lookout was close enough.

He threw the door open and lunged.

The hinges squealed as the door came all the way open, and the man with the phone looked up in surprise. He started at the sight of the big man coming for him, and while he didn't have time to notice the faint glint of light on the knife, where Wade held it low and to one side, he was still dialed in enough to recognize a threat when he saw it. He dropped the phone and grabbed for the rifle, and then Wade hit him.

He slammed into the man like a freight train, pinning him to the wall. He kept his off hand high, catching the gangster under the chin with his forearm, the impact hitting the man hard enough in the larynx that he started choking and wasn't able to scream or yell. Even as the Russian doubled up and tried to fend him off, he came in low with the knife, stabbing the man in the midsection repeatedly. The gangster choked and grunted with each impact, but he couldn't get enough wind through his battered throat to scream, even as blood flowed down his front and side.

The gangster kept trying to fight, though, pushing and hitting with ever-decreasing strength against Wade as he was stabbed to death. He was starting to sag, his knees giving way as the damage and the blood loss mounted. Wade kept him up, pinning him to the wall by his neck with that iron bar of a forearm across the man's throat, and kept going, intent on sticking the guy over and over and over until it was done.

There was no mercy in a fight like this. It was over when one of the combatants wasn't moving anymore.

He was so focused on the fight at hand that he didn't notice the movement nearby until Tackett shot the second man who had just come around the corner to the west, an AKS-74u slung at his side, still zipping up his fly.

The *crack* of the gunshots was brutally loud, even with the earplugs that Wade had in, and he almost flinched as the shockwave from Tackett's muzzle blast washed over him. He stabbed the gangster in front of him one last time, digging deep and ripping up through the man's guts and into his chest cavity, then kicked the AKM away from his now nerveless hand and stepped back.

The second man was flat on his back on the pavement, still twitching, blood spurting from his mouth. Tackett had moved, angling out to take up a semi-covered position behind a van parked next to a stack of boxes.

The echoes of the shots were still rolling across the cityscape as Wade quickly wiped his knife clean on the dead man's sleeve, folded and pocketed it, and brought his rifle up.

So much for staying quiet.

CHAPTER 16

I'm not sure how good an idea this is. Kirk had volunteered to lead the distraction element, which was supposed to cause some trouble with the guards out front. They weren't supposed to go kinetic, just create some noise and just enough of an altercation to bring the rest of the security out and open the way for the assault force. They didn't even have their weapons on them, just in case the *policie* got involved. The forged licenses *should* generally keep them out of trouble, but under the circumstances they were setting up, they'd decided that it was better to play up the unarmed dunce of an American tourist angle.

As they approached the gate and the two guards—not the same ones that Flanagan and Burgess had observed; there must have been a shift change—Kirk just felt naked.

He and Bianco still had their weapons nearby. They'd stashed them in the weeds, just in case the cops did show up and decided to search the car. They weren't immediately available, though, and the way those two meatheads in dark clothes were eyeing them, their weapons already slightly raised, was making the hackles on Kirk's neck go up. They weren't the sort of security guards who could be expected to be friendly but firm, turning people away politely.

Which went even further to suggest that they were in the right place. These weren't regular security guards. They were probably Russian mafiosi.

This could get really ugly, really fast.

For a moment, he considered just axing this part of the plan, falling back to the weapons, and calling Brannigan to let him know. The Colonel would understand. The distraction wasn't worth getting the two of them murdered, and he really didn't think this pair was going to be reasonable.

Then a pair of shots echoed from the north side of the compound and ended his internal debate.

He turned to grab Bianco, but the bigger man was already diving into the brush on the side of the road. The designated team nerd might look like a big kid, but he was just about as combat hardened as Kirk was. He knew his way around a fight and didn't need to have his hand held.

Both security guards had turned and ducked at the sound of gunfire, and one of them was still looking toward the noise, while the other had apparently figured it out and was turning back toward the two Blackhearts, his rifle coming back up.

Neither of the two mercs had waited around, though. They were already halfway back to their weapons, leaving a dark and abandoned lane in front of the mob security.

There was no getting around the amount of noise they were making, but fortunately, even as all hell broke loose in the compound behind them, the bad guys didn't just start mag dumping into the overgrown vegetation on the side of the road.

Still, Kirk could hear the man reporting on the radio and it sounded like he was demanding backup. That wasn't Czech, either. The few words he could make out were definitely Russian.

Bianco beat him to the duffel with the weapons by about five seconds. The kid was big, but he was fast. He already had the bag open and was pulling the rifles out, handing the first one to Kirk before grabbing his own.

Kirk took the weapon and pivoted toward the road, covering their backs as Bianco pulled out his load bearing vest and shrugged into it.

Something sure went wrong. The shooting wasn't supposed to have started yet. He didn't get pissed about it. It was just something that happened, especially on small-unit ops like this one. Kirk had been in combat zones all over the world. He was used to Murphy sticking his oar in at the most inconvenient time.

Movement caught his eye, and he mentally echoed Wade's complaint about the lack of NVGs. The lights in the compound behind the gate were partially blinding him, and he had to strain to see the man who was advancing carefully down the lane, his rifle up. A moment later, a bright cone of white light stabbed out from the weapon's forearm. The guards didn't have NVGs, either, but they had lights.

That was fine with Kirk. He had concealment, and now that guy had just given him the perfect target reference.

Under different circumstances, he might have held his fire. They were in the middle of a city, and Prague was hardly a Third World warzone. Still, Kirk had been in enough such places that he knew the risks were hardly that much different. Whether the cops or the local militia descended on the sound of gunshots, the end result was often much the same.

Besides, the first shots had already been fired, and these guys had been ready to shoot them rather than just turn them around.

He dumped five rounds into the dim silhouette behind the bright weapon light. The light spun crazily as the man dropped and the rifle hit the road with a clatter.

The Bren's muzzle flash wasn't as bright as the bad guy's weapon light, but it was still bright enough that he quickly moved as soon as he'd ceased fire, sprinting across the road and diving into the brush between it and the parking lot to the west.

A couple of bullets *snap*ped past his head as he moved, the second guard reacting to the gunfire with a few wild shots of his own, just before Bianco dropped him with a hammer pair from the other side of the road.

More gunfire crackled from inside the compound. Things had definitely gone south, but it sounded like the rest of the team was pressing the fight. Kirk cocked his head despite the ringing in his ears from the close-range gunfire. He'd developed a bit of a feel for gunfights over the years. That didn't sound like the other Blackhearts were trying to break contact.

"Vinnie. You good?" Speaking English where any of the locals might be able to hear them might not be the *best* idea, but things had gone loud anyway, so he figured it didn't make *that* much difference.

"I'm good. Let's push." Bianco had reached the same conclusion Kirk had. Brannigan hadn't called retreat, so they were going to push the fight.

Staying to the sides of the road, the two men hurried toward the gate, weapons up, looking for targets.

***

Flanagan heard the shot to the north and immediately changed mental gears. They were made, which meant that speed and aggression were now their only hope of success.

Not to mention survival, depending on how many shooters Garin had on site.

He still paused at the same corner where he'd spotted the two smoking patrolmen the other night. Going solo into the open ground between the scrapyard and the warehouses would be a recipe for disaster, and Joe Flanagan hadn't lived as long as he had by rushing in without covering his angles.

Gomez was right at his shoulder a heartbeat later. "High/low?"

He nodded. "I'll go low." He was already dropping to a knee as Gomez stepped up to loom over him. A second later, they both popped the corner, leading with their rifle muzzles. He heard Burgess and Puller behind them go down to a knee to cover their six.

The yard was still cluttered with junk and shadowed by the two smaller buildings that stood immediately to the west. The only lights were on the other side of the target warehouse and in the parking lot behind the Blackhearts.

That was good, and the other reason why he'd recommended the infiltration route along the tracks. They were backlit, making it that much more difficult for the bad guys to see them.

Somewhat to his surprise, there wasn't a rush to go investigate the gunshots. A light had come on inside the warehouse, visible at first as a gleam through the windows set high up in the wall, but no one ran out.

That might not be so good. If the bad guys were being cautious, it would make the assault much more difficult.

Then the door flew open, and four men came out, packing a combination of AKs, vz.58s, and a Skorpion machine pistol.

He and Gomez opened fire immediately. He felt Gomez's muzzle blast hammering at him as he dumped the man with the AK, the Bren braced against the corner of the wall, the muzzle flash strobing in his sights as he slammed three rounds into the man before he stumbled and fell against the warehouse wall. The gangster tried to bring his rifle up, but it slipped out of his fingers and fell to the concrete as he slid down along the wall.

Gomez had gotten the man to the right, who was down on his face and twitching, and now both of them shifted targets. The man with the Skorpion had returned fire immediately and indiscriminately, not even bothering to aim as he ran back inside the open door, spraying 9mm across the yard. Bullets smacked into the wall and whizzed overhead, and one smacked into the last man's back even as Gomez and Flanagan both shot him through the chest.

"Moving." Brannigan, Curtis, and Santelli rushed past the two men on the corner, dashing to the cover of the next building over. Curtis, since he didn't have a belt-fed, had

131

complained enough that he'd gotten stuck with their primary payload for the night, in a large duffel bag slung over one shoulder. He'd bitched about that, too, until Santelli had threatened to make him do eight-count bodybuilders in the back yard of the safehouse until they'd stepped off. He wasn't especially slowed by the heavy bag itself. It was what was in it that made him step a little gingerly as the three of them moved to the corner of the building.

Gomez and Flanagan held their position, though Gomez shifted to cover their back now that the last three Blackhearts had passed. Flanagan thought he could hear yelling from somewhere inside the warehouse, but it was hard to tell. His ears were ringing a bit from the gunfire. He had earplugs in, but they weren't the best, and he still needed to hear, so there were holes drilled through them. It was a balance that usually fell out in favor of more hearing loss.

"Moving." Brannigan and Santelli had their side of the yard locked down, and there was no point in hanging out and waiting.

"With you." Gomez rolled around the corner as Flanagan got up and advanced on the warehouse, both men's rifles coming up to point forward as Curtis, on the corner behind Brannigan's bulk, covered down the tracks the way they'd come.

As he got closer to the warehouse entrance, he could definitely hear voices inside. It sounded like someone was shouting into a radio or a phone, demanding backup.

"Woodsrunner, Kodiak, this is Lumberjack." Kirk's old ZZ-Top beard had earned him that nickname. "Gamer and I are coming up from the gate. Watch your fires."

"Good copy, Lumberjack." Brannigan had taken the call, since he was currently holding position. "Move on the target building and link up with Woodsrunner."

"Roger."

Flanagan didn't dare take his eyes off the door as he closed the distance, but Gomez had shifted to his left, and now flashed a red lens at their feet. Out of the corner of his eye,

Flanagan saw a similar flash, even as he wished as hard as he could that they had NVGs. That flash of light would have just lit them up for any bad guys if there were any in the doorway. They didn't take any more fire, but he stepped up his pace to get to the warehouse wall a little bit faster, hopefully denying the enemy a target.

He and Gomez reached the wall a few seconds ahead of Kirk and Bianco, and those two stacked up with them, while Brannigan and the others held their position. It might be a good idea to flood the target building with guns, but they still had to watch their backs.

Someone was *definitely* shouting inside. The Blackhearts stepped over the corpses outside the warehouse, paused just long enough to be sure they were all in place, and then Flanagan went through the door fast, his weapon up and searching for targets.

CHAPTER 17

The echoes from Tackett's shot had barely started to die away when more gunfire thundered from the other side of the tracks. Things were getting hot, fast.

Wade's first instinct was to rush to the fight, but he was far too old a soldier to do that. One of the reasons he and Tackett had cleared this side was to make sure no one came from the north to disrupt the raid before they pulled off. So, instead he moved to the corner and the next door, Tackett joining him as smoothly as if they'd worked and trained side by side for years.

The team had only worked with Tackett once before, and then he'd been a straphanger. Essentially the client, he'd contacted Brannigan, at Vernon White's request to get Mitchell Price and his guys out of Kyrgyzstan, but then he'd insisted on coming along. True to his nature, they'd found, he hadn't just been along for the ride. He'd hiked and fought right alongside the rest of the Blackhearts and done a good enough job of it that he had been accepted as an honorary Blackheart, if nothing else. Now here he was once more, proving himself all over again.

This door was latched, but Wade quickly crossed it, put his back to the wall, and donkey-kicked it just under the doorknob. It cracked but held. He hit it again, and this time the latch tore through the jamb and the door juddered open, even as a bullet caromed off the roof above them and whined off into the night. Tackett went through the door, and Wade was already halfway through his turn as the smaller man broke the threshold, riding the door to the wall as Wade slipped through behind him, covering his back.

This warehouse wasn't as empty as the first, but it was dark and quiet. Stacks of car parts and palletized boxes covered most of the floor, and the two men had to move carefully alongside them, clearing each bit of dead space in between.

There was no one inside. They were alone, except for the two dead men on the pavement outside.

So why can I hear somebody talking? The sound definitely wasn't coming from inside the warehouse, and it wasn't someone yelling up by the target building, because there was still gunfire coming from that direction, and he shouldn't be able to hear voices from that far away over that racket.

"Heading outside." He kept his voice low, moving as he spoke, and Tackett lifted his muzzle and fell in behind him.

They went out through the door the same way they'd gone in, clearing the yard and the tracks beyond. They'd barely made it across the threshold when Wade realized what he'd been hearing.

One of the gangsters they'd killed had a radio. And someone was now yelling over it in Russian.

That wouldn't be that surprising, or a cause for alarm, except that they got an answer. A much calmer answer, that had to be from someone outside the compound.

Wade couldn't make out all the words, but he recognized enough that he could get the gist.

The bad guys had reinforcements coming, and they'd be there in less than five minutes.

He moved to the corner where the second body lay, and peered around it, leading with his muzzle. He could see Brannigan and Curtis barricaded on the secondary building ahead, along with the derelict train cars on the tracks. Burgess and Puller were covering the tracks they'd followed on infil.

"On me, Dan." He had to wait to key his radio until after Kirk had deconflicted with the others. "Kodiak, Angry Ragnar. Coming from your north. Be advised, we've got hostile reinforcements inbound. Don't know from where."

"Roger, come ahead." If Brannigan was frustrated about doing mostly coordination while the rest of the team got some, he wasn't showing it.

"Moving." Wade came around the corner and sprinted toward the derelict train car. It would provide some decent cover to lock down the northern approach, which didn't seem to be nearly as secure as the southern entrance.

He and Tackett were halfway there when headlights flared on the road coming down from the north.

***

Flanagan heard Wade on the radio as he went through the door, but he had somewhat more pressing matters on his mind.

The warehouse was *packed*, shelves running east and west, filled with pallets and pallets of small bags, wrapped in plastic. They all looked roughly the same, though he didn't exactly have time to check what was in the bags.

He probably *should* have cleared the corner behind him, but he'd driven forward through the door, pursuing the man with the Skorpion. He'd last seen that guy going through the door and to the right, so that was the way he went, trusting that Gomez would adjust. They'd both come through much of the same training back in the day, as Marines. *The Number One Man is always right.*

The warehouse was dark, but that was somewhat alleviated by the fact that someone behind one of the pallets up ahead had a light on.

He paced forward, rolling his soles on the floor to make as little noise as possible, his muzzle tracking toward the white glow ahead. He sensed more than saw Kirk's muzzle over his shoulder as he moved. He wasn't alone.

The man with the light was yelling into a radio and getting a somewhat calmer reply. Another voice sounded from deeper inside the warehouse, sounding every bit as panicked as the guy on the radio.

Flanagan and Kirk faded toward the wall as they approached the corner of the shelving unit. Neither man wanted to turn that corner and end up close enough that a scared Russian gangster could grab one of their muzzles.

They rounded the corner almost together. Both weapons turned toward the man crouched behind a pallet.

The gangster saw the movement out of the corner of his eye and started like he'd just seen a ghost. He threw himself sideways, twisting to land on his back, bringing that Skorpion up to point it at the shadowy forms of the two Blackhearts.

Both Bren 2s barked at the same moment, spitting flame as the bullets ripped through the man's chest and head. One hit his gun hand, blowing off a finger and sending the Skorpion spinning off into the dark to land on the concrete with a metallic clatter.

The Russian was dead before he could scream in pain at the loss of the digit.

The other man inside the warehouse apparently decided at that point that firepower was the better part of valor. He stuck his muzzle around the corner of the shelves at the far end of the building and opened fire. Flame strobed in the darkness and bullets smacked off shelves, punched holes in the metal walls, blew bags of white powder apart, and skipped off the concrete floor.

Flanagan and Kirk threw themselves between the shelving units, diving for the dubious cover of the pallets of drugs as the Russian's rounds skimmed by them. Flanagan hoped that Bianco and Gomez had gotten out of the way, but right then was no time to go back and check. He had to kill this guy before one of them really did get hit.

Picking himself up off the floor, he moved quickly away from the settling clouds of white dust, careful not to breathe any of it in. If that *was* Roulette, that would be a very, very bad day.

The shelving units were set up in a grid, but he didn't go immediately into the first lane that would bring him around behind the shooter. The man had ceased fire and, from the clicking sounds, he was reloading.

Flanagan pushed two lanes down before he turned toward the end of the warehouse. Kirk had moved almost as fast and was on his feet and right behind him. Flanagan glided down the lane, his eyes and his muzzle quickly shifting to cover the shelves to his right. He didn't *know* that the shooter at the end was the only one left, and he still had enough presence of mind not to take chances.

The end of the lane came up fast. He could hear the Russian panting and cursing, just as he sent the bolt home and opened fire again.

This time, though, he was shooting at shadows where there were no men anymore.

Flanagan leaned out around the shelving unit, dropping his muzzle level as he moved. The sights settled right on the Russian, a short, thickset man in jeans and a dark jacket, barely backlit by the muzzle flash from his AK and the faint orange light coming in the high windows at the back of the warehouse.

Flanagan put a bullet through the back of the gangster's skull and dropped him on his face.

"Clear." Kirk had swung around the other direction, covering his six. "Let's torch this place and get out of here before we all get high on Roulette."

Before Flanagan could answer, more gunfire thundered from the north. They weren't done yet.

***

Wade held his fire, though he was pretty sure, based on what he'd made out of the radio call and the response, not to mention the time of night, that this was the Russian reinforcements.

139

In some contrast to the calm voice on the radio, the vehicle came screaming down the road to halt with a squeal of tires just before the railroad tracks. The doors flew open and men in dark clothing and carrying rifles and submachineguns piled out.

That was all Wade needed to see. These guys didn't move like cops, didn't look like cops, and he was reasonably sure that the Czech police didn't carry AK-103s and PP-19 Bizon submachineguns.

To be fair, Wade wouldn't hesitate to waste some local cops if they got in the way of the mission, but he knew that might cause them some extra problems, and Brannigan and Santelli probably wouldn't like it, either.

These guys, though, were too obviously fair game. He leaned out while Tackett covered their six, braced the Bren 2's forearm against the corner of the railroad car, and opened fire.

He rode the trigger reset, dragging the muzzle back and forth across the car as he fired as fast as the gun would let him, dumping the mag into the men and the vehicle. He wasn't really aiming, even at that range, but just hammering as many rounds through men, metal, and fiberglass as he could. Windows shattered, auto glass cascading to the ground, as men were slammed sideways into the vehicle's side or crumpled as bullets smashed through knees or hips.

Another rifle opened up from near the end of the building to his left, crashing through the hood, windshield, and anyone on the other side of the SUV.

It was all over in a few seconds. Wade's bolt locked back on an empty magazine, and he let it fall, quickly pulling a new one out of his chest rig and slapping it in before he even examined his kill zone to see if he was done or not.

A couple of the Russians were still writhing and twitching on the ground. Most of the others lay still, with that curious motionlessness that spoke of death. Santelli wasn't shooting anymore, either.

The radio crackled in his ear. "This is Woodsrunner. Warehouse is clear. We need to get the payload in here and beat feet."

***

Curtis was swearing to himself as he jogged across the yard toward the target warehouse, uncomfortably aware of how carefully and slowly he had to move. His muzzle tracked toward the opening between the building where he and Brannigan had been set up and the warehouse itself, even though Kirk, Gomez, Flanagan, and Bianco were outside said warehouse, covering both directions.

"Why did *I* get stuck with the Molotov bag?" He swung it down off his shoulder, but still very gingerly lowered it to the ground. "I haven't gotten to shoot *at all*."

"Because you drew the short straw." Flanagan was already unzipping the duffel.

Curtis stared at him bleakly. "The 'short' straw, Joseph? That's low. I mean, that's below the belt low."

Flanagan didn't even look up at him. "Not my problem that you've got a complex." He was carefully pulling out the equally carefully packaged bottles of gasoline. They'd found screw-on tops instead of stuffing the rag fuses in before Curtis had started carrying them, which was safer but now added another step.

Curtis spluttered for a moment, but still took up security, nevertheless. "Why's everybody out here, anyway? Kinda exposed in the yard, here."

"Some of the bags of product in there got shot up in the firefight." Flanagan's voice was flat and matter of fact as he unscrewed the caps and stuck the fuses in, letting them soak up the gas as he set the bottles on the ground. "None of us felt like spinning the wheel."

Curtis felt goosebumps go up on his arms and he unconsciously glanced up at the windows above and the bullet holes in the metal walls. He didn't really miss a beat. "Why's everybody standing so damned close to the warehouse?"

141

Kirk might have chuckled a little. It was hard to tell. Flanagan just shook his head as he counted out the Molotov cocktails, decided that they had enough, and pulled a lighter out of his vest.

"Let's make this quick." He lit the first and handed it to Gomez, who launched it in through the open door with a hooked throw.

"How flammable is this stuff supposed to be, anyway?" Kirk asked, as Flanagan lit the second and Gomez lobbed it inside at a different angle.

A fireball suddenly erupted inside, blowing out several windows. "I'd say, 'very.'" Flanagan lit the third, but it looked like they wouldn't need much more than that. He still finished off the next three, which Curtis was grateful for, since it meant he didn't have to repack and carry them.

Flanagan keyed his radio as he zipped up the duffel. "This is Woodsrunner. Target's burning. Time to go."

"Roger. Everyone fall back to Rally Point Sportovni." Brannigan had designated the sport center south of the actual active railroad tracks as their rendezvous point once they got clear of the target. "Steer clear of the cops and if you can't avoid the opposition, then break contact as quickly as possible."

Curtis wondered why he'd reiterated that. Sure, they were all aggressive meat-eaters, but this was a small team in a city that could turn hostile as soon as the bad guys coordinated with the local law. Even *he* wasn't so aggressive as to try to run-and-gun through freakin' *Prague*.

He glanced over his shoulder at the duffel, dreading picking it up and running with it again. It *was* going to be a lot lighter, but still…

Flanagan seemed to be thinking along the same lines. He suddenly bent, grabbed the duffel, and swung it through the open door with a heave, letting it sail inside as another fireball belched flame through the upper windows. "Let's go."

They scattered, most heading back south through the gate where Kirk and Bianco had entered the compound. Curtis went after Brannigan and Santelli, returning to the tracks, though they'd break off after a while so as not to completely retrace their steps.

Behind them, the warehouse burned, while whooping European sirens sounded through the night, and flashing blue lights began to converge on the sound of gunfire.

Garin's operation had just taken a hell of a hit. It might take some of the heat off Dalca's people. For sure it would put a crimp in the Roulette traffic.

Curtis thought about that as he slipped through the shadows, naturally following the least well-lit paths through the urban jungle. He lived in Vegas, and he'd grown up in the inner city. He knew the kind of damage drugs could do, and those were the regular narcotics, not something as openly evil as Roulette.

Even if Dalca hadn't been involved, he'd have been happy to take this job.

CHAPTER 18

"So, we need to talk about what went down last night." Santelli had been chewing on this since they'd left the warehouse. He never had been necessarily the most articulate, and compared to some men in his chosen profession, he often felt downright slow, but Santelli had never been the sort of man who'd stayed in the Marine Corps just because he didn't know how to do anything else. He was a thinker, and always had been. It might take him a while to grind his way through a problem, but he'd get through it.

The team had finally all converged back on the safehouse. The sun was just coming up, and every one of them was feeling the sleepless night, but the hot wash had to be gone through. There was more on Santelli's mind, though, than just the tactical element.

"What's on your mind, Carlo?" Brannigan was standing near the kitchen, his arms folded, looking about as solid as an oak. The Colonel could be falling down exhausted, but he'd never show it in front of the rest of the team.

"This was supposed to be a Front operation, right?" Santelli scratched his jaw with a thumb. "So, how come it looked like all the dudes we smoked were Russian mob?" He looked around the room at pensive faces. "Hell, we didn't even really get a chance to test the stuff in the warehouse. Can we be *sure*

145

that it was this Roulette stuff? What if we just torched a warehouse full of coke, or heroin, just because Dalca wanted the Russkies out of the way?"

There was no response at first. A few gazes were lowered to the floor. Not because any of them were ashamed of what they'd done. It had been pretty obvious that they'd been up against Russian mobsters, and no one was going to mourn any of those bastards. The question still needed to be answered.

"I mean, I'm fine with torching coke, heroin, meth, or whatever." Curtis was strangely serious. "'Cause fuck that shit."

"It's an important question, though." Brannigan was chewing on the question, himself. "The truth is, right now, we don't have a huge amount of proof one way or another. That was definitely a mob operation." He nodded toward the radio scanner on the counter. "We've heard enough from the Czech police to confirm that."

Santelli wasn't sure what he thought about that. Confirming the intel *after* they'd made the hit was kind of ass-backwards.

"We saw enough to be pretty sure a few nights ago, Carlo." Flanagan could have been offended at his recon being questioned, but he wasn't that kind of guy. "This was a good hit."

Santelli nodded. "I'm not objecting to smoking some Russian gangsters and burning down some drugs. Don't get me wrong. I'm just wondering if we're really doing what we set out to do. This Roulette stuff—if it's real—sure *sounds* like something the Front would be into, but where's the proof, aside from what Dalca's told us?"

"Well, as much as I hate to put it this way, Carlo, I think we're going to have to wait and see what happens." Another commander might have gotten uncomfortable over the line of questioning, but not Brannigan. "The whole point of this raid was to kick over the anthill and see what came scuttling out. That's not going to happen immediately. And you weren't there for Kozel's interrogation." His expression darkened. "I was. He

146

let out just enough that I'm about ninety percent certain that we're dealing with the Front." He shrugged. "Either that, or there's somebody else out there in the shadows who's just as dangerous."

The team was too tired to react much to that possibility, but Santelli felt a bit of a chill. What if there *was* another group as secretive and ruthless as the Humanity Front out there? *More* secretive, really. They'd known about the Front's existence even before they'd known the group's real agenda. The Humanity Front had been hiding in plain sight, masquerading as an international humanitarian NGO. *The* international humanitarian NGO, the sort of organization that celebrities and politicians the world over preened about supporting. That was how they'd built the financial and influence base that kept them functioning and threatening the world, even after they'd been exposed for what they really were.

In fact, most people probably *still* had no idea just what the Humanity Front really was. The silence over who had been running the operations in Chad and Argentina had been deafening.

"We'll keep an ear to the ground." Brannigan had apparently decided it was time to wrap up the debrief. "For now, let's set security and get some rest. I have a feeling that if Garin's as closely wedded to the Front as we suspect, something's going to be stirring soon, even if that warehouse *wasn't* full of Roulette."

***

The phone's ringtone was an electronic version of *Also Sprach Zarathustra*. It would have surprised most people who'd met the man named Winter, if they even remembered him. He took some pride in being the ultimate gray man, as hard to even recall as he was to pick out of a crowd. He was the sort of man no one would quite expect to even listen to music, let alone have the sort of tastes he did.

To anyone who did take notice of him, he looked more like a German college professor than he did a hardened killer. Which was the way he liked to keep it.

"Yes?" He kept any hesitation out of his voice—easy enough for a man with his practice at suppressing human emotions. It had been a long time since this phone had rung, and a distant, clinical part of him was somewhat fascinated at how eager he felt to answer that ring again.

He'd been out of circulation for some time, waiting for the Board to settle the disputes that had wracked it after the repeated failures in Chad and Argentina. He'd heard rumors about another disaster in Kyrgyzstan, but only rumors. His own intelligence gathering apparatus was limited, especially when it came to the Organization.

"King's Mill Park. One hour." The call disconnected.

He left the phone on the dresser as he walked out of the hotel room, shrugging into a jacket. It was finally time to go back to work.

***

Winter hadn't needed to ask where in King's Mill Park he was supposed to go. The Organization had meeting places preset around the world. It might have been impossible to memorize all of them, but he'd made contact with some of his more discreet sources within the Organization in Canada and had been provided with the list.

King's Mill Park was mostly a cemetery, which made it almost ideal for this sort of meeting. Nobody who wasn't already tracking a target would set up any serious surveillance on a cemetery.

It took a little bit of time to find the right headstone. He didn't have exact coordinates, just the name on the headstone. It was right about at one hour since the call that he walked up to the man in the long coat standing and looking down at a dark granite gravestone that read "Schofield."

The man didn't look over at him but seemed to be paying his respects. "We have a situation in Prague. A warehouse full of Project 577 was attacked and destroyed."

"I'm not aware of that project number." Winter's voice was low and deadpan.

The man glanced over at him then. "It's a disruption project, combined with the population measures. It's still technically in the testing phase, but initial reports are promising." He turned his attention back to the gravestone, as if they were talking about a deceased friend. "The product had already been handed over to the local distributor, so none of our people were involved, but someone was clearly targeting our operation. This needs to be cleaned up."

Winter's expression didn't even flicker. "There is more than one way to interpret those instructions."

The man pulled an envelope out of his coat pocket and passed it to him. Winter made it disappear into his own pocket without looking at it. "Full intel dump, dossiers for a team, travel arrangements, and instructions are there." He still didn't look at Winter but put his hands back into his coat pockets as he started to turn away to walk back toward the road. "This project shows too much promise for us to allow it to be derailed, either by greedy criminals, over-zealous counter-narcotics cops, or anyone else." He barely turned his head to speak over his shoulder. "Take care of it."

Winter didn't respond as he resumed his own study of the headstone. He didn't even pull the envelope out to look at it. There would be an SD card inside, anyway, and he'd have to read it and enter a decryption code. Even so, he'd still need to destroy it before he even got on a plane for Europe.

The brief elation at getting a mission again, after having been instructed to lay low after Argentina, had vanished as he slipped into his mission mindset. He was cold, emotionless, and analytical now. It was time to go to work.

**

The burner phone rang, and Wade snatched it up. Most of the rest of the team was still snoring. It had been a long night. "Yeah."

"This is Tomas. Yurasov is in the open. He has called a meeting of his *vory* in the city for this afternoon."

"Where?" Wade was already moving, heading for where Brannigan was sleeping on the couch, his rifle propped up next to his head. The Colonel was actually one of the quietest sleepers, though even if he had been snoring, Santelli and Curtis would have drowned him out.

"I don't know yet. I have an informant within the organization, but he's low down enough that he won't know until his boss gets them moving. I thought you should know, though."

"Good call." Wade shook Brannigan's shoulder, and the Colonel's eyes snapped open. There was no bleary sleepiness there. He just came awake. Wade offered him the phone. "It's Tomas. Says that Yurasov's called a meeting for this afternoon."

Brannigan sat up and accepted the phone. "This is John."

Wade let him talk to Tomas as he returned to his post at the back of the safehouse. Mission prep would take some time, but it looked like things were moving.

That was good. Wade didn't like sitting around and waiting.

CHAPTER 19

A hotel in downtown Prague, directly across the street from the Grand Museum, was not the place that Burgess would have expected for a Russian Mafiya meetup. His imagination had dreamed up a shadowy meeting in a warehouse, somewhere on the outskirts of town.

That would have been easier to spy on. Setting up surveillance on a penthouse apartment in the middle of the city was considerably more difficult.

Fortunately, Dalca's organization had been in Prague for a long time. And while Dalca might protest continually that her business was first and foremost information, without a lot of the sordid stuff that the rest of the global underground indulged in, she sure had a lot of resources for skullduggery.

That was why he was now walking in the service entrance of the hotel, dressed like a maintenance man, complete with the requisite tools, keys, and passcards. He even had a Czech ID with his face on it, identifying him as "Mstislav Brozik." How Dalca's organization had managed to get all of this put together in about two hours he had no idea, but they'd done it.

It occurred to him, as he started upstairs with Flanagan, similarly dressed and equipped, that Yurasov—or someone else in Garin's organization—must have used this venue before.

Probably enough times that Dalca's organization had targeted the place.

Either that, or they had one hell of a dragnet out for possible venues they might need to penetrate.

The two of them headed upstairs, Flanagan making a show of looking over a work order. No one stopped them or asked them what they were doing there. As long as they steered clear of the staff, they should be fine.

At least until they got to the penthouse. Yurasov's security was probably going to be pretty jumpy after the night before. Fortunately, they had a plan for that.

The stairs led up to the penthouse entrance, and there were two muscle-heads standing there, dressed in dark suits with far too much bling, gold chains around their necks and sunglasses on even in the stairwell. The rings on their thick fingers might have been decoration, but Burgess had been around enough to know that they were primarily there to lend a bit more damage to a punch. That was leaving aside the hardware he was pretty sure both men were packing beneath their jackets.

Fortunately, there was another door leading off the stairwell, one flight down from the penthouse entrance, and while the two hoods on the top landing glared at them from behind their sunglasses, the two Blackhearts unlocked that door and ducked through it. That would both get them onto their actual infiltration and hopefully alleviate the mobsters' concerns. Just maintenance men, going about their business.

Burgess blew out a breath as the door shut behind them. Not that he could really relax. There was every possibility that the mobsters had a way to access the maintenance areas as well, and if they were suspicious enough, they'd at least want to check the two Blackhearts out.

Sure enough, even as he and Flanagan worked their way toward the roof access, he heard one of the guards try the door. The bad guys were on their toes.

Why shouldn't they be? If I was looking at the kind of loss that we inflicted on them last night, I'd be a little jumpy, too.

Fortunately, both were carrying pistols as well as knives. There had been some discussion of taking no weapons at all. If they were stopped, it would be difficult to explain the FNX-9s and knives. They did have their forged pistol licenses, but most maintenance people didn't carry weapons.

Most maintenance workers weren't carrying laser microphones, either.

Those had been a surprise, but they shouldn't have been. Dalca's main stock in trade *was* information, after all, and if she could get it without paying for it, that was money in the bank for her and her organization. It only made sense that they'd have all sorts of spy gadgets on hand.

The door rattled again, and Burgess dropped his hand to the FNX-9 in the pocket of his coverall while Flanagan worked on getting the roof access open.

Still, neither of the thugs came through, and after a few more moments, they left the maintenance door alone. Burgess hoped that they'd given up.

Flanagan had the door open and was heading up the ladder onto the roof. This particular roof access was intended for the HVAC systems, so they would have some concealment, at least. Unless, of course, the mobsters had put two and two together and sent someone out on the roof. They shouldn't be *able* to do that, not from the penthouse, but there was always the possibility that they might get inventive. Or destructive. Burgess wouldn't put it past those two meatheads in the stairwell to bust a couple of hotel windows if they felt like it.

Well, if that happens, things are gonna get interesting.

It helped that Tomas had gotten Bianco and Kirk onto the roof of the next building over, so they'd have some overwatch. Burgess would have preferred to set up over there in the first place, but it hadn't looked like they'd have a shot at the right window from there.

They emerged onto the roof, in the middle of a maze of metal ducts and power boxes. There was certainly a lot of concealment up there, but Burgess was immediately worried about just how they were going to get line of sight on the meeting place.

Flanagan, however, seemed to have memorized the overhead imagery they'd studied, and immediately ducked beneath one HVAC duct and headed toward the northeast corner of the building. Burgess followed after securing the door behind them, holding his tool bag, which was full of tools of *their* trade, rather than the maintenance equipment it was supposed to carry, close to his side.

It took only a few moments to get to a spot where they just barely had line of sight on the window at the north side of the penthouse, where the meeting was supposed to be happening.

Flanagan got the laser mic set up quickly, training the infrared beam on the window. Burgess settled in to cover the roof access.

Depending on how the meeting went, they might be there for a while.

***

Flanagan put the headphones on and turned up the gain. For a moment, he got nothing, then he adjusted the mic's aim a little, and started to hear voices.

And promptly cursed. *Should have thought of that.* Of course *they're speaking Russian.* He pulled the headphones off. "Hey, Tom. How's your Russian?"

"Decent." Burgess glanced over his shoulder. "You want to switch out?"

Flanagan sighed and held out the headphones. "It's all yours."

***

Abrasha Yurasov wasn't a big man. He made up for that fact with force of personality and extreme violence. Which was why most of the men in the room facing him right now couldn't quite look him in the eye.

"An entire *warehouse!*" He smashed his fist into the wall, leaving a dent in the plaster. Not that he cared that much. They'd certainly paid the hotel enough, and those little *suka*s wouldn't dare complain about it, anyway. "Do you have any *idea* how much the product in that one warehouse was worth?" His voice was close to a scream.

The truth was, though he'd barely even acknowledge it in the privacy of his own mind, that Yurasov was scared. If anything, he was even more scared than the man at the other side of the table, a man whom the other thirteen gangsters in the room were trying to keep far away from.

"It wasn't my fault, *tovarisch*." The fact that the graying, portly Yevgeniy Bravikov used that term, instead of *vor*, was enough to tell anyone just how rattled he was. Bravikov was the oldest man in the room, and there had been a time when he'd been the most dangerous. He'd been a KGB officer in then-Czechoslovakia just before the collapse in 1991 and had easily slid into the role of Mafiya *vor*. He was old and tired after all these years, though, and that was why he was now on the chopping block for the massacre at the warehouse on the east side of the city. "It was a coordinated assault, and we had no warning. They left none of my men alive."

"I *told* you to eliminate this Dalca, and you fucked that up." Yurasov's voice had finally dropped, which made several of the other men in the room go even paler as they backed away as far as they could from Bravikov, while trying very hard not to make it too obvious. "This is the result. Now I'm going to have to take matters into my own hands."

Without another word, he drew the CZ 110 from his waistband and shot Bravikov through the throat.

He hadn't intended to shoot the man there. He'd intended to shoot him in the guts, then stand over him and put a bullet in each major joint while he writhed and screamed. He'd gotten excited, though, his usual cold-bloodedness lost in the rage brought on by his own fear.

Bravikov threw a hand to his throat as blood spurted from the bullet hole, letting out a sickening gurgle as he slumped backward in his chair, red flowing down through his fingers to soak his front. He was already dying, unable to even gather the breath to scream, even if there hadn't been a hole in his neck.

Yurasov cursed, his example wasted, and just dumped the rest of the magazine into Bravikov's body, the last couple rounds going high as the recoil forced his hand up, smashing into the ceiling tiles. One more thing for the hotel staff to fix, but Yurasov couldn't be bothered to care.

He threw the empty pistol on the table in front of him and glared around at the other men in the room. "The client has people coming. I don't need to tell any of you *suka blyaty* what it means if this mess isn't cleaned up by the time they get here. *Mr. Garin* is coming here, too." He stabbed a finger at every other *vor* in the room. "Find that Dalca *suka* and everyone in Prague who works for her. *Find* them and *kill* them. I want their houses and businesses burned to the ground. I want their cars bombed. I want *scorched fucking earth* on her entire operation. Am I clear?"

There were nods all around the room. No one dared say anything. Yurasov's pistol might be unloaded, the slide locked back on an empty magazine, but that didn't make him any less dangerous.

"*Get moving!*"

His screamed command had barely finished when the door to the penthouse opened, and Ignatiy stepped inside, his meaty hands glittering with rings that had borne more than one man's blood. "We might have a problem."

***

Flanagan heard the *boom*, dimly transmitted through the roof, before Burgess tore off the headset, buried the entire apparatus in the tool bag, and announced, "Company's coming."

If only we'd brought climbing harness and ropes. There hadn't been room for that kind of gear, but it would have simplified getting off the roof. If the Russians had just smashed the door to the roof, they were kind of stuck.

Not entirely, since there was, thankfully, another roof access. Whether they could get to it fast enough before the Russians found it was the other question.

He drew his FNX while Burgess finished packing up the microphone and the rest of the gear. *One of these days I'm going to come on one of these scouting missions loaded for bear.* He still only had two reloads, and Burgess was carrying the same amount.

The door to the ladder cracked open, and he put the sights on the edge of the door.

"Moving." Burgess was already heading for their exit, the tool bag on his back, his pistol in his hands. Flanagan hesitated, just for a moment, as the door continued to open. If he shot one of the gangsters right then and there, even through the door, then he might buy them some time.

Or he might just bring the whole hornet's nest down around their ears.

Finally deciding that discretion was the better part of valor, he rolled around the stack of HVAC equipment and followed Burgess, keeping his head down and hopefully out of sight of the penthouse windows.

It was a rough route and took them out of coverage from the men on top of the older building across the street. They had to sprint across the most open part of the roof, next to a three-sided, pyramidal skylight, but they didn't hear any shouts, and no one shot at them.

Then they were weaving through the ductwork on the west side of the building, heading for the roof access. Almost out.

Burgess was about ten feet away when the door burst open.

Flanagan was a couple paces behind Burgess as the door juddered open behind a savage kick. A wiry man in dark trousers, a white t-shirt, and a dark jacket came through the door, and Burgess took him low, at the midsection, slamming into him with his lowered shoulder and knocking the wind out of him as he drove him backward into the man behind him. The three of them went down in a heap as Flanagan closed in, his FNX-9 in both hands.

He didn't have a shot. Burgess was tangled up with both men, throwing knees and elbows where he could, and was blocking the way. He was also so tied up with the two of them that he couldn't reach his knife, and his pistol was off line.

There wasn't time to wait for Burgess to clear the two of them. There were at least two more mobsters coming after them across the roof. The overwatch couldn't cover them; they were on the wrong side of the building.

He cleared their six briefly. Their pursuers hadn't made it around the ductwork yet—they were probably moving cautiously, just in case the Blackhearts had set an ambush—so he had a few seconds.

Reaching down, he grabbed Burgess's shoulder and hauled him off the two gangsters. The first one still had a lot of fight in him and started to come up fast.

Flanagan put the muzzle of his FNX-9 to the man's forehead and pulled the trigger.

The report was painfully loud in the stairwell, and his hearing was immediately deadened, making the second man's scream as the bullet punched right through his buddy's skull and into his shoulder slightly thinner and weaker than it really was. The fact that the guy had a mouthful of the first thug's blood, brains, skull, and hair didn't help him in the volume department, either.

The wounded man barely had time to register the shock and the pain, though, before Flanagan shifted his blood-spattered pistol a few inches to the left and silenced him with another single shot to the face. The puckered hole that sprouted just to one side of the bridge of the man's nose splashed more gore over Flanagan's gun hand, as the pressure popped the man's eye

158

partway out of its socket. His head bounced at the impact, then lolled limply on the concrete floor.

Flanagan hauled Burgess to his feet. "We've got to move."

Burgess was looking a little battered, but he got his equilibrium quickly and stepped over the bodies, his own pistol up and at the ready. Flanagan took one last look behind them, spotting movement through the maze of ductwork, then slipped in behind him.

There was no way to secure the door. The bodies were in the way, and the latch had been broken by the bigger man's kick, anyway. They just had to move fast.

The two of them headed down the steps at very close to a run, slowed only by the necessity of covering as many angles as they could manage with their muzzles. Flanagan dimly heard excited curses in Russian above them as they pounded past the fourth floor landing, even as he keyed the radio in his pocket. "This is Woodsrunner. We have been engaged, and need extract at the ground floor, time now." He was panting a little harder than he'd expected or liked, but he still heard the reply.

"En route."

A door banged open above them, and he heard more footsteps on the stairs. Pausing for a second, he pivoted and looked up over his pistol's sights, but while he could see movement, he had no targets.

For a split second, he considered shooting up the stairwell anyway. Anyone in their right mind should have ducked for cover at the sound of those two pistol shots in the first place, and there shouldn't be anyone running toward them who wasn't a Russian mobster, but he'd also been in enough places and seen enough to know that there were always people who would rationalize the noise or just go to investigate regardless.

Better to just get the hell out. He turned back toward the ground floor and followed Burgess.

The entire way down, he expected a door to burst open in front of them and a bunch of gangsters to pour out with guns and other weapons. Yet they had apparently gotten ahead of the bad guys, and while they could hear running footsteps and shouts in Russian from above, they reached the ground floor without anyone cutting them off.

They paused for a moment at the door, first Flanagan, then Burgess covering while the other tore off their blood-spattered maintenance coveralls. Then, holstering and concealing their pistols, they ducked through the door and headed for the exit.

While most of the upper floors were taken up by the hotel, there was almost a mall on the bottom floor. It was an odd arrangement, in Flanagan's eyes, but there were enough people around the small shops that divided up the ground floor that, if they moved quickly and carefully enough, they could lose themselves in the crowd.

Both of them slowed, trying to look as nonchalant as possible. Every fiber of Flanagan's being screamed at him to run for the exit and get the hell out, especially since he had no way of knowing for sure that he hadn't gotten any blood spatter on him beyond what had splashed the coveralls. He knew he had blood on his hand, but that was shoved into his jacket pocket.

He was going to have to burn these clothes later.

No one screamed, no one gave them a second glance as they worked their way toward the exit. He saw the van pull up outside and resisted the urge to sprint for the door.

Then the door to the stairwell banged open behind them, someone shouted in Russian, and the screaming started.

He spared a glance over his shoulder, in no small part because everyone else was looking, and saw a burly man with a shaved head coming toward them, a sawed-off shotgun in his hand. The guy wasn't looking at them yet, but he had to know they were still there.

Burgess grabbed his sleeve, and they sprinted for the doors. Not a good place to get into a gunfight.

Another shout in Russian penetrated the screams, and a gunshot shattered glass as they went through the door, sending debris cascading onto the sidewalk. Somewhere nearby, a Czech siren whooped as the local cops descended on the report of gunfire.

The two Blackhearts piled into the side door of the van and Burgess hauled it shut. They were barely inside when Kirk stomped on the gas, pulling away from the curb and heading in the opposite direction of the sirens and the flashing blue lights.

Behind them, one of the Russian mobsters lunged out onto the sidewalk and fired at the retreating van. The shot went wild, and then Kirk took the next turn and disappeared around the corner.

CHAPTER 20

Boy, who would have thought we could move so much faster than a bunch of thugs who are already established in the city?

Brannigan had called Tomas to warn him, and the well-oiled machine that was Ciela International, as well as the underground organization that used the company as a mask, was already getting most of their personnel out of sight. There wasn't a whole lot they could do about the facilities themselves, but that in and of itself offered an opportunity. One that Brannigan had been entirely willing to exploit.

Kirk watched the predators gather. From the fifth floor of the Ciela building, it was easy enough to keep an eye on the street below without exposing himself, or the rifle and gear on the desk next to him.

"The wolves are circling." No one had gotten out of the sedan that had pulled up to the driveway leading toward the house immediately to the east of the semi-isolated, brick-and-glass block of an office building, but Kirk had developed a bit of a sixth sense for these things.

"They are. Two more vics just pulled up on the west side." Tackett's voice was faint and slightly tinny through the radio, mainly because Kirk hadn't bothered to put an earpiece in. The only people in the building who weren't Blackhearts were a

163

handful of Tomas's security team, and they were there as backup to the Blackhearts.

Ciela moved fast indeed.

"That makes five." Brannigan was in the building manager's office, not far from where Kirk was set in his crow's nest. "Minimum fifteen shooters, possibly as many as twenty-five."

"Easy day." Curtis sounded annoyingly chipper, as always. "If this is all they send for the big cheese, I don't know why we were getting worried."

"You had to open your mouth." The weariness in Flanagan's voice would have identified him even if Kirk hadn't recognized it anyway.

He didn't have to ask what Flanagan was talking about. From his vantage point, he had a pretty good view of the driveway leading into the building's parking lot. And the two black vans that pulled up fast, screeching to a halt with their noses toward the front doors. Their rear doors flew open and men in dark clothing poured out, splitting their columns around the vans as they crouched down and covered the front of the building with their weapons, which looked like mostly AKs and a few vz.58s.

"Here they come." Kirk heaved himself off the desk he'd been leaning on and scooped up his chest rig and his rifle.

They'd made it into position only minutes ahead of the bad guys, but those had been minutes well spent.

***

Really could use a belt-fed right now. Bianco was half-tempted to say it out loud, if only to set Curtis off. The timing could be better, but it would still be hilarious.

He really *did* wish he had a machinegun, though. There were now at least thirty or forty Russian mobsters advancing on the building, and there were only ten Blackhearts and another ten Ciela security men inside. They hadn't even had time to rig the entrances with IEDs. This was going to be rifle and pistol work

164

alone, when a few bursts of machinegun fire through those front doors would end this quick.

Unfortunately, while the Czech Republic might be one of the more permissible places in Europe for firearms, getting fully automatic weapons was still difficult, and while he was sure that Dalca *could* have gotten them, that had probably run the risk of overlapping into the Russians' network and tipping them off. So, it was what it was.

The Blackhearts hadn't had much to work with in the entryway. There was some furniture, but nothing that would provide much cover, even if they'd been able to move it. Most of it had been bolted to the floor. So instead, they'd stationed themselves in the hallways, barricaded on the interior walls, aimed in at the doors.

Hopefully, none of the other two teams they'd observed pulling up to the flanks managed to force the doors on the ends of the building, or they'd be in bad shape. His back felt awfully naked, turned toward that long, open hallway behind him.

No one opened fire yet, as the Russians closed in on the doors. Much like the night they'd hit the warehouse, there was little doubt about who these guys were. They definitely weren't cops. Their dress, armament, and demeanor all *screamed* "mobster."

Bianco glanced across the entryway at Flanagan and Gomez. They were in the same high/low position he and Curtis were in, covering the front entrance. Flanagan would open the ball, but he seemed to be taking an awful long time. The first of the Russian hit squad were already at the doors.

The lights inside were all off, but that shouldn't be that unusual, since it was the middle of the day. That alone made the hit itself unusual, though. The Russians had to be either very confident that they'd bribed just enough of the local cops, or else they were really that desperate.

The first of them yanked on the doors, but Tomas's people hadn't made it that easy for them. The doors were locked, but of course, they were glass, so that didn't last long.

One of them, a big dude with long hair tied back in a ponytail, carrying what looked an awful lot like a KP-9, stepped up to the door and smashed his muzzle into the glass.

Ciela International had some pretty good security, not all of it aboveboard or legal. The glass wasn't armored, but it was still pretty tough. It took several blows before the glass cracked, and then the big man kicked the door furiously.

The crack spread, then the entire panel of the door split in half, spiderwebbed, and finally fell, the plastic on either side still holding it roughly in shape. It crashed to the floor and the big mobster fired a five-round burst through the opening before he charged inside, practically jumping to turn and clear the nearest corner.

Bianco would have been bemused at the movement, except that he'd fought Russians—or Russian-trained—in Transnistria. He knew just how weird and sloppy Russian military training was, and he hardly expected better from the Russian mob. Most of the Mafiya had built its power base through theft, extortion, smuggling, and murder, not infantry combat.

The others poured in through the opening, all of them spraying rounds into the entryway, chipping bits off the wall in the back. More than one of them shot over the man's shoulder in front of him, and Bianco was pretty sure at least one or two got trimmed, because there was a lot of cursing and yelling, though it was mostly drowned out by the gunfire.

The Blackhearts still waited, at least until most of them were already into the foyer.

Then Flanagan opened fire, the thunder of his rifle almost as loud as the incoming shots, flame stabbing from the barrel in the dim interior of the office building. He shot the big guy with the ponytail first, walking four rounds up the man's barrel chest and into his throat and temple. He hadn't moved that far from the wall, so dark fluid splashed across the glass just before the bullet passed through his skull and punched a spiderwebbed hole through the window.

166

The other three Blackhearts were already shooting before the brass from Flanagan's first shot had hit the floor. Muzzle flashes strobed, brighter in the shadows of the back of the entryway than the flame from the AKs and vz.58s that had been backlit by the sunshine outside, and unlike the gangsters, the Blackhearts were aiming.

Bullets smashed bones and tore through flesh as the four mercenaries walked their muzzles across the knot of hapless mobsters in the entryway. Men fell, spilling blood onto the floor, some hit right through the men in front of them.

Bianco's bolt locked back on an empty mag and he let the magazine fall. It hit the floor at almost the same time Curtis's did, a faint plastic clatter on the tile.

They probably should have staggered their fire a little bit more. The sudden lull in the fire was deafening. And not all the Russians were down or dead.

A chatter of full automatic fire echoed through the room, bullets smacking into the wall just above Bianco's head as he reloaded, showering him with plaster and smashed concrete. He ducked back, grabbing Curtis by the back strap of his load bearing vest and hauling him around the corner. Down on a knee, the shorter man couldn't maneuver as quickly.

He had to hand it to the Russkies. They might just be thugs, but they were fighters. And a couple of them must have just watched their best friends get gunned down, because one of them, a short, crooked-looking man who was probably twenty years younger than he looked, roared and charged toward the back of the entryway, firing his AK from the hip.

Gomez had thrown himself backward as soon as Flanagan had ducked back out of the way, reloading so fast that he might have been running a Bren A2 every day of his life. Now, on his back, aiming his rifle between his elevated knees, he double-tapped the man through the skull. The gangster collapsed, falling on his face and skidding partway across the tile, his weapon clattering to the floor and spinning away from his limp hand.

Then Bianco stepped around where Curtis was finishing his own reload, leaning out around the corner, and shot two more near the doors. Flanagan was a split second behind him, sending a third man reeling backward, red, puckered holes punched in his upper chest across his white t-shirt.

That was the straw that broke the camel's back. The last few survivors turned and ran. Gomez flipped onto his side and shoved himself out into the foyer and shot one more in the back as he turned toward the van.

Then more gunfire erupted behind Bianco, and he pivoted toward where the gangsters were trying to push the flank.

**

Santelli didn't even glance over his shoulder as he heard the gunfire erupt in the entryway behind him. It wasn't that he was unaffected by the gunfire, or even that he was as stone-cold as guys like Wade or Gomez. He was just hard-wired from almost three decades in the Marine Corps to watch his sector and worry about his area of responsibility. The foyer wasn't his sector, and Flanagan hadn't called for help yet. The side door was his worry.

He wasn't set up in the hallway, or even in one of the offices just off the hallway. That would have both been predictable and risky, as it would have potentially put him between two fires if things got hairy. So, he was set up on the landing just above the door, since the side door opened onto a stairwell.

The gunfire from the front got intense, and then somebody hit the side door, hard.

Like the front, the side door was locked. Unlike the front, it was a solid door with a strip of wire-reinforced window, not plastic-lined glass. That would present more of an obstacle.

The door shook again as someone big slammed his shoulder into it, but it held. Santelli didn't move, didn't even twitch, but stayed on a knee on the landing, his rifle trained on the crack in the door.

The sound of the firefight behind him intensified for a moment, and the darkness on the other side of the window disappeared. Someone had decided to try a different way.

Or to find a different way in.

They were back in moments, and something hit the door, *hard*. They either had a sledgehammer, or they'd gone and gotten a crowbar to pry the door open.

They'd gotten a crowbar all right, but they weren't trying to use it like a Halligan tool. The chisel end of the steel bar slammed into the wire-reinforced window, and the glass cracked. The gangsters on the other side hammered away at it, smashing the glass in a frenzy, until a corner came loose. Several more blows opened it up further, and a hand pushed through to open the door.

Santelli might have shot the hand—he was certainly close enough—but he still waited. He needed to make this count.

The door swung open and three men, all carrying pistols pushed their way into the entryway.

Santelli opened fire.

None of them had looked up as they'd made entry. They all had their guns out and pointed, but they were all moving toward the hallway and the firefight at the entrance, hardly taking any notice of their surroundings.

He shot the first two, a pair for each, before they even knew he was there. The one with the tattoos crawling up his neck took the first pair through the shoulder and armpit and dropped like a rock. The second one survived the initial hits, but went down screaming, thrashing around as blood poured from a hole in his guts.

The third man started to turn, bringing what looked like an actual Desert Eagle up just before Santelli shot him through the forehead from about ten feet away.

The second man was still screaming as his life leaked out through the hole in his abdomen. The sound was nerve-shredding but, while he was sure that Wade might have shot the guy again to shut him up, Santelli couldn't quite bring himself to go that far.

He realized he'd gotten a little too focused on the wounded man as a fourth bad guy stuck a submachinegun in the door without aiming and sprayed down the inside of the stairwell.

***

Wade, Burgess, and Puller had been set up high, positioned to overwatch the approaches and act as a quick reaction force for Santelli or the guys at the side doors. It had meant they were out of the fight for a while, which bugged Wade, while Puller seemed to be almost relieved. He was trying hard to hide it, but the guy had seemed a little shaky from the get-go. Wade didn't like him, no matter how much Flanagan trusted him from the old days.

Now that the gunfire had intensified, Wade wasn't going to wait around anymore. The bad guys had gotten too close, too quickly to interdict them from above. "Let's go." He headed for the stairwell. Using the elevators was going to take too long.

As it happened, the firefight at the main entrance died away about the time he reached the end of the hallway, but that was when Santelli engaged the three men who'd come through the side entrance. The thunder of gunfire reverberated up the stairs, and Wade popped out fast, giving the upper roof access just the slightest look and muzzle coverage before he turned to the shaft running straight down between the flights of stairs, dropping his muzzle over the railing and looking for targets.

He couldn't seem much, but he saw movement as Santelli either fell or threw himself backward, while a full-auto rattle thundered between the enclosed concrete walls. Then he was throwing himself down the steps, a pace behind Burgess. He almost collided with Puller and snarled at the smaller man, but to the doc's credit, he didn't shrink back, but just stepped aside to let Wade past him.

They flew down the steps, even as another exchange of gunfire rattled in the stairwell. Santelli was shooting back, so he was still alive, but for whatever reason, the gunfight was still going on, even at bad breath distance.

Burgess slowed at the second to last landing, popping the opening between flights with his muzzle, and fired twice. The rattle of submachinegun fire stuttered and stopped for a moment, and Wade flowed past his teammate, his own muzzle leveled. Santelli was on the final landing, down on his side behind the second flight up, his rifle pointed at the door.

"Watch that guy, he's on the outside, just spraying and praying in through the door." Even with all the gunfire, Santelli's Boston accent was so pronounced that Wade almost laughed. Almost. When it came to killing, Wade was a deadly serious man.

He also wasn't much of one for spraying bullets indiscriminately, especially in a close-quarters combat sort of scenario, but if that was what the bad guy was doing, he was going to have to adapt. As he started to see the shadow of what looked like an Agram 2000 subgun come around the threshold, he opened fire, blowing bits of concrete and shredded metal out into the fatal funnel beyond the door, and forcing the gunman to jerk his hand and his weapon back.

Then he threw himself through the door, going around the jamb where the gunman was hiding.

It was risky, and he knew it, but he was relying on speed, surprise, and violence of action to take the gangster out fast. He'd subconsciously run through the calculations in his head, and so he was ready when he rounded the corner and slammed into a fat man with a gold chain around his neck, bleeding from his hand where a chunk of one of Wade's bullets had hit him.

Wade hit the man so hard that he went down almost immediately, letting out a yawp as the submachinegun went flying.

Having no intention of taking the fight to the ground while he was still carrying a rifle, Wade had hit the man low, leading with his shoulder, and as the gangster fell on his ass,

Wade arrested his own forward movement, brought the gun up, and blasted the Russian with three rounds from his gut to his throat.

More gunfire blasted behind him, thumping him with the muzzle blast, but he didn't hear the *snap* of the bullets going by. Giving the Russian at his feet one more round to the head, just to be sure, he pivoted toward the gunshots.

Puller had exited right behind him, going right when he'd gone left, and was now standing slightly farther out from the wall, his weapon leveled at the small SUV with the doors open sitting on the brick sidewalk outside the fence. The windshield had three bullet holes in it, centered right on the driver's side.

Maybe Puller's not so useless, after all.

***

Kirk couldn't hear, but he could see the man yelling into a radio as he ran back to the two vans. The former Special Forces soldier had climbed up onto the roof itself as soon as things had cooked off, expecting just this to happen.

He couldn't control much of what happened on the flanks, but if they were going to send a message to Yurasov and his thugs, Kirk figured they should go ahead and send a message.

As the man ran to the left-hand vehicle, Kirk leaned out over the edge of the roof and shot him through the top of the skull.

The guy dropped like a rock, and then Kirk proceeded to dump the rest of the mag through the roofs of the vans, alternating between each. Shiny holes were punched right through the sheet metal, and while one started to pull away, it did so slowly, then turned, bumped over the curb and onto the grass, then slammed backwards into the tree next to the bus stop on the main road.

The gunfire had died down, and now Kirk could hear the whoop of sirens and see the flashing blue lights in the distance. He reloaded anyway. Even if they didn't get off the X before the cops got there, they should be covered. Dalca hadn't just called in the Blackhearts. Ciela International had a small army of lawyers, too, and she'd been leaning on the local law almost as much as she had been the paid gunmen.

Still, the next couple of hours could get interesting.

CHAPTER 21

Brannigan had *almost* stayed in place. He could see some advantage in getting the *Policie* involved, but there were still too many questions about Americans with rifles that would be asked. He was sure that Dalca's attorneys had all the paperwork for a proper security contract with Ciela International worked up but getting tied up dealing with the cops—especially if questions about a few of the dead men started to get asked, including the one Gomez had shot through the heart from behind—would only give Yurasov more time to disappear.

Not that Brannigan was all that interested in Yurasov himself. Yurasov was just the string that needed to be pulled.

They didn't know exactly where he'd go once news of the disaster at the Ciela building reached him—which if it hadn't already, it would soon—but that was why Tomas had put one of his lesser-known cutouts to watching the hotel where Yurasov had held his meeting of *vors* the day before.

Wherever Yurasov went, they'd know soon.

***

Abrasha Yurasov, however, was no one's prey.

He'd felt a flush of fear when he'd answered the phone and heard the report. No one seemed to know exactly what had happened. They should have had enough killers to make that Dalca *suka* crawl, but Loban had called him to tell him that they'd heard a panicked radio call from what had sounded like Fedor, just before it had been cut short with a blast of noise, like he'd dropped the radio.

No one who had been assigned to the assault force had made contact since, and when Ilya had driven by the building, there had been blue flashing *Policie* lights everywhere.

It took a lot to make Abrasha Yurasov frightened. Yet, knowing what was at stake, and the attention that these twin disasters would draw, he started to feel a faint chill going up his spine.

He'd set his closest retainers to various urgent tasks to consolidate and bring in more shooters. Most of it was just intended to get them out of the way.

He didn't want too many circling scavengers around him right at the moment. He'd just demonstrated some serious weakness, and he knew that some of them—especially Kliment—were already sharpening their knives.

Once he was sure that no one was going to mark where he was going—at least, no one he couldn't trust to be too afraid of his wrath to keep their mouth shut—he got to his car and sped away toward the north of the city.

He didn't notice the small, unobtrusive man in the ancient, beat-up Skoda Rapid parked down the street. Nor did he notice when the man put the vehicle in drive and followed Yurasov's considerably flashier BMW.

He was careful. He still ran a surveillance detection route, as well as steering clear of any police presence—especially around the bullet-riddled Ciela International building. Still, he never quite spotted the man following him.

If he had, he would have been worried, and he should have been.

***

The estate was well hidden amid trees and hedges, and Yurasov was relieved to see there were no other vehicles parked around the outside. He drove around the back, parking under a large, ancient oak tree, and got out.

The house was red brick and black-framed glass, with a red tile roof. He didn't know whose it had been before the *bratva* had acquired it, nor did he care. He'd been to it twice, at least once without Garin's knowledge or permission. The senior *vor* had always insisted that its location needed to be protected.

Yurasov had always thought that Garin was being a bit too paranoid. After all, they had people inside the *Policie* here, so they'd have plenty of warning if the Czechs decided to come after them. There was no reason to leave the house unused.

It was an extremely comfortable house, too, with an extensively stocked bar. It was a waste to leave it sitting there.

After all, he reasoned as he went to the back door, it *was* there for special occasions and emergencies, and this qualified as a bit of an emergency.

He'd started to calm down on the drive north, thinking through his options. He still had a few other *vory* he might be able to pin the failure on. *He* had come in from his vacation in Romania to solve this. Yes. It was because of Bravikov's and Pishchalnikov's shit security that all of this had happened.

You're the problem solver. Things were just already in motion by the time you got here. Now you can settle things down.

The door opened with a *click,* and he slipped inside. The interior was dark and cool. His footsteps tapped softly on the tiles of the back room as he closed the door behind him and took a deep breath.

He considered turning on the lights, but the less signature he had in this place, the better, he decided. So, looking around and reorienting himself, he tried to remember where the bar was.

In the main room. He started through the back hallway, passing the massive kitchen on the way to the living room. He didn't want to turn the lights on, but maybe a fire in the fireplace would be nice. It was getting into autumn, after all.

The living room was huge, filling nearly half the building. A brick fireplace stood against the center wall, and the rest of the room was lined with dark wood, rich Persian rugs on the floor, and leather upholstered furniture set around the fireplace and the games table that probably cost as much as a car per piece. The bar stood to the left of the fireplace, the shelf behind it lined with expensive bottles. His eye lit on the glitter of a Ladoga Imperial Collection vodka bottle, styled like a Faberge egg, the faint sunlight filtering through the trees outside gleaming off the crystal and gold.

Yurasov took a step toward the bar and froze as the leather upholstery of one of the chairs creaked.

A match flared, and a puff of cigar smoke floated toward the ceiling. "Leave the lights off, Abrasha."

The voice wasn't familiar. The faint German accent was one he should have recognized. His hand crept toward the Laugo Alien in his waistband. "I wouldn't do that, if I were you. There is a man with an 8.6 Blackout trained on your head right now."

Yurasov eased his hand away from the pistol. "Who are you? How did you get in here?"

The man stood up out of the chair. About half a head shorter than Yurasov himself, the man didn't look the least bit impressive. Slender, brown haired, with a soft, clean-shaven face that could have belonged to a man in his late twenties to his mid-forties, he looked like an academician. Yet something told Yurasov not to take chances.

The fact that the man had a Walther PDP in the hand that wasn't holding a cigar also contributed to Yurasov's caution.

The stranger turned his back to the fireplace and pointed to the chair across from where he'd been sitting with the cigar. "Have a seat. We need to talk."

Yurasov glanced out the window, but if there was a gunman out there aimed in at him, he couldn't see him. Letting his eyes return to the pistol in the academician's hand, he shrugged and circled around him, feeling the man's cold eyes following him all the way to the chair.

Sitting back in the leather, he was careful to keep his hand away from the pistol in his waistband. He still didn't know exactly what was going on here, but he was a survivor, not one of the brain-dead enforcers who often used a bit too much of the organization's own product.

Besides, he was starting to suspect that he knew who this man represented, and that cold, panicky feeling was starting to come back.

"Again, who are you, and what do you want?" He was somewhat proud of himself. His voice hadn't cracked.

"Who I am does not matter to you." The man had sat back down and took a puff on his cigar. It was one of the Cubans that had been stored in the humidor behind the bar. "Who I represent, I think you are beginning to suspect."

Apparently he can read minds, too. It wasn't helping Yurasov's equilibrium.

"As for what I want." He pointed to the cell phone on the coffee table in front of the fireplace. Yurasov hadn't even noticed it before. "I want you to call your superior. Now."

Yurasov looked down at the phone, wondering if this wasn't one of those traps like he'd heard about Mossad setting up. Where there was an explosive charge or bullet in the phone, and answering it blew his head off.

"You don't need to worry about the phone. It's just a phone. It's *your* phone, actually."

He frowned down at it. His phone was in his pocket.

The academician sighed. "We cloned it. There is a very specific reason, as well. We need Herr Garin to answer the phone."

Yurasov glanced at the pistol in the academician's hand once more. It was just barely pointed in his direction, the small man's finger indexed just above the trigger guard.

Something warned him to go along with the man's instructions. Even if there wasn't a gunman outside watching him, he doubted he could get over the coffee table before the academician shot him. So, he reached down slowly, picked up the phone, and unlocked it. Sure enough, it even used his unlock code.

They'd even cloned all of his contacts. He felt his blood run cold as he looked down the list. *How did they get this?* These people had the entire western Czech Republic side of the organization.

He scrolled down to Garin's number and pressed "call."

The phone rang twice before Garin answered. "Abrasha Lukyanovich, what the *fuck* is going on over there?"

Yurasov gulped. He'd had his justifications and evasions all worked out on the road to the estate, but with that academician of an assassin sitting across from him, and now facing Garin's wrath, all of his excuses seemed to evaporate. "Artyom Timofeyevich…"

"Don't give me excuses, Abrasha!" The senior *vor*'s voice was an angry bark. From the background noise, it sounded like he was in a vehicle. "Do you have any *idea* just how badly you have fucked us?"

"I don't think he does, Artyom Timofeyevich." The academician had tilted his head, and for the first time, Yurasov saw the Bluetooth headset in his ear. "I needed him to make sure you picked up, though." He lifted the Walther. The flash was the last thing Yurasov ever saw.

***

Winter stayed in his seat as the phone slipped from Yurasov's nerveless, bloodied fingers, the mess from the man's shattered skull soaking into the leather upholstery behind him. If Winter had been anyone else, he might have cringed slightly at the destruction of such expensive workmanship, but Dieter Winter was not a man given to sentiment.

"Do I have your attention, Artyom Timofeyevich?" The phone had gone silent as soon as he'd shot Yurasov in the face.

"Who is this?" Garin's voice had gone quiet and calm. Winter did, indeed, have his attention.

"You may call me Dieter." He leaned back in the chair, the leather creaking under him. "I think you know who I represent. Recent events in Prague have become extremely concerning to my employers. Now, your organization has

180

provided a good buffer between ours and the product, and you have made a tidy profit along the way. I am here to clean things up if that has suddenly changed."

There was a pause on the other end. From his profile, Winter imagined that Garin was carefully weighing his options, and trying to figure out if he dared to defy the Front. Possibly by attempting to eliminate the "problem solver."

That wouldn't work out for him, but if it meant a change in leadership of Garin's organization, to someone who could both do a better job of ensuring the Organization's goals and be somewhat more pliable, so be it.

Winter had little but contempt for these Russian gangsters. They were useful tools, but messy ones. If he'd been planning this operation, he would have preferred to build the infrastructure for distribution from the ground up. It would have removed some of the buffer between the Organization and law enforcement, which even then was searching for the source of the deadly new drug, but it would have been easier to hide it, all the same.

Truth be told, he would have preferred a different distribution system entirely. The Organization had its goals, and eliminating the lower parts of society, the drug users, certainly helped, but it was slow and presented too many opportunities for discovery.

He'd simply have introduced the stuff into the water supply, and let natural selection sort the rest out. They could pick and choose which areas to target according to the advancement of the Organization's other, parallel programs, but it would be more efficient and harder to detect and interdict that way.

He wasn't in charge, though. It wasn't his project to direct. He was just the troubleshooter.

"You are right that the product has been immensely profitable." Garin still sounded thoughtful. "I am still wondering just why your people are so intent on getting this product out on the street that you take such a small cut."

"If this situation isn't fixed, we're going to take a much larger cut, and I am not just speaking about money, Herr Garin." Winter's tone hadn't changed at all. He was always a bit deadpan anyway, and he'd never felt the need to really attempt to get intimidating. "I am speaking to you to give you one last chance to fix this. My associates and I will lay low for the time being. However, if the situation continues to deteriorate, understand that we *will* intervene before the product can be captured or linked to our organization. Do I make myself clear?"

There was another pause. While he had never met Garin, Winter could imagine the gang leader grinding his teeth at being addressed like a wayward subordinate. Winter didn't especially care. He had his own team of shooters on hand, and if things got really desperate, the Organization was going to send the "special" package, whether he wanted it or not.

He was determined to fix this before that became necessary.

"I understand your message." While Garin was still calm and hadn't gotten audibly angry, there was a heaviness in his voice that told Winter all he needed to know. The mobster had a vested interest in maintaining the business arrangement as it was, but he wasn't happy, and if he could manage to drive Dalca and her allies out of the picture, keep the product coming, *and* eliminate Winter for his insolence, he'd do it all in a heartbeat.

Winter wasn't scared. He'd expected as much from a Russian mobster. He was ready for it.

"Good. I look forward to continuing our relationship." It was about as close to sarcastic as Winter ever got.

He hung up the phone and leaned back in his chair, taking another deep draw on the cigar. He'd destroy the phone before he left, to make sure there was no way for Garin to track him, but he had security set, and it would be a crime to waste such a good cigar.

CHAPTER 22

It was just past midnight. The lights alongside the road were lit, but they didn't cast much illumination into the trees and fields on either side.

Tackett had welcomed the chance to take point for the assault element. He'd generally kept his head down and his mouth shut so far, but his determination to stay out of the private military contracting business after the Anambas—with the notable exception of missions like this, where he got to stick it to the people who'd captured and tortured Vernon and Max—was waning. He *liked* this team. They were *pros*. Part of his not quite vow to stay home after the mission with Price had been simply because he'd had almost as much to worry about from his teammates as he'd had from the enemy on that job. He didn't think he had to face that with Brannigan's Blackhearts.

He didn't think he was a Blackheart *yet*, but he was discovering that he wanted to be.

It had probably been inevitable. It had been easy to forget just how crushing he'd found "normal life" once he'd gotten home. As time had gone by, though, he'd found himself thinking about combat again. Thinking about the brotherhood that he'd shared with Vernon and Max, if not with many of their other teammates. Thinking about how alive he'd felt when he was in hostile territory with a gun in his hands.

He'd thought the Anambas had gotten it out of his system, but maybe there wasn't any such thing as "getting it out of your system." Not for him, anyway.

They'd parked the vehicles on the far side of the Hvězdárna Ďáblice observatory, with the overwatch and assault teams splitting up and curving around to either side of the observatory building. The trees were pretty thick on that hill, though not so densely packed as to hinder movement. The darkness also provided plenty of concealment, thanks to the very presence of the observatory.

Tackett was ahead of Brannigan, with Wade, Bianco, Flanagan, and Gomez spread out in a wedge behind him. He was pretty sure that it would be an awfully tight match between him, Flanagan, and Gomez in any contest of fieldcraft, but he was holding his own, and that was gratifying.

He lowered himself carefully to a knee under the drooping branches of a large, gnarled tree, just on the other side of the road from the target house. Feeling around to make sure he wasn't about to put his weight on a dead branch and give their presence away with a loud *snap*, he eased himself to the ground and peered through the shadows at the house.

There wasn't much to see. The lights were all out, and the house was set far enough back in the trees and hedges that it practically disappeared in the darkness.

That wasn't good. The power was on. The nearby streetlights, and a few lights still on in or outside nearby houses told him that much. If this place was completely blacked out, it might mean that the bad guys knew they were coming.

While the rest of the assault element cat-footed their way into a perimeter behind him he stayed perfectly still, listening and watching. He hadn't been particularly impressed by the gangsters' discipline or tactics so far. If they were in there—and Dalca's spy had insisted that he'd followed Yurasov to this estate—then they were being uncharacteristically patient.

184

Brannigan took a knee next to him. The big man didn't speak at first, but did the same thing Tackett was doing, listening and watching.

Finally, Brannigan gave his shoulder a squeeze and stood. Tackett pulled himself to his feet using one hand on the tree trunk, hoping that the older Brannigan hadn't noticed. He'd been training, but not consistently, and he wasn't exactly a young buck anymore.

With Brannigan beside him, both of them watching to either side of the narrow road that led past the estate's main entrance, they moved on the house.

The front door was framed by more hedge, the door itself apparently all iron-bound timber. That could be an issue, except that it had a large, framed window set in the door.

There was a chance that, if this place was as secure as someone like Garin or Yurasov would like, the glass was armored, or at least as sturdy as the doors and windows in the Ciela International building. But when he thumped the glass pane with his Bren's muzzle, it shattered nicely.

It took a moment to sweep the glass out of the frame, then he reached inside, unlocked the door, and pulled it open, stepping out of the way as Brannigan and Wade made entry.

No gunfire thundered in the entryway, but he still fell in with Flanagan as he went in after the lead shooters.

Lights flashed around the inside, revealing glimpses of a lavishly furnished living room, with a brick fireplace, dark wood interior, and a bar with quite a collection of liquor bottles behind it. The lights, however, quickly converged on the figure sitting in a chair next to the fireplace.

Gomez and Bianco swept past, heading into the back hall, as soon as the bloody bullet hole in the man's cheekbone registered. He wasn't going to get up and shoot them.

It took about two more minutes to sweep the rest of the house. Empty. They converged back on the living room, and while Gomez, Bianco, Wade, and Tackett set security on the inside, watching the entrances or the hallways that led to the entrances, Brannigan and his second in command looked down at the corpse, their weapon lights illuminating the bloody scene starkly.

"That's Yurasov, all right." Flanagan sounded disgusted. "Somebody got to him before we did."

"Dammit." Brannigan didn't sigh, probably because he was trying to avoid breathing too deeply. The place stank of death. Even the faint remnant of cigar smoke couldn't cover it. "There goes our lead." He looked up at Flanagan. "Our friends from the Front, you think?"

"More than likely." Flanagan bent and picked something up off the floor. It was a phone, or what was left of one. It had been shot at least twice. "I don't think they're too happy about their drug project getting disrupted."

"Probably not." Brannigan looked around. "Nobody touches anything else. If the Front's been here, who knows what kind of nasty surprises they might have left."

Tackett couldn't help but feel a bit of a chill at that. He'd been lucky not to have set anything off when he'd broken the window and opened the door.

"Let's get out of here." Brannigan keyed his radio. "Guido, Kodiak. Dry hole. Coming out."

Right back at Square One.

***

"No, this is good." Dalca had taken the news with surprising equanimity. "Yurasov would have known more about the operation locally, but if he's dead, then that means one thing." She looked up at Brannigan with a gleam in her eye that was decidedly different from her usual flirtatiousness. She'd been targeted, was still a target, and she wasn't the sort to shut down over it. She had blood in her eye, now, and with the Blackhearts on her side, she saw a route to vengeance. "Garin will be coming here. He might have left things to Yurasov, but there are no others in Prague he trusts to fix this. Besides, if he *doesn't* handle this personally, he's going to invite a power play, probably from the likes of Ugolev."

186

"So, Garin's probably coming to Prague." Brannigan folded his arms. They weren't in the Blackhearts' safehouse—he had refused to potentially burn it if Dalca's organization had a leak—but were sitting in a place remarkably like the estate where they'd found Yurasov's body, and, in fact, not all that far away from it. This place was smaller, and far less ostentatious, but it was still fairly traditional compared to the blocky modern buildings in the subdivision across the road. "Do you have any idea where he might be setting up?"

She smiled, and it was as bloodthirsty an expression as the gleam in her eye. "Oh, he's much more a creature of habit, Artyom Timofeyevich, than Yurasov was. I know *exactly* where he'll be." She waved at Tomas, who was leaning against the wall near the door leading toward the bedrooms in the back. "Tomas? Bring the map of the city, will you?"

"Hold on a second." Brannigan lowered his voice warningly. "Something needs to be entirely clear here. I know you well enough to know that whatever we do, you're going to find a way to make it profit your operation. *But*." He lifted a finger. "We're here because of the Front. If taking Garin down *doesn't* stop the Front, then we're out."

She pouted a little. "I had *hoped* you were here for *me*, John. After all our history together."

His heavy-lidded stare was not amused. She smiled anyway and leaned forward to pat him on the arm. "I'm joking, John. You *do* remember what a joke is, don't you?" When he didn't break the stare, she settled back in her chair with a sigh, accepting the map from Tomas, who had kept his own expression carefully neutral. "Someday, John, I'll find a way past that reserve of yours. But you're right. To business."

She pointed to the map. "He has his own suite in the Andaz Prague Hotel. It's on the top floor. I've even met him there. He can be slightly charming, from time to time."

Brannigan didn't even look at the map. "The *Front*, Erika."

187

She didn't back down, either. "Garin's the key. He's the façade they've been using to spread their poison in Prague. He's the buffer. Don't you see? If you take out Garin, they're going to have to move to protect their operation. Ugolev wants the money, but he's a barbarian, not that far removed from a Dagestani. There is *no way* the Front will trust Ugolev with this sort of thing. They'll *have* to send someone to sort things out, presuming that someone isn't already here."

Brannigan finally lowered his eyes to the map. She had a point. He wasn't sure he liked it, but she had a point.

He'd seriously considered approaching the Czech police about this. They had to be after Garin's organization anyway. The security risks, however, were simply too high. There had already been several indicators that Garin, at least, had the local law penetrated. If they were going to destroy the Roulette operation, they needed to move against the Front quickly, and if word got out, he could expect the whole thing to disappear in a heartbeat.

They'd already done it before. For most people, even if they'd heard about what the Front had done in the Southwest or Africa, they'd forgotten it in the deluge of PR that the organization had put out over the following months.

That factor alone made going up against them extremely dangerous. There were a lot of very wealthy, very powerful people who were in the Front's pocket, even if they weren't true believers themselves. Even if they didn't have the cops penetrated—which seemed unlikely—they'd have well-meaning but uninformed forces coming down on the Blackhearts' heads pretty quickly.

Secrecy was their only advantage.

"That's going to be a hell of a hit." The hotel was right smack dab in the middle of the city, just outside of Old Town and only about half a mile from the river. Getting in there, hitting Garin, and worse, getting out, would be a nightmare. "We're going to have to get *really* sneaky, or else find a way to draw him out somewhere he can be hit without pulling far too much

188

attention." He raised an eyebrow as he looked up at her. "Your organization's extensive capabilities aside, I don't think even you can quite pull that off."

She shrugged. "You're probably right." She sipped her drink. Something fruity and alcoholic, by the look and the smell, though he didn't doubt that the alcohol was low enough that it didn't affect her in the slightest. She was too in control. "You're hoping that drawing him out draws out the Front, too, aren't you?"

"Naturally."

"Well." She leaned back in her chair. "Last anyone in my organization knew, he was in Paris. He should arrive at the airport tonight, provided he doesn't come by train. We can have someone in place to shadow him."

"We can do that." Brannigan looked up. "Tom, you feeling up to a surveillance mission?"

Burgess nodded. "Any day, boss."

"Good. The rest of us will start looking for the Front's operation." He grinned wolfishly. "They're who we're after, anyway, and if they get hit, that will for sure draw old Garin out."

Anyone else might have gotten annoyed. Dalca just smiled at him.

CHAPTER 23

Kliment Yurievich Ugolev waited by the limousine, his hands clasped in front of him. He was a short, thick, ugly man, his shaved head melding almost seamlessly into his shoulders without much of a neck in between. His thick, calloused hands had beaten or wrung the life out of more than a few men.

If not for the current circumstances, he would have been ecstatic. Yurasov was dead, and that put him, Kliment Ugolev, second in line to be the senior *vor* in Prague. Now he just had to figure out how to get Garin out of the way.

Except that no one knew exactly who had murdered Yurasov. His absence hadn't even been noticed at first—he was always gone until the worst possible time, when he'd show up just to scream at you for fucking up, and possibly kill someone just to make sure it didn't happen again—and then it had taken some time to figure out where he'd gone. Only when Garin had called and briefly described the phone conversation—probably leaving out more than a few details—had they even known that Yurasov was dead.

Even though Garin hadn't said much about the rest of the conversation, Ugolev had been able to put the pieces together. He knew Garin didn't think much of his smarts. He was the sort of *vor* who was always much more comfortable with straightforward violence and extortion, rather than complicated

191

mind games, which led many of his rivals to underestimate him, but he saw more than he let on, and thought more than he said.

The guys who bring us the Roulette. That has to be who killed Yurasov. And now they have Garin running scared. He wouldn't rush down here otherwise.

Another man might find that a reason to be concerned. Worried. Even frightened. Not Ugolev, though. Kliment Yurievich did not frighten easily. He didn't know who was behind the drug, but he knew that they were one of two things. Either they were a tool he could leverage to his advantage, or they were an obstacle to be eliminated. Preferably in such a way that he could take over the Roulette operation, of course. The *bratva* was making a killing on that stuff.

The plane taxied over to the side of the terminal, and the stairs were wheeled out. Garin, a portly, jowly man wearing a black shirt and red suit jacket, lumbered down the steps and toward the car. Ugolev greeted him, shaking his hand with both hands, and then his own bodyguard, Lavrenty, escorted both men into the back of the limousine.

"To the hotel, boss?" Girom, the driver, looked back over his shoulder as Lavrenty went around the front to get into the passenger seat.

"No." Garin's voice was heavy and there was vodka on his breath. "Take me to the house in Klukovice."

Ugolev blinked, though he managed to suppress any other reaction. He hadn't even realized that Garin had known about the house. It was a hangout and staging area for the killers who worked for the *bratva*. It wasn't a place that the upper echelon of the organization would *want* to know about, let alone go to visit.

Girom and Lavrenty looked at each other for a moment.

"Did I fucking stutter?" Garin snarled. "Get fucking moving!" Ugolev blinked again as Girom and Lavrenty hastily turned forward, Girom putting the vehicle into gear and starting them out of the airport.

No one said anything as they raced down the streets. It was getting late in the afternoon, and the dappled sunlight through the clouds played across the Russian *vor*'s sagging, jowly face as he glowered out the window.

Ugolev was trying hard to rationalize his own silence. He wasn't really afraid of this fat old man. At least, that was what he kept telling himself. Yet he didn't dare meet the *vor*'s eyes when Garin turned his baleful stare on him. It ate at him, even as he realized, to his growing rage, that he simply didn't have the balls to do anything differently. Yurasov might be out of the picture, but Garin was in a black rage that would probably result in his death if he crossed the old man.

Garin got out without waiting for Lavrenty to open the door and stormed inside. When he looked around at the couple of gunmen hanging out in the kitchen, smoking Petras, he seemed to get even angrier. The two younger men just stared for a second, one with his cigarette burning down toward his fingers, then scrambled to their feet.

He whirled on Ugolev, stabbing a thick finger in his face. "Get the rest of the *brodyagi* and *shestyorki* in here. I want everyone in the city who can use a gun, a knife, or a bomb, and I want them here *now*." He started to pace the room, the gunmen moving away to stay out of his reach. He looked more and more like an angry bear. "These *mudila yobaniy* drug pushers think they can threaten *me*? I'll show them."

He stopped and stared at Ugolev, and for a moment, the younger man thought he'd made a terrible mistake, standing there in shock as his boss, whom he'd held in a degree of contempt for a long time, finally showed his fangs. "We're going over to that lab. We're going to take it. And we're going to show that Dieter *govnyuk* that we don't need him and his 'organization' to make this Roulette *govno* profitable."

***

Following the limo had been easy. Staying out of sight as it had headed into a small cul-de-sac on the south side of the city, sheltered among trees and hills to the point that it may as

193

well have been a medieval village with cars, had been considerably more difficult.

Setting up anywhere on that road would have been immediately detected. Burgess had been in too many places like this around the world, either in the Middle East, Africa, or Eastern Europe. The locals knew who belonged there and who didn't, and a stranger just parking in the area was going to draw attention. If the mob had a hold on this place, it would only make it worse.

So, while he saw the limo pull through a gate into an ancient, walled estate in the middle of the tiny suburb, he kept rolling past, heading down the road and around the Černy Kohout Restaurant. He had a map on his lap, allowing him to see what hopefully was a route to a spot he could park and find a new vantage point.

Continuing around the bottom of the hill, he drove beneath the railroad bridge and found a small park in the valley, surrounded by trees and granite cliffs. It was well out of sight of the little cul-de-sac, and as good a place to stage as any.

He pulled over, watching the few people in the park. There were a couple of families with their kids playing on the equipment, and he saw about three single people just walking the road, but that was it. None of them looked like Mafiya spotters.

Shutting off the engine, he opened the door and got out. There were enough people around that this *might* look suspicious, but he needed to get eyes on that place. He locked the car and headed up the hill, into the trees.

No one paid him any mind.

It didn't take long to get across the tracks and up over the hill. It got a little steep in places, but nothing like some of the mountains he'd climbed in his day. The trees were thick, but not enough to hinder him.

The difficulty lay in finding a spot where he could watch the compound. He eventually settled into the bushes at the end of the lane, hoping that none of the locals had dogs.

***

Within the first two hours, he was already convinced that they weren't going to be able to hit Garin here.

He'd seen no fewer than ten vehicles show up. Not all of them could park on the street, so some had dropped off what were unmistakably more Russian mobsters. The gathering had to be up to thirty men by now, and more kept coming. Garin was calling in the army. By the time the Blackhearts could move on this place, the disparity in numbers would be too much to overcome. *Especially* in a spot like this.

He could have pulled off and sent the warning to the rest of the team, but he stayed where he was. Something was definitely happening, and Brannigan and the others needed to know about it.

While he could have sent a text, there was the risk, despite his apparently good concealment, that the light might show. So, he eased back into the brush and risked a call.

"Send it." Brannigan was as terse on the phone as he was on the radio.

Burgess kept his voice as low as he could while still making sure the mic picked it up. "Garin is in a walled, stone house in Klukovice, along with at least thirty of his goons. More keep coming, too. He's setting up for something."

If Brannigan was having a hard time hearing him, he didn't say anything about it. "Roger. Any prospects on taking down the house?"

"Inadvisable." He'd been thinking it over several times during the last couple of hours. "It's all stone, and there's a timber gate outside that we'd have to breach to even get to the front door. The place may as well be a fortress, or one of those Afghan compounds. There's also only one good approach. I think it's probably best to wait and see what they're doing. They're not gathering here permanently, I don't think."

"Good copy. Keep me posted. I'm sending Joe and Dan to stage nearby. They'll back you up if you need help."

Burgess felt an immense wave of relief at that that he hadn't expected. It *was* nerve-wracking, sitting out here in the weeds by himself, watching a growing mob of killers gather. He hadn't quite realized *how* nerve-wracking until he'd heard he had backup.

"Roger. Thanks, Colonel. I'll be in touch."

***

Fortunately, he was in contact with Flanagan when things started to move.

More of the vehicles that had dropped men off and then departed started to come back. They weren't just picking their passengers back up and leaving, though. They were lining up on the road, forming a convoy of vehicles that quickly curved out of sight around the bend in the road. More than a few of the Russians were hanging out by the vehicles, clearly unafraid of outside interference.

More than a few of them were openly armed, too.

"They're getting ready to move. Big convoy is forming up on the road." He'd already talked Flanagan onto the main road of Do Klukovic, so he and Tackett were in position to pick up surveillance if the Russians moved before Burgess could get back to his car.

"Good copy. We can already see some of them. Damn, that's a big convoy." They were on the phone, both burners, so neither man was all *that* worried about someone listening in. The Front probably *could*, but it still looked like they were just up against the Russians.

"If you've got eyes on, then I should probably break off and get back to the car." Burgess peered through the leaves in front of him at the group coming down out of the gate. Garin himself was in the middle of a large knot of Russians, carrying what looked like an over-under shotgun over his shoulder.

Whatever was about to go down, the man himself wanted a piece. He reported that to Flanagan.

"Good copy. Get back to your wheels. I'm calling in the rest of the team." Flanagan sounded a little pensive. "We could interdict on the road, but I think we might just see where they're going."

196

"On my way." Burgess hung up and faded into the trees.

There were a couple of possibilities. The worst case was that Garin was going after Dalca. He shouldn't have any way of knowing where she was, but he also might be going after every Ciela International asset the Russians could find. Which might make this a *very* interesting evening.

On the other hand, it hadn't been Dalca's people who had killed Yurasov. They were pretty sure about that. There was another power play going on.

Either way, it was going to be an eventful night.

CHAPTER 24

Flanagan watched the convoy pass. Skoda sedans, GAZ SUVs, a couple of vans, and even a limo rolled by. There wasn't a lot of dispersion; no one was going to mistake this for anything but a convoy.

"They're sure not worried about keeping a low profile, are they?" Tackett was leaning back in his own seat, his elbow propped on the door, his chin on his fist. His hand rested on the Bren at his feet, a jacket thrown over it to conceal it from prying eyes.

"Nobody ever accused the Russians of being particularly subtle, *especially* not the mobsters. They're not professional soldiers, even the ones who were KGB."

Tackett snorted softly. "I'd say *especially* not the ones who were KGB. Secret police ain't soldiers."

Flanagan nodded as what looked like the end of the convoy went past. "There's an interesting thought." He put the car into gear. As much as he hated it, he and Tackett were back in the Fabia. "I wonder if Garin was one of the KGB guys who just sidestepped into the mob back in the 90s."

"Does it actually matter that much at this point?" Tackett asked, as they turned onto the main road and followed the convoy at a distance, hopefully far enough back that they weren't immediately obvious.

199

"If he's old-school KGB, then it might." Flanagan was chewing on it as he drove. "How much you want to bet that they maintained contacts in the Kremlin after they 'changed careers?'"

Tackett tilted his head as he glanced around them. The man was clearly a thinker, and Flanagan was finding he was glad he'd come aboard. He and Tackett seemed to be of similar minds and temperaments. It was too bad he was still holding back from being a full-fledged Blackheart. He was definitely an asset and could be a good friend.

"I hadn't actually thought about it that much before, but it makes sense." He shrugged. "Got to be honest, most of my career was focused on the Middle East. Then I had to learn about the Chinese the fast, quick, and hard way in the South Pacific. The Russians were my dad's adversaries."

Flanagan took the next turn, slowing deliberately to open up a bit of space. The convoy seemed to be heading south, toward the E50 highway, but he still needed to balance maintaining contact and avoiding detection. "Same here. We had some experience with the Russkies in Transnistria, though. Even their soldiers tend to be thugs."

Tackett nodded thoughtfully. "I guess that fits what I've heard about them." He looked over at Flanagan, taking his eyes off their surroundings for just a moment before turning back to hold security. "Transnistria, huh? Not sure I know where that is."

"Moldova." Flanagan slowed further to avoid catching up to the convoy as they turned onto the highway. "It's a little wannabe Soviet Union between Moldova and Ukraine. We actually had our second clash with the Front there, though we didn't know at the time who they were."

Tackett didn't reply at once, only speaking once they were on the highway, hanging several hundred yards back from the end of the convoy. It was getting darker, the sun going down ahead of them, though the clouds had thickened over the last couple hours, so Flanagan didn't have to squint into the sunset, at least not yet.

"You guys really get around." There was a note of what might have been wistfulness in Tackett's voice.

Flanagan glanced at him. "You know you're always welcome to join up all the way. You handled yourself well in Kyrgyzstan, especially given how long you'd been out of the game. I'm sure the Colonel wouldn't turn you away."

Tackett lapsed into silence again. After a few moments, still looking out the window, he said, "I'm thinking about it."

That was probably the best they were going to get, particularly mid-mission, but it was better than Flanagan might have hoped. He just nodded and concentrated on driving and not getting them burned.

He frowned as they kept going. He didn't *know* about any Ciela International holdings out on the west side of the city, but that didn't mean they weren't there. Still, he would have expected Dalca to read them in if there was something sensitive enough in the area that the bad guys might want to hit it. He'd never put it past her to play both sides against the middle—and he'd seen her flirt with Brannigan enough that it made *him* uncomfortable—but this seemed a bit counter-productive.

They turned off the highway, taking several long, sweeping curves toward the 606. It looked like they were heading for an industrial park just off the highway, just south of the airport.

Sure enough, they hadn't gone a mile from the turnoff when the whole convoy turned right and headed into the complex of massive warehouses sitting just outside the airport fence. Flanagan pulled over rather than following them in. The map didn't show too many ways in or out of that area. *What's going on?*

*   *   *

Ugolev couldn't quite believe what was happening. While he insisted mentally that he wasn't afraid of the people they were doing business with, he'd seen just enough—and the fact that they'd gotten to the extremely careful Yurasov, despite his contempt for the other man, was something that kept nagging

201

at the back of his brain—the idea of trying to seize the Roulette operation by force seemed insane. It just wasn't the way things were done.

There was no going back, though. One look in Garin's eyes after he'd declared their mission had made that clear enough. Garin *would* kill anyone who gainsaid him, and he'd do it personally.

Ugolev had too many plans in motion to want to risk it. He'd have to wait and bide his time, get Garin out of the picture when the old man wasn't as alert and pissed off.

Still, this seemed absolutely insane, even to a man as comfortable with violence as Ugolev. The entire way there, he had convinced himself that Garin was just going to try to scare their partners, renegotiate things with some bluster and threats. It was what he'd do.

But as they pulled up into the parking lot, and the first vehicles raced right up to the doors, the first *shestyorki*, the low-level, expendable soldiers who hadn't yet advanced far enough in the organization to be true "thieves" yet, rushed out with their AKs and shotguns ready, he realized that he wasn't dreaming, that this really was happening.

He pulled his own Skorpion onto his lap as Garin glared at him, the mob boss's own thick fingers clenched around his own shotgun. He opened the limo door and got out as the first bursts of gunfire thundered from the open door.

***

Winter wasn't especially surprised when he got the call. He'd long considered himself a good judge of men, even though his perspective often seemed to be from the outside looking in, much like the academic people often thought he resembled. He'd read Garin as best he could during their brief conversation, and while the Russian had *seemed* to go along with what he said, he'd noted the resentment barely disguised in the man's tone. He'd more than half expected him to do something desperate and stupid.

"The lab is under attack." The man on the other end of the line was calm, thankfully. There was no screaming, no panic. That was to be expected, given the degree of security that the Organization had put on that facility. It was easily as good as what they had at an Indigo Lithium site. Granted, while he hadn't been told the classification level of this lab, he expected that it wasn't too much lower. This was nearly on the same level as the genetic research labs in Africa, Central America, and Eurasia. "A large force of irregulars, armed with automatic weapons and shotguns."

"Can you eliminate them, or will you require intervention?" Winter didn't want to commit his team any earlier than he absolutely had to. He was fairly sure there was another player involved here. This sounded like Garin. He was there for whoever had hit the Mafiya's warehouse and destroyed the Roulette shipment. From what he'd gathered, those people were *far* more dangerous than the Russians.

He was still irritated. With Garin turning on them, they'd need to take a hand in rearranging the underworld environment in Prague to replace him. Either that or pull the operation out entirely and set up elsewhere. He'd always thought Amsterdam would have been a much better place to start this project, at least once he'd been read in, but he already knew that he'd be tasked with overseeing security for such a move, and it wasn't a job he relished.

"We should be able to handle the situation." The man was all business. "However, they do have greater numbers than we do, despite our advantage in defensive preparations."

Winter sighed silently. He didn't know the man on the other end of the phone, and that man probably didn't even know the name of who he was talking to. But he could tell that he wasn't a soldier, wasn't anything like Winter. He talked more like an engineer.

"We will be on standby." As a matter of fact, they already were. He'd had his suspicions after his conversation with Garin. Now they were confirmed, which was why he was sitting in a van, dressed in black fatigues, body armor, and helmet, armed with an HK 416, surrounded by five other men in the same gear.

He was still hoping that they could handle this without bringing in the men waiting on standby at the airport.

Hanging up, he briefed the rest of the team on what was happening. They took it in impassively. None of these men were ideologues. They were professionals. He'd hand-picked them himself, this time.

They didn't fidget. Didn't even talk amongst themselves. They just took in his words and waited for the time to kill.

Winter got on the phone again, to make sure that the Czech police did not interfere. Sometimes there was a distinct advantage to working for an organization with influence that went so far…

***

The rest of the Blackhearts' vehicles pulled up behind the Fabia as the light got dimmer. Flanagan and Tackett had stayed in place, listening to the firefight to the northwest get more intense. The Russians were pushing hard, but it sounded like somebody was pushing back.

Flanagan glanced in the rear view mirror. The rest were staying put, but Brannigan got out of the lead SUV, some mid-size thing that Flanagan couldn't identify right off, and moved up to join them. He hadn't brought his rifle. It was still too light out, and they had too far to go to expose themselves just yet. This was still a covert operation, which seemed weird when there was gunfire booming only half a mile away, but it was what it was.

He rolled down the window as Brannigan got close. "Dalca's confirmed that it's not one of her places. If Garin's having a falling out with his partners, this might be the time to move."

Flanagan scratched his beard and looked toward the thunder in the north. "That's an awful lot of shooters."

"It is." Brannigan followed his gaze through the windshield. "We'll have to move carefully and pay a lot of attention to angles. But they're not expecting us. It might be the opportunity to take Garin *and* the Front's operation out."

Flanagan thought it over. He was fairly sure that the fight was happening somewhere on the other side of the two large warehouses in front of them. There wasn't a whole lot of cover and concealment there, so they'd have to use fire and movement a lot. Even then, the disparity of numbers was going to make that touch-and-go.

"We'll be better off if we drive right up on them." Tackett had gotten decidedly more comfortable voicing his tactical opinions. "I know these aren't exactly armored, but we can drive a lot faster than we can walk, and it might help us get on target before they know we're in the neighborhood."

Flanagan nodded. "It's a good point." He glanced at Brannigan, then pointed at the narrow lane between the big warehouse complexes. "Speed is security."

Brannigan wasn't entirely sold, though. He was looking around and comparing their surroundings to the map. "I don't want to just rush in there without overwatch." He grimaced. "Doesn't look like we've got any high ground nearby to work with, though."

Flanagan craned his neck to look at the map. This was a bad spot to do final assault planning, but it was what they had. "Put a team with a vehicle here to cover the exit route. Send the rest up this road here, get onto the railroad tracks, and approach from the east. Should be able to get shots on any outer security Garin might have thought to put out there."

He could see the wheels turning in the Colonel's head. It was far more half-baked than any of them liked, but it was what it was. They probably weren't going to get another chance. If what was going down up there was what he thought, they had to move now if they were going to get any shot at the Front's drug operation before it disappeared, one way or another.

205

"I don't have a better plan. You boys are with me." Brannigan headed back toward his vehicle and his weapons.

CHAPTER 25

Santelli was torn. A part of him thought that he really should have gone with the assault team. It was still quiet back by the road, and that nagging, depressing voice in his head was immediately whispering in his ear to tell him that he was old, fat, and just slowing the team down now. *Why did you even come along?*

He knew better. He knew that Brannigan had put him back at the vehicles with Curtis and Puller because he needed someone solid and dependable to hold down the support position. Just running into the middle of a firefight with the whole team was amateur hour, and Brannigan was no amateur.

So, with Curtis *still* grumbling about his lack of a belt-fed machinegun, and Puller silent and earnest—he hadn't said much lately—Santelli headed up the road and toward the towering warehouse with "Expediters" in big, black letters on the wall.

He could hear the gunfire beginning to slacken to the north. No, not slacken, he realized as he puffed his way to the fence. It was muffled. The fight must have moved inside. That was bad news for whoever the Russians were hitting. Potentially bad news for the assault team, too, if they had to go dig the Front out of another warehouse.

He paused at the base of the fence. There were lights in the yard beyond, starting to come to life as the evening turned to twilight, but not very many of them, and it looked like everyone who worked in either of the huge warehouses—or cargo terminals—had gone home. Everything was quiet...except for the gunfire.

The fence was a good seven feet tall, and he sighed tiredly. He *was* getting old, but he still reached up, grabbed hold of the chain link, and started to haul himself over. Fortunately, it was just a chain link fence, without the usual barbed wire across the top. It still wasn't all that stable, and it wobbled and rattled as he labored to get his bulk over the fence and down to the ground.

A part of him wondered if umpteen burglar alarms weren't going off at that moment, but he hadn't seen any extra wires.

Puller and Curtis both beat him over the fence, even though he'd been in the lead. Curtis was covering the road while Puller had dashed to a small European truck with a snowplow attached, that looked like it hadn't moved since spring, and took a knee, covering toward the far end of the long stretch of pavement between the two huge buildings.

Santelli dropped to the ground with a grunt. For a moment, he looked around, wondering if they shouldn't push up to the end of the pavement, where they could provide some support by fire.

A look at the angle of the hill over there precluded that idea. Support by fire doesn't work very well when it's shooting uphill. Besides, Brannigan had specified that he wanted them in reserve, watching the exit and covering the assault team's six.

"Let's set in but be ready to move." He might be there to watch the vehicles and keep anyone from intervening from the south, but that didn't mean Carlo Santelli had any intention of sitting the fight out if things got hairy.

*　*　*

Gomez had taken point, essentially shouldering his way in front of Flanagan. The two men had had a certain rivalry going from the beginning—though until Childress had been crippled, it had been more of a three-way contest—over who was the better hunter. You wanted a man on point who was stealthy, perceptive, and accurate, and he and Flanagan were both very good at it.

But Flanagan was the team's second in command now. That meant he didn't belong on point anymore. Or so Gomez told himself, quietly. The truth was that roles in the Blackhearts tended to be pretty loose.

Speed was security at that point, so he moved up alongside the fence outside the Expediters warehouse at just short of a jog. There was zero cover out there, and lights about every thirty yards or so, so there would be no careful, bounding movement.

And with gunfire already having split the evening, there was no hiding the weapons, either.

The assault team had split up in a staggered column across the street and moved up fast. Flanagan was off to his right, not far behind him, since the bearded woodsman wouldn't let Gomez get the lead by *that* much.

He slowed as he got close to the intersection and the railroad overpass beyond. The gunfire had become muted, echoing from inside the target building, but that didn't mean Gomez was going to let his guard down. They were in the open and the fight had already started.

The hill eclipsed most of the parking lot of the target warehouse, which provided a little cover, but while he considered just sprinting across, he decided to do it right. He dropped prone in the grass on the corner, getting behind his rifle and covering down on the road.

Wade sprinted across the street behind him, his boots pounding on the pavement. A moment later, the big man had thrown himself down on his belly on the other side. "Set!"

Gomez got up and sprinted to join Wade. Flanagan, Brannigan, and Kirk were already across on the other side, with Burgess and Tackett still watching their six. They waited just long enough for Gomez to get across the street, then ran to link up with the rest of the team.

There were more trees up on the hill alongside the tracks, providing at least some concealment and a little bit of cover. Gomez was already up and moving before Burgess and Tackett had finished crossing, slipping from tree to tree, his rifle in his shoulder.

At first glance, it looked like the entire force of Russian gangsters had gone inside the warehouse. More gunfire still slammed inside, the sounds like distant hammer blows reverberating through the concrete walls. But as he got closer, he saw movement in the parking lot.

The vehicles that Flanagan and Tackett had followed were parked in a chaotic sort of fan around the main entrance, many of them with their doors still open. But the Russians weren't being complete retards. They *had* left a rear security element.

He settled to a knee behind a bush, letting his eyes focus through the leaves while he had to admit that he kind of wished they'd gotten ACOGs or something on the Brens.

Two. It wasn't much of a rear security element, but that was fine with him. He laid the front sight post on the nearest man and let his finger tighten on the trigger. The rest of the team was behind him, so it was go time.

The shot broke with a much louder *crack* than the muted gunfire from inside the warehouse, and the muzzle flash was painfully bright in the dying light. His round hit the Russian thug high in the chest, punching across his torso and through his lungs. He dropped as Gomez shifted to the second man.

Then a voice yelled in Russian, and a stuttering burst of automatic fire ripped into the hillside.

Shit. There were more than two.

Only the fact that the Russians weren't that accurate with their weapons saved the Blackhearts' asses. Bullets *snap*ped overhead and thumped into the dirt, showering Gomez with shredded leaves and splinters as he threw himself flat. The rest of the Blackhearts did the same, though Wade was already moving, crawling as fast as he could past Gomez and toward the fence.

Bianco might not have had a belt-fed, but fire support was almost in the kid's blood. He stood up as the incoming fire slackened—the Russian must have mag-dumped and run dry—and ran out to the flank, where he hammered most of his own mag into the parking lot. He was shooting so fast that he probably wasn't aiming that much but was just suppressing the bad guys.

Gomez surged to his feet as the enemy bullets stopped coming for a moment and raced past Wade toward the fence. Flanagan was right on his heels, and the two of them reached the fence, barely a couple of yards from the warehouse wall, at nearly the same time.

Wade hadn't followed but had taken up the fire as Bianco reloaded and moved. As soon as Wade ran dry, Burgess opened up. The rest were moving fast to catch up with Gomez and Flanagan.

Flanagan had immediately let his rifle hang on its sling, putting his back to the fence and cupping his hand for Gomez's boot. They *could* both scale the fence, but this would be faster, and speed was life.

Putting his foot in Flanagan's hands, Gomez jumped for the top of the fence, grabbing the wire with both hands and almost losing it as the fencing bowed under his weight. Without a bar across the top, there wasn't a whole lot of structural integrity to the cyclone fencing. Just enough to make getting over it a pain in the ass.

He felt himself start to go backward, threatening to take Flanagan down with him, and he pulled hard, throwing his leg up over the wire. It still almost left him hanging upside down—an awful feeling when there were bullets flying around—and he was pretty sure he'd just kneed Joe in the face. Then a hand caught him in the back and pushed up, and he hauled himself the rest of the way over, letting go and hitting the ground like a sack of rocks.

211

Should have just climbed it straight.

The rest of the team seemed to have learned from his mistake and, except for Tackett, who was still laying down cover fire toward the corner of the warehouse, they were spread out along the fence and climbing it as quickly as they could.

Gomez, for his part, pressed forward toward the parking lot. The Russians were out of sight beyond the corner at the moment, sheltered from Tackett's fire.

Flanagan had been quick. His muzzle dropped over Gomez's shoulder as he took a knee behind the corner. "With you."

The two of them rounded the corner as Tackett ceased fire. More gunshots rumbled from inside the warehouse, but the parking lot had gone quiet.

Another body sprawled in front of a bullet-riddled Audi SUV. That made two. Gomez got up and moved quickly to the front of the vehicle, taking a knee behind the engine block as best he could, while Flanagan swept past, clearing the other side before moving toward the next, another blocky Ataman.

Gunfire roared, bullets shattering glass and punching through metal. Flanagan dropped to the concrete, returning fire but failing to silence the shooter.

Gomez couldn't see where exactly the fire was coming from, so he dropped to his side, putting his feet against the wheel and rolling to his shoulder, craning his neck to pick up the sights as he laid the Bren on its side on the pavement.

There. He saw shoes moving from several vehicles away and fired. His first shots missed, but he dumped another six and finally blew out the man's ankle, dropping him screaming to the asphalt. Three more shots silenced him.

Then Wade opened fire from the rear of the Audi, dropping yet another Russian as he showered Gomez with hot brass. The otherwise taciturn half-Apache mercenary cursed and brushed the casings off as he rolled to his right and started to get back to his feet.

"You're welcome." Wade rolled away from the Audi and slapped Gomez on the shoulder as he moved, muzzle high, toward where the front doors of the warehouse hung, shattered and twisted, from their hinges. "On me."

***

Winter glared at the phone as it rang insistently. He could hear the change in the sounds of the gunfire from down the road, and what he could hear did not speak well of the site security's performance. This should have been over ten minutes before.

While another man might have cursed, he simply picked up the phone and with a voice even more deadpan than usual, answered it. "Status."

"They have forced the door! The Russians are inside the facility! We need support!" The man's previous professional detachment seemed to have fled. The Russians, thugs though they may be, seemed to have been more than the site security was prepared to deal with.

That was unacceptable. While his expression remained bland, Winter's fingers tightened on the phone. He *should* just leave them to their fate. With such an important operation to secure, a bunch of Russian mafiosi should *not* have been such a problem.

Yet the fact was that the operation was far too important to leave it to the Russians just because the Board had put a pack of incompetents in charge of security. "Copy. We are on the way. Do try not to let them breach the laboratory before we arrive."

He hung up and tapped on the divider between the back and the driver's seat. "Take us in."

CHAPTER 26

Wade ran up the steps, pausing by the smashed doors just long enough to make sure that Burgess and Brannigan were behind him, and then he went in fast, his muzzle dropping level, his weapon-mounted flashlight strobing in the dim interior as he looked for Russians to kill. Not for the first time, he thought that it would have been nice to have some NVGs, but he'd gone white light on just about every hit in the sandbox he'd been on, once the first shot was fired, so this wasn't that out of his comfort zone.

John Wade's comfort zone was a very dangerous place.

He found himself immediately in a small entryway, with shredded, bullet-riddled benches against the equally destroyed cloth-paneled wall, and another shattered glass door leading deeper into the warehouse itself. Two bodies lay on the floor, leaking what was left of their blood onto the cheap carpet.

He pivoted as he moved out of the fatal funnel of the second door, while Burgess and Brannigan moved toward it and pushed through. Wade had taken the number one spot out of an innate sense of aggressiveness and the need to kill as many Russians and Front goons as possible, but he was far too much of a pro to get butt-hurt about taking the wrong turn and having to give up the lead spot.

There were plenty of targets inside, he had no doubt about that.

He fell in behind Gomez and Flanagan as Kirk and Tackett made entry and held on the doors.

They found themselves in a hallway of sorts. It looked like the entire warehouse was filled with cargo containers, stacked two to three high. There was a narrow corridor between the outer wall of the warehouse itself, including the rollup doors for the cargo docks, and the stacks of containers.

Several bodies were scattered on the floor in that corridor, both obvious Russian gangsters and men in jeans and black plate carriers. Brass casings littered the concrete floor between them.

Three more bodies, all Russian, lay outside another broken door set into one of the containers. As Wade pivoted to cover the corner behind him as he came out of the door from the entryway, he saw at least two more such doors, both with windows set in them, leading deeper into the container stack. So, apparently, the containers weren't containers, but prefab rooms.

That meant they had a maze of tight spaces to clear. Joy.

More gunfire sounded from inside, ringing through the steel of the containers like somebody was beating on them with a hammer. The complex of containers explained why the fight was still going on. The Russians were having to fight their way in, room by room, which gave the defenders a hell of an advantage.

Burgess stacked on the smashed door just long enough to get a shoulder squeeze from Brannigan, and then he went in fast, disappearing through the opening as Wade moved to close the distance with Flanagan and Gomez. He'd thought about pushing to one of the other rooms, but that might just get them split up and at a disadvantage. Better to keep the team together.

The first room was clear as he entered, at least it was now. Two more bodies lay on the floor, both the plate-carrier wearing security men. There were two doors leading deeper in, one straight ahead, the other to the left. The one to the left had

216

clearly been breached, and Brannigan was already on it, while Burgess covered the one straight ahead.

More gunfire hammered from deeper in. Wade found himself hoping that the bad guys didn't all kill each other before the Blackhearts could get some.

Brannigan went through the door with Wade on his heels. They found themselves in yet another room, this one apparently made from two containers set side to side, the intervening walls removed. It looked like something of a storage room, with boxes stacked against the walls, some of them full of bullet holes.

There weren't any bad guys in there, as the Blackhearts quickly spread out from the door and cleared the room, but judging by the increasing volume of the firefight, they weren't far away.

Wade moved quickly to the next door, which had partially closed, though it looked like it had been kicked open. These weren't security doors, but simple hollow-core wood jobs that would splinter if you leaned on them too hard.

This one opened outward from the double-container room, so he just set in at the doorknob, waited for the squeeze from Flanagan, then battered his way through the door, his muzzle dropping level as he rode it to the stops.

He almost ran into one of the Russians, a guy wearing dark trousers and an actual tracksuit jacket, who was crouched behind a couch of all things. Wade didn't even hesitate, but double-tapped the man in the side before quickly transitioning to his head and splashing his brains across the already partly shredded remains of the couch. The Bren's thunderous reports were painfully loud in the enclosed space, but they almost didn't even register, considering how much noise was echoing around that room.

Wade pivoted, taking in the scene over his sights as he looked for his next target.

The Blackhearts flowed into a large room, the walls on each side made up of three containers set end-to-end, with

217

dividers closing off a couple of small recreational areas set back in two of the opposite corners. Much of the rest of the room seemed to have been devoted to desks and computers, and the Russians were currently hunkered down behind those desks and some of the other furniture, exchanging fire with someone barricaded on the other side of the big double doors on the opposite side of the room from where Wade himself had made entry.

He and Gomez opened fire on the Russians at the same moment, blasting two more AK-wielding mountains of muscle off their feet and spattering two smaller men with blood and brains. One of them reached up to wipe the blood off his face, at which point Gomez shifted aim and shot him, too. Three rounds walked up his back and blew his throat out. He slumped, sliding down the side of the desk he was hiding behind and leaving a dark red smear on the metal.

The second man whipped around, bringing his submachinegun up, and Wade shot him through the eye.

Then several of the Russians deeper into the room figured out what was going on, and with shouted warnings that were too late for a few of their fellows, started blasting the rest of the room.

Wade dropped flat as bullets, slugs, and buckshot tore the couch to shreds. The Russians had simply turned and unloaded on the Blackhearts' side of the room, and for a moment the air was full of flying metal, impacts tearing up the walls of the stacked containers behind them.

Never one to just let himself get pinned down, Wade rolled to the side, pushed out along the floor, and started to return fire, aiming to cut more than a few of their legs out from under them. He shot underneath the desks, and was rewarded by a scream, that was nevertheless drowned out quickly by the thunder of shotgun blasts and automatic rifle fire.

The room went quiet for a moment, and he eased his head up a little, just in time to see movement by a door. The

Russians, realizing they were caught between the hammer and the anvil, had fallen back into some of the side rooms.

Great. Now we've got to dig them out of there, too. While these other assholes are still barricaded in the lab.

This was not going smoothly.

***

Kirk could hear the gunfight going on deeper inside the warehouse, and while a part of him did not envy the rest of the assault team, going into that meat grinder, another part was busily beating him up for holding on the door while the other guys went in to fight.

On the other hand, that van that suddenly came roaring up over the hill from the small neighborhood to the southwest was probably not friendlies, so maybe there was a good reason he and Tackett were sitting there.

He snapped his rifle up as the vehicle bumped and rolled over the grassy hillside and smashed into the cyclone fence. There had to be quite an engine in that thing, because even with as little room to build up speed as it had, it still tore through the fence and bounced onto the pavement, racing toward the cluster of Russian mafia vehicles. It screeched to a halt, the rear doors flying open, and he decided that this was *not* some of Dalca's people coming to back up the Blackhearts unannounced.

He opened fire, and promptly discovered that the windshield was made of ballistic glass. None of his shots penetrated.

Definitely not Dalca's people, as rich as she was.

He shifted his fire to the dark-clad, armored figures getting out of the back. His first shots hammered into the lead man's chest, and he staggered but kept moving. Unfortunately, he wasn't such a motarded dunce that he kept charging forward across open ground toward a man barricaded on a doorway, but threw himself flat, making Kirk miss high on his follow up shot.

The others ducked back behind the van and returned fire, bullets smashing into the concrete above Kirk's head, as Tackett leaned around the doorjamb and added his own fire to Kirk's.

The concussion of the muzzle blast was punishing, and he didn't hit any of the bad guys, but they ducked back behind the van and the Russians' cars as bullets smashed through metal and glass and punched more pits in the van's armor.

Kirk ceased fire as he no longer had any targets. They might be armored, but that didn't mean they were invincible, and while there was something to be said for suppressing fire, he wasn't going to sit there and shoot at nothing all night. He didn't have that many mags.

Sure enough, as soon as he'd stopped shooting—and Tackett had done so a split second before he had—the guys in the SWAT gear started to try to move. He definitely hit one, but again, the guy's plate stopped the round, and he ducked out of sight.

They could stay here all night, except Kirk didn't think that either the Blackhearts or the bad guys had all night. "Guido, this is Lumberjack. We've got what appears to be somebody's react force trying to crash the party. Armored van with at least five shooters. I'm reasonably certain that they're not cops. No lights, no sirens. We've got them pinned down in the parking lot, but I'm not sure how long that's going to last. Could use some maneuver backup."

"Good copy, Lumberjack. Guido and Company are on the way."

Kirk grinned tightly. Santelli was an old-school Sergeant Major in many ways, but he was starting to mellow in his old age. At least, he was mellowing in terms of radio discipline. Kirk had gotten to know the man well enough to know that the bad guys weren't going to get to meet Friendly Carlo.

He braced his weapon against the smashed and bent doorjamb and waited for one of the bad guys to stick his head out again while another crash of gunfire echoed from inside. Sirens were already starting to whoop in the distance, though curiously, there didn't seem to be any nearby.

Hurry up, guys. I don't think we've got all that long to finish this.

CHAPTER 27

Flanagan rose cautiously from where he'd thrown himself flat on the floor, just inside the door, as the Russians had proceeded to hose down the entire room. He was pretty sure they'd shot a few of their own in the process. But now they'd moved deeper into the complex of cargo containers, which was just going to make this harder.

Worse, he was on the wrong side of the double doors where the Front's security had barricaded themselves.

Rolling away from the fatal funnel of those double doors, he got back up on a knee and scanned the room. Smoke drifted through it, and most of the lights were out, but he could still see that there were two doors leading off either side, not including those double doors in the center of the far wall. Which meant, hopefully, that there was a way around.

It also meant that if they didn't act quickly and aggressively, they might find themselves getting flanked.

Wade and Gomez were down behind the remnant of the couch on that side of the room, but both were focused on the double doors, though not so exclusively that they couldn't immediately engage anyone coming through the side doors. Flanagan decided to take the bull by the horns and moved behind them, tapping Wade on the shoulder as he passed. "On me."

For his part, Wade didn't hesitate, but got to his feet, his muzzle going high as he swung around behind Gomez and joined Flanagan on the way to the first door. They stacked for a moment, Flanagan pointing his weapon at the crack while Wade reached around him and tested the doorknob, then the big former Ranger ripped the door open and Flanagan went through, fast.

It was a storage closet. He almost tripped as he dug the near corner, barked out, "Small room!" and turned back toward the door. Wade had halted as soon as he'd seen the same, and backed out, moving to the next door. Flanagan came out and joined him, lifting his own rifle toward the ceiling as he leaned around to reach for the doorknob, reversing roles as the geometries required.

Maybe there isn't *a way around. Which could suck.* They didn't have any grenades. Not even smokes or flashbangs. They'd have to try to storm the double doors by main force, which could get messy, fast.

The door was unlocked. He ripped it open, swinging it so hard that it bounced against the wall and rebounded, juddering toward him fast enough that he had to shoulder it aside as he went through the doorway on Wade's heels.

They were in hallway, all right. Wade was moving forward at an easy glide, his weapon up, when another door about three more containers ahead of them opened, and two men in jeans, blue shirts, and plate carriers came out, carrying what looked like HK 416s.

Wade opened fire immediately, and Flanagan threw himself across the narrow container hallway, adding his own fire to Wade's. Speed, surprise, and violence of action are the keys to winning a close-quarters gunfight, especially when outnumbered three to two. The Blackhearts used all three.

Flanagan's first shots were slightly low, punching into the number two man's stomach below his plate carrier. The Front shooter doubled over, and Flanagan's next two punched into his collarbone, and then the top of his skull. The bullet in his

222

brainpan didn't quite kill him, though he dropped to the floor, spasming and sending a burst of 5.56 into the wall.

Wade hadn't bothered with a lot of precise shooting but had just hammered a third of his mag into the figures in the hallway as fast as he could press the trigger. He cleaned up number three as Flanagan's target hit the floor, his last bullet catching the man in the neck, just below his ear, and ripping its way out through the side of his skull.

The two of them pushed forward toward the open door. Neither one wanted to have to stack up and breach it if the bad guys got to it and barricaded it first. Gomez was right behind them, his own weapon pointed at the ceiling in the narrow, cramped quarters.

Wade was closest to that side of the corridor, so he was the first one on the door, while Flanagan covered down the long axis. The door was still open, and he could just hear a voice on the other side yelling. They'd seen the security team go down, and someone in there was panicking.

He gave Wade a thump, and they went through the door together, Flanagan needing to fall back a short way to get through the door, his muzzle dropping past Wade's shoulder. He hooked left as Wade went right, dug his corner, and swept back toward the center of the room.

There wasn't anyone in the room, which appeared to be another office of some sort, but there was another door on the other side, with a narrow strip of window that had been covered over. When Wade moved to that door and tested the knob, it was locked.

Apparently, the bad guys had figured out that locks could help shape the battlespace in this sort of a fight. It had taken them long enough.

Gomez had entered with them, and was currently covered down on that door, his muzzle and eyes locked on the uncleared part of the corridor outside. "What's the plan?"

Flanagan looked at Wade, keeping his voice low just in case. He didn't trust these walls to stop bullets, so giving the enemy any more indicators of their location than they could help would be a bad idea. It didn't often get trained for, but with thin walls, whether they were sheet metal or drywall, all it would take would be someone with half a brain to pour a burst through the wall to ruin everyone's day. "Should we try to breach this one, or keep going around?"

Wade glanced at him. "You're the 2IC. I'm just a trigger puller."

Flanagan shook his head. "Fine. Let's keep pushing. I don't want to try to breach that door by kicking at it for five minutes, anyway." He turned toward the door where they'd made entry. "On you, Mario."

***

Bianco dumped another mag at the double doors, giving Burgess a chance to dash across the room toward the doors the Russians had disappeared through. Only when the bolt locked back and he reached for a fresh mag did it occur to him that he was burning through his ammo awfully fast. *Don't have five hundred rounds on me this time around. Gonna have to be a little more careful and a little more accurate.*

He got up and surged toward the door, where Brannigan and Burgess were now stacked up and waiting for him. He'd lost track of where all the gunfire was coming from. The whole warehouse sounded like they were on the inside of a snare drum, and his head was starting to hurt abominably.

Still, he kept his muzzle on the double doors as he ran past, finally getting a glimpse at the other side. Desks were piled up behind the doors, desks currently pocked with bullet holes, but still otherwise intact. They made for a decent defensive position, and there wasn't any way for an assault team to get through them quickly.

The only question in his mind, as he joined the other two and Brannigan went through the door with Burgess almost right beside him, was why the Russians had bothered just sitting there trading shots with the guys on the other side, instead of trying to go around in the first place.

224

Brannigan and Burgess both engaged as they went through the door. Bianco came in after them, unable to squeeze his bulk in until the other two Blackhearts had cleared the doorway.

He could just hear yelling in Russian and more gunfire up ahead. He remembered at the last moment to pivot around and check their six through the door before turning to join Brannigan and Burgess as they pressed on through the corridor.

For a brief moment, he wondered, somewhat whimsically, how it had worked out that three men with last names all ending in "B" had ended up on one element.

The corridor didn't go far before it opened on a larger room that looked like it was some sort of barracks. The Russians had worked their way in there, and as the three Blackhearts moved to the door, another mobster, skinny, bald, and with an Adam's apple almost as big as his nose, popped out behind one of the dividers between bunks, leveling what looked like a Mini-Uzi. He was a bit too slow, though, the weapon pointed at the ceiling when he popped out and, in the time that it took him to drop the little submachinegun level, Burgess had twitched his own muzzle about an inch up and cored out his brains with a double tap. Blood, hair, bone, and brain matter sprayed out onto the floor as the thug toppled backward.

Things might have gotten *really* hairy at that moment, since there were probably a dozen remaining Russians in that room. Except that they breached the next door on the other end at the same moment, and took fire from the site security through it, blasting yet another Russian off his feet with a storm of bullets.

The big fat guy in a red suit coat was bellowing in rage, shoving men ahead of him as he pushed through the open door, shooting a big over-under shotgun over one thickset man's shoulder as he went. Whatever was going on, the Russians were currently more focused on the interior of the facility than the mercenaries coming in behind them.

Two of the Russians did turn around to confront them, one carrying an AK, the other a vz.58. Brannigan shot the AK gunner in the stomach and throat, while Bianco, having pushed up to cover Burgess as he kicked the Mini-Uzi away from the first thug's hand, just to be on the safe side, hammered probably half his mag at the other guy. He missed twice, the first round going past the man's ear and the second low, but he got the rest on target, blasting the unarmored man back against the doorjamb, where he bounced off and fell leaving a spatter of red on the metal.

Bianco almost looked around, shamefacedly, to see if Brannigan and Burgess had seen his misses, but there were more pressing matters at hand.

Brannigan moved up to the doorway, only to have to jump back as a long burst of 7.62x39 fire hammered bits off the door and the doorjamb. The Russians hadn't all abandoned their six. And with that door covered, this was going to get rough.

CHAPTER 28

Santelli's ears perked up at the sound of gunfire in the open. He'd gotten somewhat used to the more distant sound of gunshots hammering inside the warehouse, but the decidedly different tone of rifle fire in the open meant something had changed. He didn't even need a radio call. "Let's move." He was already on his feet and heading up the inside of the paved yard between warehouses, his rifle up, looking for targets.

Unlike some of the other Blackhearts, Santelli wasn't wishing he had NVGs. Not that he had anything against the advantage they could provide. He just wasn't the sort of man who bothered expending the mental energy to wish for something he couldn't possibly have. Instead, he concentrated on maintaining his footing as he moved up through the shadows along the cargo docks, his rifle in his shoulder, doing what he could to avoid looking directly at the orange sodium lights that illuminated the lot.

Curtis, true to his character, had shut down the class clown part of his personality as soon as the shooting had started. Even the complaints about the lack of a belt-fed had stopped. He moved alongside Santelli at a fast glide, his own weapon pivoting to cover any door or other cover where bad guys might be lurking. Puller, for his part, was doing a good job of keeping up while still covering their six o'clock.

So far, none of the gunshots had come down the gap between the two big cargo terminals, but Santelli wasn't all that comfortable that they weren't. He could see the muzzle flashes occasionally from what he figured was probably the doorway to the target warehouse. He hoped that was the Blackhearts, because otherwise, things were going to get weird, fast.

They still might.

He cut across the open yard to the second building, cutting off a lot of his view of the hill ahead and the target warehouse atop it, but giving his little element a bit more cover. He'd always hated this sort of urban combat, with parking lots and streets creating far too many open danger areas. The least he could do was get some cover to establish what was going on before they exposed themselves.

Taking a knee, more out of sheer habit than any immediate tactical necessity, he eased his head and his weapon out around the corner to get a look at the situation, then cursed. All he could see from there was the low concrete wall along the road and the fence above it. Even the front door to the target warehouse was out of sight. He couldn't see any of the parking lot.

Whoever had flipped the table on the situation was out of sight, too, and he hadn't seen them cross the gap between the two warehouses, so either they had some squirters from a previously unknown door in the target warehouse that were trying to flank the Blackhearts, or else someone had pulled one hell of an end run.

That left him with the need to do some quick planning, but Santelli wasn't the sort to try to put together a plan without intel. And he wasn't going to go running out into the open to get that intel when there was probably someone else with eyes on whom he could coordinate with.

It was at that point that Kirk called over the radio. "Guido, this is Lumberjack. We've got what appears to be somebody's react force trying to crash the party. Armored van with at least five shooters. I'm reasonably certain that they're not cops. No lights, no sirens. We've got them pinned down in the parking lot, but I'm not sure how long that's going to last. Could use some maneuver backup."

"Good copy, Lumberjack. Guido and Company are on the way." In fact, cops had not been Santelli's first thought. He knew cops, even European cops. They wouldn't have come in shooting without identifying themselves.

He didn't pass the word along, because Curtis and Puller both had radios, and should have heard it all. There was no time for a powwow in the parking lot, either. He dashed across the road, slamming into the concrete wall with his shoulder. He wasn't nearly as athletic as he'd been thirty years before. It wasn't as easy to stop on a dime anymore.

Puller beat Curtis to the wall by a split second, but still took up rear security while Curtis caught up, quickly falling in behind Santelli. For his part, Santelli barely waited for the other two to join him before he was moving along the wall toward the parking lot.

He crouched down a little as the road rose to meet the level of the lot. The concrete didn't provide a lot of cover, but it was still cover, and it sounded like there were a lot of bullets flying around.

It wasn't far before he had to either get down and crawl or pop over the top and engage. Seeing little to no need to close the distance any more than necessary, he popped up behind his weapon.

The van looked like it had already been shot to hell. The windshield was starred and cracked, and it looked like it would be next to impossible to see through the ballistic glass. The grill was even smoking. Kirk and Tackett had put some serious fire on the vehicle.

The rear doors were open, and a cluster of men in black SWAT gear were huddled behind the van, popping out to either side to try to engage the men at the door of the warehouse. He didn't have a great angle on them; the van was still partly facing

229

him. But it was about as good as he was going to get without leaving cover.

He braced the rifle across the top of the low wall and opened fire.

The muzzle blast blew grit back into his face, and the flash was momentarily slightly blinding. He still saw his rounds chop into at least one leg, and a man dropped screaming to the pavement, silenced a moment later as Santelli pumped several more rounds into the dark silhouette.

Then another man in black leaned out from behind the rear doors and opened fire, hammering bits of dirt, pavement, and concrete into his face, forcing him back below the top of the low wall.

***

Another man might have cursed as Iota went down, the man letting out a scream of pain as his ankle was shattered by a bullet, choked off a second later as several more rounds hit him with a series of meaty *thuds*.

Winter wasn't that sort of man. He was even colder under stress than he was under ordinary circumstances, and he took in Iota's death with a stoic detachment that might have struck a normal person as psychopathic. Even if he'd thought about it, he wouldn't have worried about these men thinking that way. If anything, they were probably worse than he was.

The Organization selected for a certain personality profile, or at least within a certain window of that profile. The fact that the late and unlamented Flint had passed it was a matter of annoyance to Winter, though not a reason to question his own choices and attitudes.

He quickly located where the fire was coming from. The men in the entryway had friends, and they'd come up on the van's flank. They didn't *quite* have his team in an L-shape; they'd gotten impatient and hadn't closed off all the angles.

Leaning out around the door, he flipped his HK 416 to full auto and dumped the mag at the only spot where the enemy could find some cover. "Fall back to the hill!" They might not

230

have been completely flanked, but they still couldn't hit that entryway without exposing themselves to fire from one angle or another.

While he kept up the fire, Gamma leaned out around the other side of the van, staying low to the pavement and shooting underneath the open rear door. Meanwhile, the rest of the team turned and sprinted for the flattened gap in the fence where they'd driven through, and the low ground beyond it which would provide some cover.

Winter's mag ran dry and he let it fall, turning away from the van and checking the position of the rest of the team before he put his head down and sprinted for the edge of the parking lot. Even though Beta opened fire a moment later, from where he'd fanned out to the flank, shooting through the fence, taking up the cover for him, he figured he'd still have just enough time to get to the low ground before the enemy behind that low wall was able to stick his head up and shoot him.

His boots slid slightly on the grass as he threw himself down the slope, pivoting to land on his stomach facing the parking lot. He'd over penetrated a little bit and had to crawl back up nearly half a meter toward the pavement before he could return fire at the men across the parking lot.

Before he popped over the curb, however, he had a call to make.

It was time to call in the other team, as much as he didn't want to. He didn't trust them. He never had. They might be the only way to change the balance in this situation, though. If they were all killed in the process, so much the better, but even that would take some doing.

"Kappa, this is Alpha."

The tinny voice that came back through his headset sounded almost eager. Kappa had been far too excited to be put in charge of the secondary team. He probably wouldn't live to regret it, not if he tried to keep up.

"Bring the Type Ns up."

231

CHAPTER 29

Brannigan paused just long enough to take a deep breath. The element of surprise had been lost, and the bad guys definitely knew the Blackhearts were out in the hallway. Those sheet metal walls weren't going to stop bullets, and sooner or later the Russians were just going to mag dump through them, wherever a body might be hiding.

To rush into that room meant very probable death. To stay put meant *certain* death.

So, he threw himself across the threshold and into the room.

Under different circumstances, he might have stayed upright, moving quickly to a point of domination as he engaged every threat he could see. With the enemy already alerted and zeroed in on the door, however, that didn't seem like that great an idea.

Instead, he flung himself across the doorway, taking two steps and dropping flat to the floor, rotating to land on his side with his rifle leveled underneath the cots set up along the wall.

He felt and heard Burgess open fire from the doorway as he moved, seeing the gangsters deeper into the room tracking him with their muzzles. They were all ever so slightly too slow.

One of them jerked as Burgess shot him, red painting the white wall behind him, and he slumped over, triggering a burst of 9mm into the floor. The next one froze, caught between following Brannigan and engaging the threat at the doorway, and both Brannigan and Burgess shot him at the same moment, their shots crossing through his lungs and dropping him to the floor, pink froth spraying from his lips.

The last gangster might have stood his ground and fought, but more thunder came from the doorway behind him, and he decided he'd rather face death with the rest of his *bratva* than alone in an already bullet-riddled, corpse-strewn barracks room.

Burgess and Bianco flowed into the room as Brannigan started to pick himself up off the floor. Both kept their weapons trained on the door the last mobster had disappeared through, though Bianco quickly transitioned to cover the door they'd just entered. He might be a machinegunner first and foremost, but Vinnie Bianco still knew the score. Always cover the six.

Burgess didn't look at Brannigan as the elder Blackheart got up. "Not the most orthodox of entry methods, but it worked."

"That's the key word." Brannigan fought to keep the ache out of his voice. He'd hit hard and almost knocked the wind out of himself. He wasn't the young door kicker he'd once been. "It worked. And I didn't get my head blown off."

He had to use one of the cots to lever himself to his feet. He was *definitely* not a young buck anymore.

The door the Russians had gone through was still open, though all three Blackhearts had eased toward the wall where they weren't immediately visible through it. It sounded like things were still pretty hot up ahead, though the gunfire had died down and given way to a pounding that sounded like somebody was trying to kick in a door.

Brannigan moved up to join Burgess, though the other man had taken the lead as soon as he'd stepped in front of Brannigan to cover him while he got to his feet. They had to step a little bit farther out into the room than he thought either of them liked, just to get around the cots, but going over them wasn't exactly practical.

He paused over one of the dead Russians. The man wasn't wearing gear, but he did appear to have something in his pocket that caught Brannigan's attention. Letting Burgess move on the door, he bent and fished around until he came out with an RGD-5 grenade.

It wasn't a flashbang, but at that point he wasn't inclined to worry too much about taking anyone in the warehouse alive.

Moving up behind Burgess, he let his rifle hang on its sling and held the frag out over Burgess's shoulder where he could see it. It was pretty standard close quarters battle procedure, but Burgess still started a little. They hadn't had frags, so he hadn't exactly been expecting it. He caught himself quickly, though, and nodded.

Brannigan had used the RGD-5s before. That other Russian gangster, Dmitri, had gotten them the frags for the Khadarkh mission, the Blackhearts' very first rodeo, back before they were the Blackhearts. He gripped the grenade, holding the safety lever with his fingers, pulled the pin, and lobbed it into the next room, hard enough to bounce it off the wall.

He didn't want one of the gangsters to throw it back, but he also didn't trust a Russian fuse to actually be long enough to justify cooking it off before throwing it into the room.

There was a yell, and then the frag went off with a *wham* that immediately deadened his hearing, even with the electronic earpro they were all wearing. An ugly black cloud billowed through the room, and frag pattered and scraped off the walls and the ceiling.

A moment later, in the sudden quiet, the moans and screams started.

Burgess was moving then, and Brannigan followed him through the door.

***

Gomez was starting to think that he had the layout just about figured out. The three Blackhearts were working their way down a corridor that circled the outside of a large, central room or set of rooms. There were a few offices and supply rooms along that corridor, but as they swept through the next three, all with blacked out and locked doors leading deeper in, he thought he was starting to pick up the pattern. The goons who ran the facility, the guys with the security in plate carriers and carrying HK 416s, had fallen back into the central part of the maze of containers, locking themselves in.

Which told Gomez that they were expecting reinforcements.

They came to the corner. Judging by the lack of doors on the outside, he figured they were probably at the far end of the warehouse.

"Hold up." Wade and Flanagan had switched places several times, in a smooth, almost effortless flow that came from years of experience in close quarters combat. "We're just circling around at this point." A heavy *thud* shook the whole building. "That was a grenade, unless I'm mistaken. I really don't want to circle around and end up on opposite sides of a room from the rest of the team."

Gomez nodded, though he didn't take his eyes or his muzzle off that corner. "What do you want to do? We don't have breaching charges."

A distant *boom* sounded as if in answer to the question. Wade grinned tightly, though it wasn't an expression that reached his eyes. "Some of these clowns have shotguns. You and Joe have done shotgun breaches before, haven't you?"

"I think I saw one back in the first room." Flanagan was already facing back the way they'd come. "On me."

Gomez pivoted to follow as Flanagan led the way back to the living area just inside the entryway.

***

Brannigan and Burgess burst into the room, which looked like some sort of prep space, before the smoke from the frag had dissipated.

Three of the remaining Russians were on the floor, bleeding. Two were motionless, one very obviously dead, the side of his neck and his face ripped open, one eye mangled, the

236

other staring sightlessly at the ceiling. The other was lying face down in a rapidly spreading pool of blood.

The third man was trying to crawl away. For a brief moment, three rifle muzzles moved toward him, but he was clearly a heartbeat away from death.

Brannigan still hesitated, just for a moment. He remembered some of the jihadis he'd fought over the years, and the Marines he'd lost, often when those jihadis played dead, or really were on their last legs and decided to take at least one more infidel with them.

He'd known men who could make the case that the "insurance round" was prudent. There were places where he knew that it was. He wasn't sure about this Russian gangster, though. The Russians didn't really seem the type.

A moment later, the man breathed his last, slumping onto his face in his own blood, and ended the dilemma.

The smoke was starting to clear as the three Blackhearts swept through the room. It was subdivided into several sections, with what looked almost like an airlock at the far end, leading inward toward the central part of the warehouse and the conglomeration of containers.

Several of the gangsters were still trying to get through that door, which seemed to be sturdier than they were prepared for. The fat guy in the red jacket was yelling at them, a full-length over-under shotgun in his hands.

Two of the Russians were on the floor behind the dividers, having apparently thrown themselves there as the grenade had come sailing into the room. The dividers themselves were shredded and pocked with shrapnel, but they'd still somewhat shielded the Russkies from the frag.

As the three Blackhearts loomed out of the smoke, a man in a dark jacket, gray t-shirt, and black jeans started and grabbed for the AK-74 that he'd dropped as he'd dived for cover. Brannigan walked three rounds up his chest and into his throat. He jerked, blood spreading quickly from the holes blasted in his shirt and began to shudder as his life drained out. He was already dead before he stopped moving, his nerveless hand falling away from the Kalashnikov.

Burgess pivoted the opposite direction, hammering four shots into the man on the other side of the room. Bianco flowed between the two Blackhearts, taking forward security immediately. As Brannigan turned from the AK-wielder he'd just smoked, he saw Bianco dump two Russians who'd noticed the figures looming through the smoke and had pivoted toward the oncoming Blackhearts, bringing up their own weapons. The big man double-tapped the first, pivoted toward the second as the first staggered, punched five more rounds into that one, then shifted back to the first, who hadn't fallen yet, and put a single round through his skull.

Vinnie Bianco was better with a rifle than his preference for belt-fed machineguns would suggest.

The fat guy in the red suit jacket roared and swung his shotgun toward them, triggering one barrel up into the ceiling. Half the surviving Russians scattered toward the walls, just to get away from that big bastard and his shotgun.

The Blackhearts did much the same, Brannigan going right while Burgess and Bianco went left. Incoming fire always has the right of way, and none of them were wearing armor, anyway. That had been a bridge too far for even Dalca's organization in the Czech Republic, at least on the timeline involved.

The second blast tore a chunk out of the divider over Brannigan's head, and then one of the other Russians opened fire, just holding down the trigger and spraying his mag across the room. The ragged holes in the divider walked up and away as Brannigan made himself as small as he could against the wall.

He glanced across at where Burgess and Bianco were piled on the other side, just in time to see Burgess throw himself flat on the floor and push out from the wall, his eye already seeking his sights as he pivoted over onto his side.

The former SEAL didn't push himself all the way out into the middle of the room but engaged as soon as he had a target. Brannigan moved to do the same, though he didn't lie down on the floor, but instead started to pie off the edge of the divider, moving as fast as he could without overexposing himself. He caught a glimpse of a Russian in a tracksuit pointing a sawed-off shotgun toward Burgess, and blasted the man off his feet, the first round going low into his side but the second punching between his ribs and obliterating his heart.

Brannigan hadn't broken stride as he'd shot the Russian and continued his glide out around the corner, even as a second shotgun blast *boom*ed painfully in the small space, ripping through the divider *behind* him.

The fat man apparently wasn't that great with the weapon, which was a good thing.

Burgess fired twice more, as Bianco moved to the edge of the divider, barricading on it even though there were still plenty of bullet holes in it to serve as a graphic illustration of the difference between cover and concealment. His own rifle barked, and then Brannigan went for broke.

He stepped out from behind the divider, just in time to see the fat man duck behind yet another at the back, desperately trying to fumble two more shells into the over-under. Brannigan shot the last Russian through the skull from about ten feet away as he came around the edge of his own divider, then advanced on the fat man.

With a shouted curse in Russian, the fat man flung the shotgun around the edge of his barricade and fired, hardly looking. Brannigan *felt* the buckshot go past his ear, then he was advancing on the divider, leaning into his rifle and pumping rounds through the fiber wall and into the corpulent mobster behind it.

The man yelled as the bullets punched into him, but he fired again anyway. This time, Brannigan felt a fiery *thump* in his shoulder as one of the pellets hit him, but he kept moving, kept firing as fast as the trigger would reset, hammering round after round through the barricade and into the gangster.

The fat man jerked and groaned under the onslaught, but he didn't give up, didn't lie down and die. He stumbled out from behind the divider, bleeding profusely as he tried to reload the shotgun. His fingers were shaking, and he jerked again with every new impact. Brannigan kept shooting him. The fact he was reloading meant he was still a threat.

The shotgun fell as shells spilled from his fingers. The big man stumbled, going down to one knee as the weapon clattered to the floor.

Brannigan held his fire for a moment, as the other two Blackhearts stepped out to join him, the gunfire going quiet. The rest of the Russians in the room were down. It was just the fat man, blood turning his red jacket a darker shade as he went down onto all fours, more gore dripping from his mouth. He must have taken a round through the lung, but he wasn't going down just yet.

For a brief few seconds, he just stayed there, holding himself up with his beefy hands, dripping blood onto the floor. Then he looked up at Brannigan.

The fat man's face was a mask of hate. "*Yub tvoyu maht!*" He lunged to his feet, swaying drunkenly, and dove for the AK-47 that one of his men had dropped.

Burgess and Bianco opened fire immediately, at least a dozen more rounds ripping through his massive girth, but then, as his sausage fingers closed around the Kalashnikov's grip, Brannigan put the sights on his head and pulled the trigger.

The gangster's head, balanced on a column of fat and muscle that almost didn't qualify as a neck, barely moved at the impact. He froze for just a second, as if his sheer mass wasn't quite ready to fall yet. Then, rather like a collapsing balloon, he slumped to the floor.

"Kodiak, Woodsrunner."

Realizing his chest was heaving, Brannigan keyed his radio. "Send it."

"We've got a couple shotguns for breaching, but this main entryway is a non-starter." He could remember the barricaded double doors leading deeper in from the first big room. "Have you got a breach point?"

"Affirm." He looked at the blacked-out door in front of him. There wasn't a lot of space between it and the dividers to either side, but there was enough for a breach. However, it was also almost certain that the bad guys inside would know a breach was coming there. The Russians had already tried to get in. "We'll meet you at the first door around the corner." He turned back the way they'd come. There was another way in from the barracks, so that was probably the best bet.

"This is Guido. Best make it quick. I think we've got more company coming."

CHAPTER 30

"We've sealed the lab, but we need help *now!*" The voice on the other end of the radio was increasingly panicked. "The Russians have control of the rest of the facility."

Winter found that unlikely. There was another player at work here. The men who had driven him and his team to cover were far more professional and deadly than any Russian mafiosi. It could be hard to tell once bullets were flying, but Winter had been in combat all over the world. It was part of why he was in the position he was. He had experience that the Organization valued. That he believed in the Organization's goals was an added bonus.

He was sure that if he hadn't, they still would have managed to pay him enough to make up for it. And to keep his mouth shut.

Dalca? Possibly. She certainly has the money to pay mercenaries to back up her organization. He had, as was his wont, studied the situation before he'd even arrived in Prague. He was all too familiar with Dalca. The Organization suspected that she might have been involved in a few setbacks they'd suffered over the last few years, though they had never put together enough solid intel to justify a target package.

If Winter had been more like Flint, he might have resented that.

He eased his way up to see over the smashed fencing, looking for the enemy. If he was lucky, they'd gotten overconfident at his team's retreat, and might have exposed themselves.

He wasn't that lucky. They were definitely professionals, and therefore definitely *not* Russian thugs.

Which presented some problems when it came to the lab. If those idiots inside realized that the opposition weren't the Russians…

"This is Alpha. There is a second opposition force that is not the Russians. Do not allow them access."

There was a pause, even as Gamma and Beta started to move down the flank to the right, looking for an angle on the men who'd blindsided them from the south. None of *his* team were the type to sit there and wait while there was a fight to prosecute.

"Do I understand that right? There is a *second* opposing force?" The man on the other end of the radio sounded like he didn't quite believe it.

Clearly, the Organization had gotten sloppy with the security for this operation. Probably because it was in Europe. They hadn't thought extensive security measures were necessary. So, they'd hired bottom-of-the-barrel security men.

"That is what I said." Winter's tone was still so calm that he sounded bored. "Secure the laboratory, seal the entrances, and hold your position until I can reach you. Do not open to anyone who cannot provide the appropriate recognition code."

Once again, there was that pause. "Acknowledged."

A burst of gunfire echoed off the walls of the warehouses. A stray round must have hit one of the streetlights, because it flickered and went out. Those newcomers who'd nearly flanked them weren't going to be caught asleep. They had that road locked down.

We'll see how long that lasts.

"Kappa, Alpha. What is your estimated time of arrival?"

"Thirty seconds."

244

***

Curtis couldn't help but curse his luck silently. No machinegun, stuck on outer cordon while the rest of the team went in on the target, then pinned down in a sunken street. None of it added up to his idea of a good night.

Granted, his idea of a good night didn't include the work. It tended to include booze, gambling, and women. Okay, one woman, now, but at least he could still go with the booze and the gambling.

Even the first contact with the Front's react force—and he didn't need to ask Santelli to come to the conclusion that these guys in black were Humanity Front—had been disappointing. Santelli had gotten most of the shots in while Curtis had been taking cover.

Now, though, he had maneuvered to put Santelli between him and Puller, so he'd get first crack if they tried to maneuver on them.

Sure enough, at least one was trying to creep around the side of the low hill where the warehouse sat. Curtis lined him up and fired, rocking eight or ten rounds at him. He might not have a machinegun, but he could still do support by fire. It just wasn't quite as fun.

The man in black ducked back behind cover and disappeared. A moment later, though, more fire came from a little higher up the hillside, chipping away a little more at the low concrete wall that was the three Blackhearts' only cover.

"Carlo, I think we might want to relocate." Curtis brushed bits of concrete off his scalp before leaning out and returning fire, albeit not quite as accurately as he might have hoped. There *were* houses down that way, but his own survival and that of his teammates trumped concerns about collateral damage.

Santelli popped up over his head and fired at the men who'd fallen back from the van, the muzzle blast slapping at Curtis as he did so. "I think you're right."

Then all hell broke loose.

The growl of a helicopter had gone unnoticed in the thunder of gunfire, but now, as the bird came around the corner of the big warehouse to the south, flying low over the houses to the west, it couldn't hide its approach anymore. It swooped toward the parking lot, already starting to flare as it passed over the neighborhood just beneath the railroad tracks.

After Kyrgyzstan, Curtis half expected to face one of those hybrid pusher helos, but this was just a normal medium duty utility helicopter. It was even painted white and blue, looking to a passing observer like it was just another civilian helicopter out for perfectly peaceful purposes.

Curtis would probably have agreed with anyone who said that he wasn't always the most intuitive of individuals, but even he could tell that this wasn't that. The bad guys had just brought in reinforcements.

For one thing, no regular civilian pilot worth his salt would willingly and knowingly fly a civilian helicopter right into the middle of a firefight. And that was exactly what this pilot was doing.

The doors slid open, and before he could react, Santelli had grabbed him by the back of the jacket and hauled him away from the wall, dragging him as fast as possible toward the shed just outside the fence to the bigger Expediters cargo yard.

Muzzle flash flickered in the open helicopter side doors, and bullets smacked into the pavement and the dirt around them, sending up little puffs of pulverized asphalt, concrete, and earth. The crackle of the rounds ripping through the sound barrier was almost deafening, and Curtis felt a bullet pluck at his sleeve just before he threw himself behind the shed, following Santelli's lead. Puller tumbled to the grass behind him, and for a second he thought their new doc had been hit, but the former Corpsman scrambled back up and into the shelter of the structure a second later.

More rounds hammered into their cover but didn't make it all the way through. Curtis moved to the corner, trying to get a shot at the helicopter, easing out as carefully as he could.

He got a glimpse of fast ropes dangling from the bird and black-clad shapes sliding rapidly down them, but then was forced back by another long burst of fully automatic fire.

The bad guys had reinforcements, all right.

***

Tackett had been barricaded on the doorway, while Kirk moved back out into the parking lot, using the Russian mobsters' vehicles for some cover and concealment once the Front shooters in the van had been forced back. He spotted the helicopter even before Curtis did and came to the same conclusion.

While he hadn't had the experience with the Humanity Front that the rest of the Blackhearts did, Dan Tackett had developed a very finely tuned sixth sense for threats while fighting through the jungles of the Anambas Islands. He recognized the threat immediately. The bird was too low, too fast, and coming right at them.

He already had his weapon trained on the oncoming aircraft as it flared and slowed, coming to a hover above the parking lot. "Kirk! Get back here!"

The retired Green Beret took one look at the helicopter, pivoted, and ran back toward the entryway, as Tackett's finger tightened on the trigger. He didn't have a target *yet*, but fractions of a second could matter in a firefight.

Even before the helicopter's nose had dropped, its forward momentum all but completely arrested, the side door was sliding open. Tackett got a glimpse of a weapon as the door gunner swung out through the opening, and he got two shots off before the gunner opened fire.

A stream of machinegun fire tore through the front of the warehouse and the closest vehicles, tracers chasing Kirk toward the door. The older man sprinted the last few yards, throwing himself in through the door as Tackett returned fire for a few moments before he was forced back deeper into the entryway, dropping to the floor to avoid the stream of high-velocity metal punching holes in the wall.

The murderous suppressing fire kept up for a long time, presumably keeping the men fast roping out of the helo covered until they could close on the doorway. Tackett knew he was vulnerable, but he also knew that if they gave up the door, they were going to get slaughtered. He stayed prone and crawled toward the opening, easing out just far enough that he could get his muzzle and his sights around the doorjamb.

Half a dozen men in black fatigues and body armor were working their way through the maze of parked vehicles, weapons up and moving fast. They all looked big, like roided-out bodybuilders in tactical gear. He got a shot at one of them, but while he was pretty sure he hit the guy, his target showed no reaction, except to immediately snap his rifle up and send a withering storm of fire in return that tore through the doorjamb and shattered more of the remaining glass in the open door.

Kirk grabbed him and hauled him back out of the doorway. "We can't hold this door with that bird providing fire support. Come on." He headed deeper into the warehouse, his weapon up, and got on the radio. "Kodiak, Kodiak, Lumberjack. We've got a hostile react force about to make entry. They've got air support, and they've forced us and the security element to cover. We need to barricade and get ready to repel an assault."

***

Winter watched the Type Ns fast-rope down out of the helicopter. It was a much more high-profile than he would have liked, but he couldn't expect much else from the products of that program. The strike on the facility in Argentina had put the research back several years, but it hadn't stopped it. Unfortunately, the weaknesses in the original experiments hadn't been ironed out, and that meant that while he had a semi-useful wrecking crew, the combination of performance-enhancing drugs that had turned the professional soldiers into hugely strong and tough specimens meant that they were almost mindlessly aggressive along with feeling no pain. They weren't ever going to take the subtle route.

248

He was already thinking ahead. The Type Ns would more than likely clear the entire warehouse, at the very least killing everyone who had a weapon. That was fine. He had decided that the facility was probably going to have to be burned to the ground. It was simply too exposed at this point. For the moment, however, he had the opposing forces outside to worry about. "Come with me." He fell back from the parking lot and headed south along the railroad tracks.

He'd caught a glimpse of those shooters running across the road toward the cargo yard ahead of the first aerial gunfire from the helicopter. They would have to be neutralized. No one could leave this place who wasn't working for the Front. Not alive, anyway.

CHAPTER 31

Flanagan heard Kirk's radio call just as he was about to move through the door that Brannigan and Burgess had taken out of the central living area, following the trail of spent brass and dead bodies toward the rest of the assault team. It made him stop, reconsidering the next step. He had a shotgun slung over one shoulder, taken off a dead Russian gangster, but if they were about to get hit from outside, trying to breach the central part of the complex might be a bad idea.

Brannigan had apparently come to the same conclusion. "Good copy, Lumberjack. Fall back to the first big room and link up with Woodsrunner. Break, break. Woodsrunner, Kodiak. Hold what you've got. We're coming to you."

Flanagan held on the door, hardly bothering to glance over his shoulder to make sure that Wade and Gomez were covering the other danger areas. Both men were pros, and Flanagan knew he didn't need to worry about either one of them. They were all used to looking for work wherever it might be. No Blackheart was going to fall into the attitude of a junior enlisted just sitting on his hands because no one had told him what to do next.

"Friendlies," Burgess called out from the far side of the door.

"Bring it in." Flanagan stepped aside for him just as Kirk and Tackett came in from the front with the same deconfliction call, punctuated by an explosion from the entryway that rattled the walls. Either that had been a hell of a flashbang, or else the enemy react force was leading with frags.

Kirk was already turning back toward the entryway. "We have *no* time."

He hammered three shots back toward the entryway, then he was moving, Tackett right at his shoulder, pressing deeper into the main room.

Flanagan had turned from the doorway as soon as Burgess, Brannigan, and Bianco had come through, and now he kicked over a sofa, dropping to a low crouch behind it. It wasn't cover, but concealment had a place in a gunfight anyway. When life or death hinges on fractions of a second, getting the drop on the enemy by that much might be the difference between winning and being a rapidly cooling corpse on the floor.

He leaned out around the arm of the couch just as another flashbang sailed through the doorway and clattered to the floor just inside the threshold.

Flanagan didn't have time to get his head out of the way, but he squeezed his eyes shut as the bang went off. The concussion was ear-splitting even with his electronic earpro in, and he felt like he'd just been punched in the head. He could see the flash even through his eyelids. But at least he could still see when he opened his eyes, and his sights were almost right on the big man in black SWAT gear who came charging into the smoke roiling up from the detonated concussion grenade.

The assaulter was massive, and while Flanagan had compartmentalized everything in that moment, something about that big bruiser seemed uncomfortably familiar.

Keeping his eyes shut, along with hiding behind the sofa, had bought him a couple of precious seconds. The assaulter was pivoting as he came through the door, digging his corner just like every CQB school had taught for as long as Flanagan could remember. He was so fixated on that corner that he was facing

252

exactly the wrong direction as Flanagan shot him through the side, the rifle's report sounding dimmer than it should have after that flashbang had gone off.

The man didn't even flinch. He swung back toward Flanagan even as the black-bearded mercenary pumped more rounds into him, walking his fire up the man's torso toward his head.

More gunfire thundered and rattled across the room, as the other Blackhearts engaged the men in black. The entire room reverberated deafeningly.

At first, the bad guys' Number One man had barely even reacted to the bullets punching into him, almost as if he didn't feel anything. Even the force of the rounds tearing into his flesh barely staggered him, and when they hit his front plate, he was already moving his weapon toward Flanagan's face.

Only when Flanagan and Wade both double-tapped him in the head, two of the four rounds going through his black balaclava, a third through his eye protection, and the fourth clipping the rim of his helmet before it punched into his skull, did he finally topple, his entire body going limp as a 5.56 round obliterated his brain stem. He collapsed like a puppet with its strings cut, hitting the floor on top of his weapon.

The gunfire fell silent for a moment, just before another heavy object hit the floor just inside the doorway. Tackett let out a bellowed, *"Grenade!"* and every Blackheart hit the floor.

The concussion was brutal, and frag tore into the couch in front of Flanagan, pattered off the walls and the ceiling, and more smoke roiled through the doorway and over the furniture.

More gunfire clapped through the room. Kirk had rolled out from behind the desk where he'd taken cover and was mag-dumping at the doorway. A third black-clad figure lunged into the opening as the smoke began to dissipate, only to take a burst of fire from Kirk and crash onto his back as his head snapped back from the impact that had just painted the back of his helmet with his brains.

"Fall back." Brannigan had gotten to his feet, hauling Bianco up off the floor. The big, baby-faced man was clearly bleeding. He'd taken a hit.

Kirk, Tackett, and Gomez sprinted across the room, guns up and still covering that entryway. They had a brief second to move. It looked like the rest of the assaulters might have paused just for a second, having seen the first three go down. The Blackhearts would take full advantage.

Flanagan and Wade popped over the top of the upturned couch, weapons trained on the entryway, waiting for a target. The smoke swirled through the room and bit at the back of Flanagan's throat.

"Move!" Brannigan was at the doorway. Flanagan and Wade surged to their feet and ran.

As they hit the doorway, another black figure plunged into the open room, and Brannigan opened fire, spitting 5.56 rounds at the man as he ran at an angle across the room.

***

Puller crouched behind the shed, wondering how long it was going to take for that helicopter to circle around and light them up from the air. They had some cover where they were, but it wasn't going to last if the bad guys got any kind of better angle on them.

The pitch of the rotors had changed, and he craned his neck, tracking with his muzzle, as he could hear the helicopter start to move. He had a sudden nightmare image flash through his mind of the bird suddenly overflying the parking lot and shooting them to shit from a hundred feet above.

The helo was moving, starting to circle. Santelli cursed, then pointed to the office entryway into one of the Expediter warehouses. It was the only overhead cover anywhere around.

Unfortunately, there was a fence between them and the warehouse. They had to expose themselves even more to get to cover, and that helicopter was coming around.

Puller took a deep breath. He didn't think about what the other Blackhearts might think. Didn't even think much at all. He just moved.

While he hadn't been able to see it, he'd figured out that the helicopter was coming around to the east. So, he stepped out onto the grass until he could see it around the corner of the shed, put his rifle in his shoulder, and opened fire.

He'd barely aimed at first, so it was sheer, dumb luck that his first couple rounds took the door gunner in the goggles, throwing the man back into the fuselage before Puller really got on his sights and shifted his aim toward the cockpit. His bullets punched through aluminum, fiberglass, and Perspex, and the helicopter suddenly veered away, the pilot unwilling to put his own personal skin on the line to get a shot at the Blackhearts.

He turned as he lowered his weapon, dropping the empty magazine and slapping a reload in. The sheer stupidity of having just run out into the open to shoot at a helicopter with machineguns in the door had just sunk in, and he was starting to shake. Santelli and Curtis were already at the entryway, and Curtis was waving at him. "Hurry up, Doc!"

Puller put his head down and ran for all he was worth. It sounded like the bird was coming back around again, and he did not want to be in the open when the surviving door gunner set out to avenge the one Puller had shot.

He got there just in time. The helicopter swept past and machinegun fire peppered the pavement behind his heels, as well as punching a train of holes through one of the handful of semis parked at the loading docks. He threw himself through the open door. It looked like Santelli had broken the glass, reached through, and opened it.

Skidding on the tile floor, Puller rolled to his back, pointing his rifle between his knees, breathing hard. The roar of the helicopter's rotors shook the building, then receded.

Curtis reached down and helped him up. "That was some action movie shit, Doc. You did good, but don't ever do that again. You gotta stick around to patch the rest of us up, remember? We already lost two docs as it is."

Santelli was covering the doorway. "Get up here, Kevin."

Curtis gave Puller a slap on the shoulder and then hurried to the other side of the door from Santelli, covering down on the far side, back the way they'd come.

Puller sucked in a breath, annoyed by how hard his heart was beating. *You did okay on that counter-piracy mission. Suck it up. This is what you signed on for.*

Then, as Curtis opened fire, he started, shook his head, and turned to look for work to do. They were in the main office of the warehouse, and it looked like there was a door leading deeper in. He had no idea if there was another entrance in the back, but it was probably a good idea to set security on it. He moved quickly to the door, opened it so that he could see deeper into the darkened warehouse, stacked with shelves and pallets of cargo, and sank to a knee, watching the open area over his sights.

***

Winter rounded the corner right behind Beta, moving fast. It had taken longer than he'd liked to get the team over the fence, and even from the other side of the warehouses, he could still hear the muted hammering of gunfire from within the lab complex. They needed to clean this up quickly. It had already taken far too long.

The team spread out into an echelon formation as they glided up the strip of pavement, checking beneath and behind each truck as they moved. Kappa's voice echoed in his ear. "They shot Sigma. We are down to one door gun, and the pilot thinks that we've taken some damage to one of the rotor blades. Be advised, they appear to have gone inside the western warehouse." With a growl of engines and rotors, the H160 came around over the top of the lab complex and toward the cargo yard. "We are coming around for another pass."

Beta picked up the pace, moving toward the awning over the entryway ahead. As he rounded the front of a parked semi, however, another burst of fire caught him mid-stride. He staggered, half-turned, and then slumped to the pavement.

Winter threw himself behind the semi's front wheels, even as the helicopter went past overhead again, spraying down the front of the building with machinegun fire.

The helicopter kept moving, continuing to circle. For a moment, he wondered why they didn't just hover and hose down the building, but after taking accurate fire, he suspected the pilot didn't want to risk it.

He *could* order him to. Even threaten his life and his family. The Organization had all the information on everyone. It wasn't hard to get to anyone, once they were identified.

He'd be a lot more worried about identifying this strike force if he wasn't already planning on ensuring that none of them left Prague alive.

He started to ease around the front of the semi but had to quickly duck back as another burst of fire blew out the headlight and chewed into the hood and the grill. They not only weren't dead; they weren't even properly suppressed. That building had provided them with more cover than he'd hoped.

"Alpha." Gamma was at his elbow. "There's a loading dock that wasn't secured back here. We can make entry and get behind them."

Winter nodded. Better to get on their flank. They could command the open pavement in front of them too easily.

They quickly turned away from the front door and headed back toward the rear of the warehouse.

CHAPTER 32

Brannigan's breath was heaving, and the blood was pounding in his ears. He hadn't been this worn out by a fight in a while. Nothing was going right.

The corridor didn't present much in the way of defensive possibilities, and the barracks room beyond it wasn't much better. The cots weren't even concealment, let alone cover, and it was becoming evident that they were going to have to slow these roided-out monsters down long enough to put enough bullets into them to put them down. Headshots worked, too, but it was hard to rely entirely on them in the frantic chaos of a close-quarters firefight. There was a reason most gunfighters trained to shoot center mass.

The containers shook as yet another grenade was lobbed into that big central room, further shredding papers and dead bodies, and filling the air with even more smoke. A light flickered, damaged by the shrapnel, through the door to the corridor.

Flanagan, Wade, and Gomez were already in the barracks room, with Flanagan holding on the doorway. "Turn and go."

Something about the tone of Flanagan's voice brooked no argument. The quiet man had a plan, so Brannigan surrendered the lead for the moment and pivoted away from the central room to sprint down the corridor.

He heard movement behind him before he reached the door, however, and stopped, turning just in time to eat the flashbang that hit the floor with a *thunk* just inside the door, a split second before it detonated.

He'd squinted but hadn't quite managed to get his eyes all the way closed before the bang had gone off. The electronic earplugs kept him from being deafened and protected him from a lot of the disorienting effects of the bang. There was still a glowing green blotch in the middle of his vision as the smoke roiled in the doorway and the first black-clad figure darted through, an HK 416 swiveling toward Brannigan's face.

Then Gomez opened fire just over his shoulder, having been shielded from the blast by Brannigan's considerable bulk. Gomez being Gomez, he hit what he was aiming at, his first round taking the black-masked man in the throat, the second punching through the balaclava and his teeth, tearing out a chunk of his spine. He still triggered a burst of 5.56 into the wall as he toppled.

Then Gomez was dragging Brannigan back toward the door with him, his own rifle pointed at the doorway.

Two more burly shooters burst through the door then, but Flanagan had laid down in the prone behind the doorway, only his muzzle and his head protruding out into the corridor, and he shot the first one in the foot as soon as he broke the threshold. It was a testament to whatever those guys were hopped up on that the guy didn't even slow down.

As Flanagan continued his barrage, Gomez and Brannigan dove for the deck, the first spray of 5.56 rounds punching new holes in the metal over their heads. Brannigan was half blind and out of position, so he landed on his back, his rifle pointed between his boots, and he opened fire as soon as he hit, even though he didn't have much more than silhouettes to shoot at.

He felt a fiery impact in his side, but kept riding the trigger, dumping his mag into the two men who were still advancing quickly down the corridor. One wasn't moving that well anymore, and as Brannigan walked his rounds up the second man, that one took a series of five or six shots to the upper chest and head and fell on his face.

Brannigan crawled backward and into the barracks room, only rolling over and getting painfully to his feet as he cleared the doorway. A hand to his side identified the wound as just a graze along his ribs. It hurt like the devil, but it was hardly fatal.

Flanagan had ceased fire, though he still held his position on the floor, lying on his side along the inside wall, aimed in down the corridor. Gomez was on his feet on the other side of the door, even though there was hardly any space there.

Burgess had dragged Bianco back to the far corner, not far from the prep room, still littered with Russian corpses, and was doing blood sweeps while Bianco held a hand to the hole in his shoulder. Brannigan wasn't the only one who'd gotten trimmed. Wade was on the door leading toward the prep room, watching their six.

Things had gone quiet, but Brannigan wasn't sure they were out of the woods yet. He didn't have a count on the Front's bullet sponges, but he suspected there were more than just six.

He dropped his mag and slapped in a new one. It had taken entirely too many rounds to drop those three in the corridor, but that was clearly par for the course. These guys reminded him of some of the Al Qaeda fighters in Iraq, who'd been so drugged out of their minds that they'd felt no pain as his Marines had shot them to ribbons. Except these guys were also on so many steroids that they had considerably more mass and strength than those poor saps had had, and they clearly had a lot better training and equipment.

"Those look like the freaks we ran into in Argentina to you?" Gomez kept his eyes and his muzzle down the hallway as he spoke.

261

"Yeah." Flanagan started to pick himself up. "Apparently, we didn't shut the program down when we dropped a mountain on the lab."

"Makes sense that we wouldn't have." Brannigan took a deep breath and immediately regretted it. "Question right now is, did we get all of them?"

"I doubt it." Wade sounded more irritated than anything else. "They're just recalculating because they got their teeth kicked in. I say we stack up and go kick their asses, rather than waiting for them to come to us."

Brannigan thought about it, watching the faint, flickering light of the damaged lamp play over the dead bodies in the doorway down the hall. If the Front's roid monsters hadn't followed up, it told him one of two things. Either they *had* killed all of them, or the survivors were looking for another way at them.

He made his decision. "Wade, on you." There was something to be said for the advantage of the defender in this sort of close-quarters fight, but with only six men, he hated to be on the defensive. He'd long ago taken to heart the purported general order issued by General Rommel to his troops: "In the absence of orders, find something and kill it."

They'd go on the hunt.

***

Wade couldn't quite restrain a tight, wolfish grin as he held position just long enough for Gomez to stack up with him and give his shoulder a squeeze. *Finally*. If Brannigan didn't like being on the defensive, Wade positively *hated* it. He got antsy sitting on security for ten minutes.

And these Front assholes really needed to die.

He swept into the prep area, moving fast, checking the corner and then moving to the edge of the first divider, clearing his dead space right alongside Gomez, even as the rest of the team made entry behind them, Burgess and a freshly bandaged Bianco taking up rear security.

Wade suppressed a whistle. The destruction in that room was impressive, as was the sheer number of bodies on the floor. As he pied off the door leading deeper into the complex, he came up on the corpse of the fat man in the red jacket, and a single glance showed him the sheer amount of punishment the gangster had soaked up before he'd gone down. Wade wasn't a man who was easily put in awe of much, but that fat bastard had taken as many rounds as one of the Front's super-soldiers before he'd dropped.

He reached the far wall, where yet another door stood closed, though unlike the inner doors, this one didn't have its window blacked out. He glanced through it, keeping well back so as not to expose himself in the window, making sure that his muzzle was between his eye and anything on the other side, but he saw no movement. The room on the other side was dimly lit and looked like a kitchen, but there didn't seem to be anyone in it.

Moving to the edge of the door, he kept his weapon pointed at it, while Tackett moved up behind him, reached around to the door handle, and yanked the door open.

They went through fast. It was indeed an industrial kitchen, albeit a small one, packed into a cargo container. There wasn't a lot of space, so they moved just as fast to get to the next door, before they found themselves in the proverbial knife fight in a telephone booth.

They reached the door a moment later, just in time to see the handle start to turn.

***

Puller flinched as he heard the helicopter make its second pass, spraying down the side of the building with more machinegun fire. He'd been pretty sure he'd killed at least one door gunner, but it sounded like he hadn't put the guns out of action. Maybe they were even remote. From what the others had told him about the Humanity Front—presuming that was who was running this operation—he wouldn't be surprised if they had the tech to do that.

263

He couldn't help but feel like he was hiding, back there on the door leading into the dark and quiet interior of the warehouse. Santelli and Curtis were facing the helicopter and the shooters who were trying to maneuver on them. He was sitting back there staring at shelves.

It ate at him for a few moments. Rear security was absolutely necessary. He knew it. He was the lowest man on the Blackhearts totem pole, though, and if he was going to prove himself, he couldn't just be hiding on rear security.

For a second, he was about to do something stupid. Then he heard something. A distant *bang*, somewhere in those shadows. Maybe a door slamming.

All thought of abandoning his position to try to get some vanished. He was suddenly that young Devil Doc again, ready and willing to apply the adage that, "The best medicine is lead downrange."

He eased the door open a little wider, giving himself a larger window to see and shoot through. Santelli and Curtis were shifting in the main doors, the sounds drowning out what little he could hear through his door. He lowered his profile still more, bracing his rifle against the doorjamb with his support hand, searching the darkness over his sights. Was there a little bit more light in there?

Movement. He leaned out a little farther and saw that he'd been looking a little too deep.

Five men were moving up the gap between the loading docks and the stacks of stored cargo, all in black SWAT gear, their HK 416s in their shoulders, looking over their sights. They'd closed half the length of the warehouse already, in the brief time since he'd heard that *bang*.

Puller didn't hesitate. He leaned out just a little bit more to bring his weapon to bear and opened fire.

He was barely aiming. It was almost too dark to see his sights, anyway. He just pointed the rifle and started squeezing the trigger, holding the forearm clamped against the doorjamb to keep it steady against the recoil.

His first shots missed, and the man in the lead flinched as the bullets *snap*ped past his ear, his weapon tracking toward the muzzle flash in the doorway, but Puller hadn't just defaulted to a pair of shots at a time. His next round hit the man in the side of the head, sending him reeling, and then he sped up the mag dump.

Bullets tore through shoulders, necks, guts, and legs as he hammered fire into the stack. He saw at least two go down hard before the bolt locked back. The others had already been moving to cover behind the stacked cargo before he'd even run the mag dry, and he thought he'd clipped another one as the survivors had scattered.

He ducked back behind the doorjamb as he dropped the magazine and reloaded as fast as he could. His hands were shaking a little. That surprised him, but he fought through it, dragging the recalcitrant mag out of his chest rig and struggling to get it lined up on the mag well.

Fortunately, he wasn't alone. Santelli had rolled off the front door as soon as he'd started shooting and was now on the other side of Puller's door. He fired twice, the concussion battering at Puller where he knelt, flame stabbing into the darkened interior as brass clattered to the floor. Puller thought he heard a yell and another body hitting the floor. Then he was up and back on target, searching the dimness of the warehouse for any of the other targets.

Good thing you held your sector, huh, Doc?

CHAPTER 33

Wade took in the situation in a heartbeat. The door opened outward from the kitchen, so he raced forward and slammed into it, driving through the door at the man on the other side.

He had just enough time to register two big, black-clad figures on the other side of the door as he tackled the first one. Going hands-on in a gunfight was hardly what he'd consider ideal, but they were too close to do anything else.

He drove the first man's rifle up and away as he hit him with the door, driving forward with his legs as he pushed him back toward the second man. That one tried to take a step back, but Wade kept up his assault, shoving his forearm into the first man's neck as he twisted around to force him back against the second man, tangling both of them up.

For the moment, neither could get a shot at him. The second man tripped and went down, tangling the first man's legs, and all three of them went down in a heap.

Wade could only ride the tiger. The man he'd hit was *strong*, and he wasn't just going down. He'd clamped a hand on his rifle as he swung an elbow at Wade's head. Wade cranked his own neck back to avoid the strike, even as he brought a knee up to get some leverage. The elbow strike grazed his chin and still rattled his brain.

He heard the door hit the wall as Tackett came through after him, but he was a little busy. The big man beneath him wasn't that great a fighter, not on the ground, anyway, but he was so powerful that it didn't matter. Even from his somewhat advantageous position on top, Wade could already feel the fight turning against him.

The big man bucked, almost dislodging him, but he grabbed the man's collar and held on, cranking down as he did so. With only one hand, he wasn't sure he could choke the guy out, especially not if he was as hopped up as these monsters seemed to be. But it kept him from being thrown off. Wade wasn't a lightweight in the strength category, either. He held on, pinning the man's weapon and weapon arm against his chest, tucking his head as the wannabe super-soldier pummeled him, keeping his other hand up to fend off the blows. It meant his weapon was out of action, and he couldn't exactly hit the guy back, but right then he was trying to stay on top and just keep those two from getting up and killing all of them.

He hadn't reckoned on the second man, though.

With a roar, the bad guys' number two man suddenly threw the two struggling combatants off him, lifting both bodily and throwing them across the narrow container. Wade hit the wall hard, and only sheer grit kept him conscious and holding onto his opponent.

Tackett had moved fast, dodging the two flying bodies, and now he pivoted and put a double tap right into the number two man's face from less than four feet away. The roid monster's head bounced, and blood and brains painted the wall behind him.

Wade still had a hell of a fight on his hands, though. He was too entangled with his antagonist for any of the others to risk a shot, so he had to win this fight on his own, and with the other man on top of him now, that was suddenly a lot more touch-and-go than it had been a second before. The big man had abandoned any attempt to get to his weapon and was now trying to get all the way on top of Wade, still swinging at his head. Wade, for his part, had managed to twist around so that he was in his guard, his legs wrapped around the giant's waist, still holding onto that collar and fending off strikes with the other hand.

The coked-out bodybuilder in tac gear wasn't getting tired, and his strikes felt like they were getting harder. Wade had his body somewhat in control, but if he didn't do something quickly, he knew he was going to lose. It would be small comfort to him if the other Blackhearts shot this guy full of holes *after* Wade was dead.

Another elbow strike got past his guard and rattled his teeth. He might even have blacked out for a split second, though he was still holding onto the guy's collar with a death grip. He could vaguely hear voices yelling, presumably telling him to let go so they could haul the Front commando off him and kill the bastard.

Wade wasn't giving up, though. He gritted his teeth, tightened his grip on the bad guy's collar, tucked his chin, and headbutted the man in the nose.

He put almost all he'd had into it. These bastards had taken round after round of 5.56 and kept coming, so he knew he had to hit this guy as hard as he could. Fortunately, while whatever drugs were probably coursing through his veins must have reduced any pain he felt to almost nothing, there's only so much that drugs can do to counteract having your brains sloshed against the inside of your skull.

The guy went limp, just for a second. It was enough.

Wade shoved him over to the side, dropped his hand to his holster, and shot him six times in the guts from retention with his FNX-9.

Then he pushed off, sliding across the floor and bumping into the second man's corpse, punching the pistol out and blowing the commando's brains out from almost contact distance.

His breath was heaving and everything ached. He kept the pistol trained on the suddenly deformed skull in front of him for a long moment, as Brannigan loomed over him, rifle in his shoulder and pointed down the corridor.

"You good, Wade?" Brannigan lifted his muzzle toward the ceiling and held out a hand to help him up. Tackett and Gomez had both pushed forward to cover down the long axis.

Wade took his hand and accepted the help up. He felt battered and exhausted. *Not in my twenties anymore.*

It took a second to check his weapon. "I'm good."

"Let's make sure these were the last ones, then we're breaching that lab and shutting this place down." Brannigan moved up behind Gomez. "With you."

Before anyone could move, however, a radio on one of the dead men's chest rigs crackled. "Team Venganto, this is Alpha." There was a faint German accent in the voice. "Team Venganto, this is Alpha. Report."

Wade couldn't help himself. He reached down and picked up the radio. "This is Angry Ragnar. Sounds like Team Venganto has taken a bit of a dirt nap. We'll see you soon, 'Alpha.'"

***

Winter stared at the radio for a second, though he couldn't spare too much attention from the threat at the end of the warehouse. He didn't doubt that those foreign shooters were about to maneuver on him soon.

Beta and Gamma were both dead, lying sprawled on the floor halfway between their breach point and the main entrance. Omicron was in a bad way, nursing a bullet in his guts. That left Winter and Epsilon still on their feet.

He stuffed the radio back into its pouch. He wouldn't give the enemy the satisfaction of a reply. He had all the information he needed, anyway. If any of the Type Ns had been conscious, they would have responded. They were dangerously unpredictable and tended toward what he'd once heard described as "Active Stupid," but they followed procedures like radio protocols. The only reason any of them wouldn't have answered would be that they were dead.

He peered around the pallet of plastic-wrapped cargo where he'd taken cover. Sure enough, three gunmen were working their way toward where they were hiding. He leaned out and fired, forcing at least one of them back behind piles of crates just inside the warehouse proper.

Flint would doubtless have taken the risk to make sure he killed these men. Winter, however, wasn't Flint. If he killed them in the process of making his escape, so much the better, but the odds weren't good, especially not if these men had already killed the entire team of Type Ns. It was far more important to make sure that he and what was left of his team got out.

And that the lab was completely eliminated.

He leaned out again, flipping his HK 416 to full auto. "Get out as soon as I open fire. Rendezvous with the helicopter in the field to the south."

"What about Omicron?" Epsilon kept his voice hushed, but the full meaning of the question was fairly obvious. The man was dying and would probably expire before they could get him to medical help.

Yet, once again, Winter was not Flint. "He's still alive, so he still has a chance. Take him with us."

His rifle stuttered deafeningly, flame spitting from the birdcage muzzle device, and the shooter who had suddenly appeared only about five rows down the array of shelving ducked back into cover. Epsilon heaved Omicron to his feet, throwing one of the wounded man's arms over his shoulders, and ran as fast as he could drag the other to the still-open loading bay door.

Winter fired two more bursts as Epsilon struggled to get Omicron down to the ground, then he got up and ran for the opening himself, sending the rest of his magazine roaring down the length of the open interior of the building. He threw himself out, helped Epsilon get Omicron to the pavement, then pulled a grenade off his load bearing vest, pulled the pin, and threw it in the opening.

Then they were running for the fence as the fragmentation grenade exploded with a heavy *thump*.

Winter turned and dropped to a knee behind the corner of the building as Epsilon let Omicron down and went to work cutting through the fence. He had one more task to complete. The Type Ns had failed, but the lab could not be allowed to fall into either the Czech police's hands, or anyone else's.

He took out a small tablet, tapped a couple of keys, entered his authorization code, and then it was done. It was a pity about those personnel still inside, but they were replaceable. The Organization's mission came first. Always.

Winter took one more look around the corner, making sure the opposition wasn't in pursuit, then he turned and moved toward the gap in the fence, as Epsilon hauled Omicron back up, the wounded man groaning in agony, and headed for the rendezvous point.

***

It didn't take long to sweep the rest of the outside corridor and rooms and determine that they'd taken out the last of the Front's chemically enhanced soldiers. The team gathered back in the prep room, Bianco, Burgess, Tackett, and Wade on outer security while Gomez, Flanagan, Kirk, and Brannigan got ready to breach the door.

The electronic earplugs they were all wearing had the ability to amplify most ambient sounds while automatically deadening anything above a certain decibel level. That was the only reason they heard the sudden commotion on the other side of the door, as something *pop*ped loudly, followed by the crackle of what sounded like several explosions. Screams erupted from inside, and the door suddenly rocked as something or someone hit it from the other side.

A frantic pounding started to shake the door, but it appeared to be locked. Magnetically locked, from the looks of it, since it wasn't shaking that much, and appeared to be affixed to the doorjamb. Flanagan hefted his captured shotgun and placed the muzzle against the top hinge. "Step away from the door!" He wondered briefly at the wisdom of issuing the warning, but it sounded like all hell was breaking loose in there. Besides, if they

272

could take any of the Front's people alive for interrogation, it might be a good thing.

The shotgun *boom*ed, cratering the door but failing to penetrate. He gritted his teeth as bits of metal flew off and peppered his cheek. That hadn't worked. And they didn't have heavy breaching tools, either.

Brannigan was looking around for a pry bar of some sort, but Flanagan knew that if the door was solid, and mag-locked, they were never going to get it open with anything short of a cutting charge or a torch. He set the shotgun muzzle against the hinge again. Maybe he could get through with multiple shots.

Before he could fire, though, Gomez grabbed his shoulder. "We need to get out of here." Another series of *pop*s sounded up and down the corridors to either side, and even before he saw the flickering light, he could smell the acrid odor of incendiaries.

That was why the people inside the lab were screaming. They were about to be burned alive. And they were locked in.

Flanagan tried one more shot, but it still didn't break the hinge. The doors were too solid. This place had been built to be hard to breach.

Brannigan grabbed him. The smoke was getting thicker, and the temperature was already rising. Flames licked at the dividers at the walls. "They set this place to self-destruct. We're not going to get anything useful out of it. Let's go."

Flanagan took one more look at the door, the beating of fists on the other side getting more frantic, faint though they were.

"I don't like it, either," Brannigan said. "But they chose their path. I'm not going to mourn Front drug dealers for long. Let's go!"

Another series of *pop*s sounded, and a sheet of flame erupted along the floor. Acrid smoke filled the room, and Flanagan let the shotgun fall, turning to follow as Brannigan went after Bianco and Burgess, heading back out through the barracks room. Several of the cots were already blazing, and smoke roiled along the ceiling, as flames ate away at everything flammable inside. The heat hit them in waves, and it got increasingly difficult to breathe. Bianco was stumbling, the pain and the blood loss making the heat hit him even harder. He stacked on the door to the corridor, and Gomez moved up. "I've got it, brother." Gomez and Burgess pushed into the corridor, and Kirk grabbed hold of Bianco, hauling him along like a little brother.

The living spaces were fully involved, and at first glance, it looked like they were cut off. Flames licked up the walls and roared on the furniture, and the smoke was so thick that it was impossible to see all the way to the other side. Flanagan could only follow the rest, hoping that they found the way out and that there weren't more shooters waiting for them outside. He hadn't heard any radio calls from Santelli in what felt like a very long time.

Fortunately, Gomez's sense of direction was unerring. The entire team was practically crawling by the time they got to the exit, but as they burst out into the relative cool of the night, he looked around while he coughed and saw that all eight were out. They spread out into the parking lot, taking what meager cover they could behind the cars, looking for more threats.

The flames were starting to eat through the roof, and Flanagan realized he could hear sirens in the distance. Whatever had kept the Czech police at bay seemed to have run out of time. Which meant the Blackhearts were out of time.

"Guido, Kodiak." Brannigan's voice sounded raw and hoarse even over the radio.

"This is Guido. We're secure. We have shooters in the wind, somewhere to the south of us, but they might have gotten on the helicopter. It did a touch and go to the south of us about five minutes ago."

"Get to the rendezvous by the railroad tracks," Brannigan croaked. "We need to be gone in five minutes."

Flanagan looked over his shoulder and got the nod from Brannigan. He got up and led out, jogging toward the shot-up Front van and the breach in the fence.

Behind them, the drug lab burned, and blue lights flickered in the night as the Czech authorities closed in.

EPILOGUE

"You seem awfully relaxed, after everything that's happened." Brannigan watched Dalca as she sipped her champagne. His own whiskey sat untouched for the moment. "Seems to me we should be getting out of Prague posthaste."

She smiled. "Don't worry, John. I have friends in high places. An advantage of my position with Ciela International. No questions will be asked about any Americans who might have been involved. Or any Ciela International personnel. As far as the *Policie* are concerned, this was a dispute between Garin's gangsters and his drug suppliers that went very, very bad." She took another sip. "Everything is taken care of."

"Seems a bit unethical." Brannigan wondered if he was objecting because of the ethics of having a local police department infiltrated, or because he simply didn't want to accept much in the way of favors from this woman. Any such favors were likely to come with some significant strings attached. Even if they were of a more personal nature.

She dimpled behind her glass. "John." She tilted her head as she leaned back in her chair. "Which is more unethical? Using my connections to help those who have helped me, or allowing you to be punished for taking out not only a notorious Russian gangster and any number of his murderers, as well as a massive, and dangerous, new drug lab?" She beamed at him. "You must keep perspective about these sorts of things."

Brannigan scowled. She was working on him, and he didn't like it. She was stunningly beautiful this evening, and he knew that it was all aimed at him. To make matters worse, he had to admit that she had a point. They'd put down some very evil people and getting slapped in jail for it was hardly the definition of the word "justice."

"I just hope that the lab's destruction actually put a dent in the operation." He swirled the whiskey in his glass, staring grimly at the amber liquid. "We already know that destroying that facility on the Altiplano didn't stop their little super soldier program."

She sobered. "I've had my feelers out. So far, my sources haven't reported any other appearance of Roulette outside Prague. It seems that this was their testbed. A strange place to pick to develop and test a new narcotic, to be sure, but I suppose they wanted to maintain strict control over it, instead of possibly allowing the narcos in Central and South America to copy it. We'll keep looking and listening. It's possible—one might almost say probable—that they'll restart it, but it will take time."

The music changed, and Brannigan suppressed a sigh as Dalca's smile got wider. He recognized the tune. She set her glass down and reached across the table to take his hand. "You know how much I love this song, don't you, John?" She got up. "Come and dance with me. Just for tonight."

***

"You've been hard to find." The man leaning against the railing, looking down into the River Spree, was about as nondescript as the meeting place. He was younger than Winter's usual contacts, his hair slicked back and a thin mustache over his lip.

Winter joined him, leaning one shoulder against the dingy, pitted, and graffiti-covered brick column that held up the structure of the Oberbaum Bridge. "I've had my reasons to be."

278

The man looked over at him. "If you are concerned about the Board taking the loss of the Roulette lab out on you, you needn't be. You cleaned the situation up, which was the mission. Frankly, most of the current Board, ever since the last purge following Flint's series of spectacular screwups, was against the project in the first place." He turned back to the water. "It was too haphazard. Eliminating the dregs who are prone to street drug use has its time and place, but hardly as a lower-tier phase." He snorted as he shook out a cigarette. "It would end up eliminating too many useful engines of chaos, on both ends of the socioeconomic scale."

"So, all is well, then?" Winter wasn't convinced. "An entire Type N team eliminated, a multi-million-dollar secret facility—and all its personnel, I might add—destroyed, and a useful ally in the Russian underworld dead. That hardly seems like a win to me."

The man turned to him with a crooked sort of look on his face. "You can accept what I've told you, Herr Winter, or you can attempt to force this into a loss, which will not work out well for you. You know what retirement from the Organization entails."

Winter subsided, turning to face the river, though not before double-checking his surroundings, just in case the man's calming words were a trap, and there was a kill team closing in on him.

He nodded, reaching over to take a cigarette from the other man's pack. He was something of a perfectionist. That was why the Organization retained him. He was also, however, pragmatic enough to put that aside, if only for the sake of his own self-preservation.

"Someone came after the lab, and they weren't gangsters. Garin and his people weren't anywhere near as well-trained or well-equipped to take on an entire team of Type Ns."

"We're looking into it." The man glanced at him sideways, then pulled a thumb drive out of his pocket and handed it across. "That's our worry. There's another situation that requires your attention. In India…"

LOOK FOR MORE HARD-HITTING ACTION SOON, IN:

BRANNIGAN'S BLACKHEARTS

LEGACY OF TERROR

AUTHOR'S NOTE

Thank you for reading *Concrete Jungle*. This was a story idea that was kicking around as far back as the *American Praetorians* series, in which The Broker was going to be targeted by some of the underworld elements he'd dealt with in the course of helping the Praetorians. I thought it worked out better here, though adding the Front just made sense along the way. I hope you enjoyed it.

To keep up-to-date, I hope that you'll sign up for my newsletter—you get a free American Praetorians novella, *Drawing the Line*, when you do.

If you've enjoyed this novel, I hope that you'll go leave a review on Amazon or Goodreads. Reviews matter a lot to independent authors, so I appreciate the effort.

If you'd like to connect, I have a Facebook page at https://www.facebook.com/PeteNealenAuthor. You can also contact me, or just read my musings and occasional samples on the blog, at https://www.americanpraetorians.com. I look forward to hearing from you.

Also By Peter Nealen

The Brannigan's Blackhearts Universe
Kill Yuan
The Colonel Has A Plan (Online Short)
Fury in the Gulf
Burmese Crossfire
Enemy Unidentified
Frozen Conflict
High Desert Vengeance
Doctors of Death
Kill or Capture
Enemy of My Enemy
War to the Knife
Blood Debt
Marque and Reprisal
Concrete Jungle

The Maelstrom Rising Series
Escalation
Holding Action
Crimson Star
Strategic Assets
Fortress Doctrine
Thunder Run
Area Denial
Power Vacuum
Option Zulu
SPOTREPS – A Maelstrom Rising Anthology

The Lost Series
Ice and Monsters
Shadows and Crows
Darkness and Stone
Swords Against the Night
The Alchemy of Treason

The Rock of Battle

The Unity Wars Series
The Fall of Valdek
The Defense of Provenia
The Alliance Rises

The American Praetorians Series
Drawing the Line: An American Praetorians Story (Novella)
Task Force Desperate
Hunting in the Shadows
Alone and Unafraid
The Devil You Don't Know
Lex Talionis

The Jed Horn Supernatural Thriller Series
Nightmares
A Silver Cross and a Winchester
The Walker on the Hills
The Canyon of the Lost (Novelette)
Older and Fouler Things